Driven to Distraction

Stuart Bone

Novel - © 2016 Stuart Bone

Front cover coach design - © istock.com/jameslee1

Printed by CreateSpace, an Amazon.com Company

For Mum, Dad & Dave who have always been there for me since the day I was born.

Chapter 1

"This drizzle is getting on my pissing nerves," the old lady said, as she sat down beside me at the bus stop, "Look at my new cardigan; it's ruined. Three quid I paid for this at the charity shop."

Great Derek, I thought, you've managed to attract another eccentric that likes to chat.

The old lady wriggled uncomfortably as she pulled her suitcase nearer to her side.

"Ooh, that damp's gone right through to my bra. That's all I need on a long coach journey; soggy tits!"

I wrinkled my nose. "Yes that does sound unpleasant."

She pulled a small handkerchief out of her sleeve, shoved it inside her blouse and began dabbing.

"This'll have to do for now until I can get the hairdryer on them," she told me.

I suppose that was better than swinging them in the breeze.

"Are you going to Tenhamshire as well?" I asked, trying to move the conversation off of body parts.

The old lady shook her head as she extracted her hand. "Ooh no," she told me, "I went there once, about thirty years ago."

"Did you?"

"Yes. Never again. I was bored shitless the entire time."

"Oh."

That wasn't exactly an endorsement of the county where I was going to be spending the next week but then I wasn't really looking for excitement anyway. A relaxing holiday is what I was after, a distraction from all of my recent upsets. The brochure promised a luxury spa break and that's what I was looking forward to; a bit of pampering alongside a few

1

excursions to various local places of interest. I'd read the itinerary so often I knew it by heart.

"So where are you going to?" I asked the old lady.

"Amsterdam," she replied, "I'm off on a Swingers holiday."

"Really?"

I looked down at this tiny, grey-haired, woman sat beside me, a silk headscarf pulled around her head and tied under the chin, her arm resting on the crutch she was using as a walking stick. I couldn't picture her cavorting sexually with a group of strangers; not that I particularly wanted to.

"Yes," she continued, "I've always been a swinger. I particularly love a bit first thing of a morning. It sets me up for the day."

"I imagine it would," I replied.

"You can't beat a bit of Glen Miller or Benny Goodman with breakfast. They don't make music like that anymore."

Oh my God, she thought a Swingers holiday referred to the style of music!

"Erm, where did you see this trip advertised?" I asked her, tentatively.

"It was on the back page of a holiday magazine I found on the bus," she replied, "'Hot and Sticky' I think it was called."

"Right. Are you sure it was a holiday brochure? Did you look through it at all?"

"I didn't really need to once I'd seen this trip," she told me, "I just ripped the page out. Oh look; here comes a coach now."

A luxury, double-decker coach had just come into view from around the corner. I really hoped it was my one. It was due to arrive about now; nine o'clock. I didn't want to be here to witness the fall-out from the old lady's mistake. What on earth would happen when she found out the truth?

As it pulled up into the bus bay in front of us I noticed all of the blinds at the windows were down…on an overcast day. Damn, I didn't think this was the coach taking me to Tenhamshire. What was going on inside? Couldn't they wait until they arrived at their destination? A heavily made-up woman walked down the steps as the doors opened. Her outfit of thigh-length, black leather boots and red, rubber basque was actually quite practical for today. She wasn't going to suffer with soggy tits.

"Mrs Crabtree?"

The old lady waved over at her.

"I'm off then," she said to me, and stood up, "I wonder if someone will hold my crutch for me while I get on."

"I don't think you'll be short of offers," I told her.

She smiled and headed off.

I guess I should have tried to stop her but my attention was diverted by another coach that had just come into view. Well I say coach; looking at the age of it I estimated it was about five years off from being called a Charabanc. That was quite a cloud of smoke coming out of the exhaust pipe and the noise from the engine was very reminiscent of a death rattle. Scarily I was the only person left at the bus stop. Surely this wasn't for me. The brochure had said, *'Our superior coaches come with reclining seats, toilets and coffee-making facilities and each member of our professional staff is highly trained so that your holiday starts as soon as you board.'*

There was no way anyone could describe this vehicle coming down the road as superior.

A scream pierced the air. I turned my head just in time to see Mrs Crabtree come flying off the coach she'd just boarded, her headscarf pulled down over her eyes. I ran over to her.

"Dear God," she called out, "I've not seen one that size since I lived on the farm."

She leaned back against the coach and took a couple of deep breaths.

"Talk about swinging; he almost had my eye out."

"I'm sorry," I told her, "I should have tried to explain to you what a Swingers holiday was."

She looked up at me as she straightened her headscarf.

"I'm guessing I won't be doing the jitterbug."

I whispered a quick explanation to her.

"Really?" she said, looking up at the coach, "So they'll be having sex…all week…with each other…and everyone else."

"I believe that's the general gist," I replied.

"Hmm."

The courier appeared at the top of the steps.

"Are you getting back on, Mrs Crabtree?" she asked, "Mr Jefferies has strapped it down again now."

The old lady patted my hand.

"Oh what the hell," she said, "In for a penny, in for a pound," and she re-boarded the coach.

Just before the doors closed I heard her say, "Can we stop at a charity shop on the way. I think I'm going to need a whole new wardrobe."

I shook the image of Mrs Crabtree in a rubber basque out of my head as I made my way along the pavement to where the ragged-looking coach had just chugged into the bus bay. Was this really going to take me all the way to Tenhamshire? My fears evaporated as the doors opened and a vision of loveliness appeared, holding a clipboard. Tall, blonde and wearing a short skirt that showed off fabulous legs, she slowly descended from the vehicle. Her long, blonde hair fairly shone in the gloom of the overcast day as it bounced from side to side in unison with her perky bosom. The drizzle ceased and I swear I could hear music. Her mouth opened; her tongue protruded and gently moistened those luscious, full, red lips. Then she spoke.

"Nobber?"

"Erm, it's Noble actually; Derek Noble."

"Fuck me, the state of my writing," she said, squinting at the clipboard, "Should have been a doctor. Anyway, I'm Shauna. Is this your case?"

The music vanished, my fears returned and the rain teemed down.

"Yes it is," I said, and she picked it up, "Er, shouldn't the driver be doing that?"

"He should," Shauna replied, as she effortlessly threw my case into the hold, "But he's got a bit of a problem."

"Bad back?"

"No, he's a lazy tosser. Anyway, hop on Dirk and find yourself a seat."

"I prefer Derek."

"That's what I said."

Shauna closed the door to the storage area and saw that I was still standing in the rain.

"Are you getting on or are you still enjoying an eyeful of all my talents?"

"Erm, this doesn't appear to be the luxury coach described in the brochure," I said.

"Oh; yeah. Bit of a snag there I'm afraid, Dirk. The superior coach wouldn't start this morning. We had to resort to a slightly older model."

"Slightly?"

"Scrimshaw Travel is allowed to make last minute amendments to your trip without incurring any penalties or reducing the price of your holiday in any way, as stated in the small print of the brochure, which no one ever reads. Hop on Dirk."

I stepped onto the coach. The driver was sat up on a cushion, staring out of the windscreen through glasses with the thickest lenses I'd ever seen. He was trembling and sweating quite profusely through his uniformed shirt. *'Your holiday starts as soon as you board.'* I really wasn't feeling that vibe.

"Hello," I said to him, as brightly as I could.

No response.

"When do you think it's going to stop raining?"

The driver jumped in his seat. "Is it raining?" he asked, narrowing his eyes as he strained to see through the windscreen, "I guess I should switch the wipers on."

Run Derek, run. Get on the other coach with Mrs Crabtree and let your hair down.

Shauna climbed the steps behind me, blocking my exit.

"Sit Dirk," she said. It sounded more order than request.

I looked around at my fellow passengers as I resignedly made my way down the coach…all twelve of them. How many more pickups were there going to be? I was surprised to see two young couples sitting in the first two rows on the left hand side. At forty-five, I thought I'd probably be the youngest on this trip. Coach tours did have the image of being the preferred holiday for pensioners. When I'd first booked my seat I did worry that I might end up spending the week looking at photographs of grandchildren or be forced into playing in a Rummy tournament. Perhaps an excursion would be cancelled because an old dear named Elsie wakes up with a leg cramp which means a violent storm is on its way.

The girl in the first row smiled warmly at me, her boyfriend didn't look up. As I smiled back I noticed she was heavily pregnant. From the second couple it was the guy that smiled and said, "Alright Geezer." I responded with a very hip and trendy, "Good Morning."

On the opposite side behind the driver a large, elderly lady was sat in the aisle seat. She was asleep with her head lulling to one side, glasses askew and mouth wide open. Squashed tightly into the window seat beside her was, I presumed, her daughter. She looked really uncomfortable and I saw her trying to free a hand to wave at me. She gave up and smiled instead.

Further down behind them was an elderly couple and thoughts of that Rummy competition ran through my head again. He nodded but she was too busy nagging him to notice me.

"Did you pack the Antacids?"

"Yes dear."

"Because you know how irritable you get with heartburn."

"Yes dear."

"Did you remember to put your vest on this morning like I told you to; it's still chilly for May?"

"Yes dear."

"I bet you didn't pack a spare."

"No dear."

My God, I hoped 'dear' would cheer up before we arrived at the hotel. She was wearing an expression on her face that said, 'Come too close and I'll bite.'

Right behind them was a man leaning his head against the seat in front and groaning quietly to himself. He was holding a paper bag up to his mouth. I gave him a wide berth and kept moving towards the back of the coach, past a couple of old ladies who were dressed in matching rain hoods. I sat down a few rows behind them, just across from a rather attractive looking woman who nodded and smiled at me. I nodded and blushed back.

We kangaroo-hopped away from the kerb and Shauna's dulcet tones resounded through the speakers.

"Is this shitting thing on? Right, hello again. Now that we've made our final pickup, we'll be making our way down to Tenhamshire."

What? Was this it; thirteen of us?

"I'm Shauna and the sweating vision of loveliness at the wheel is Jim. I should point out that we are a little thinner on the ground than originally planned. One old wrinkly had to cancel at the last minute…because she died; and a family of four dropped out as one of their children has just been electronically tagged by the police and isn't allowed to leave the house. We would have had another couple here with us but unfortunately Jim managed to reverse over their cat this morning and so they felt they couldn't continue on with their holiday, choosing instead to stay behind with Fluff's remains. Seeing as most of him is still stuck to the wheel I don't think there's a lot left back at home to mourn."

Oh well, it didn't really matter about the number of passengers. The main thing for me was spending time relaxing at, '…*the beautiful Manor Park Spa Hotel set in rolling acres of traditional English countryside where each sumptuous bedroom has a balcony and luxury en suite facilities.*'

"Now because we're thinner on the ground, I'm afraid that means we can't get the group booking at the Manor Park Spa Hotel."

Oh bollocks.

"So instead of charging you extra we're now booked into a smaller hotel near to the spa town of…hang on; I can't remember the pissing name."

Shauna bent down and retrieved a small piece of paper from her handbag and squinted at it.

"Cunnilingus? That can't be right. No wait; Cunden Lingus. That's still quite a mouthful. Anyway, we're staying there.

Scrimshaw Travel is allowed to make last minute amendments to your trip without incurring any penalties or reducing the price of your holiday in any way, as stated in the small print of the brochure, which no one ever reads."

I felt I'd be hearing that sentence quite a lot over the next seven days.

"But as a goodwill gesture, we have organised an extra excursion this afternoon on the way to the hotel. That's all for now, so sit back and relax."

I really needed a coffee.

Shauna switched off the microphone and disappeared down into her seat. She jumped up again suddenly and shouted out, "And the coffee machine ain't working."

Great. Well it was all going swimmingly so far. The holiday I'd envisaged when reading the brochure was already starting to disintegrate and we hadn't even left the high street yet. I sat back and closed my eyes, picturing in my mind the tiny, cold, lonely one bedroom apartment that I'd recently been forced to move into. I'd left it only half an hour ago but was already missing it dreadfully. I was missing Mrs Crabtree too; or was it just the big, beautiful coach she'd got onto? I sighed to myself and was just wondering whether I could jump out of the emergency exit (although that probably wasn't working either) when I felt someone sit down beside me. I opened my eyes. It was the attractive woman from across the aisle.

"I hope I'm not disturbing you," she said, "I'm Angela."

"Dirk, I mean Derek. My name's Derek. Definitely not Dirk."

Smooth Derek, smooth.

Angela smiled.

"Here," she said, getting a thermos flask out of her bag, "You look like you could do with some coffee."

She poured the nectar into the cup and handed it to me. I must have looked puzzled as she added, "I've travelled with this firm before so I've come prepared."

"You've travelled with them before and still come back for more?" I said, "Are you a sucker for punishment?"

Angela laughed. It was a beautiful, melodic sound that I felt I'd never get tired of hearing.

"It's a cheap holiday and the excursions are good so why not," she said, "I guess you get what you pay for, although last time I did at least manage to stay in the hotel that was advertised in the brochure."

"That must feel like winning the lottery now," I told her.

Angela laughed again. She looked to be around my age; probably a bit younger, late thirties perhaps and she obviously kept herself in shape. Her light brown hair curled gently at the shoulders and the cut suited the profile of her face. Her ice-blue eyes sparkled the whole time we were talking.

"I travel abroad a lot with work," Angela continued, while I downed the coffee, "And so for me a holiday is somewhere in this country. I love historical buildings. My degree is in History and it's a real passion of mine. I've never been to Tenham House and that's the excursion on the last day of this tour, which is why I risked booking another trip."

"I really want to see the gardens at Tenham House," I told her, "I've heard they're spectacular. I've recently begun a garden design course at my local college. I'm hoping to set up a little business doing it."

Angela nodded, looking impressed.

"Is that a big change of career for you, Derek?"

"It's part of a whole life change really," I confessed, "It all started when my divorce came through several months ago. My wife had pushed for it and got custody of the house and the friends."

"Your friends took sides?"

"Not took sides so much as it was just easier to stay mates with her. We were all in couples you see and would only ever meet up together as a group; never individually. We'd go for meals or would all holiday abroad somewhere. My ex is already with someone else so she still fits in with the rest of them. Even if I was included I'd just be an extra seat at the dinner table; stuck up the end where I could be stared at and pitied."

"That doesn't seem fair."

"Yeah, but what can you do," I told her, "At least I don't have to listen to all those endless, boring stories anymore; like Tom's one claim to fame when he got an angry letter printed in The Telegraph, how prissy Sarah's latest sponsored fast for disadvantaged cats in Corfu is going; the adventures of Janice and her overactive colon."

"Wow, you guys really know how to party," Angela said.

I laughed. "It does sound awful doesn't it? These friends mostly started out as work colleagues of my wife's and there's a constant game of one-upmanship being played out between them."

"I know the type."

"But anyway, after the divorce, about two months ago now; the firm I was working for as an Accountant went bust and so I lost my job as well."

"You have been through it," Angela said, putting her hand on top of mine and gently squeezing. It felt nice. I couldn't remember the last time I'd received that level of intimacy from a woman.

"It has been a bit of a struggle," I admitted, adding in a little sigh for some extra sympathy, "Starting over again in my forties was never part of the grand plan but losing my wife, my job and my home has left me with no other choice. I've spent a lot of time feeling sorry for myself and looking back at my life, probably through rose-tinted spectacles; but now I'm trying to see things clearly."

Angela was screwing the stopper back onto the thermos but it was obvious she was still listening to what I was saying and seemed genuinely interested. I couldn't stop myself from continuing on.

"It's difficult but I'm trying to look at this as an opportunity rather than a chore," I told her, "For example, I realised I'd never particularly liked my job. It was a good income that helped to pay for the lifestyle my wife wanted us to have but now I only have myself to please and can do whatever I want; hence the new business as a garden designer. I've always enjoyed gardening and I loved the garden back at my old house. I created it from scratch and it was the one place I could escape to where I could be on my own and really relax. It's probably the only thing from my marriage that I still truly miss."

"There were no children then," Angela asked, hesitantly.

I paused before admitting, "No. It was something we were always going to get around to eventually. Leanne kept telling me she wanted to wait until her career was on track first. I've just heard she's pregnant with the new fella's baby."

I couldn't believe I'd just blurted out all of my problems like that. I was supposed to be trying to forget them on this trip. Not that that was easy. I hadn't actually discussed the divorce or redundancy with anyone before now. Well, who did I have to talk to seeing as Leanne had taken all of the friends? She'd chased off my old mates from Uni years ago. There was my mother of course, but she worshipped the ground Leanne walked on. Angela was a complete stranger but didn't feel like one. I must admit it felt quite good to finally say all that I had out loud. Mind you, it was a depressing conversation to have the first day of a holiday. I decided to move the discussion on.

"Anyway," I said, handing back the empty cup, "How about you? Why are you on this trip on your own?"

Oh yes, nice one Derek. That's a great way of changing the subject. Why not ask straight out if her life has turned into one big mess like yours has. Fortunately, Angela didn't take offence at the question.

"As I said, I travel a lot with work and so there's very little time for marriage or romance or children," she told me, placing the lid back onto the thermos, "It would have been nice, I suppose but I don't really dwell on the subject. I don't think anyone can have it all, Derek and to be honest, I'm not too bothered. Anyway; I should let you get back to your snooze."

She got up, gave me another lovely smile and crossed the aisle back to her seat. I'd rather have carried on talking than gone to sleep, but making a grab for her and yelling, "Please stay" might have come across as a trifle desperate.

It was a while before I eventually nodded off. I guess it was the coffee but when I finally woke up I was in desperate need of a wee. This decrepit, old coach didn't even have a toilet on board, which I wasn't sure was legal. Mind you, even if it did have one there would probably be a sign on the door saying, 'Out of Order.' I looked at my watch. We'd been driving for ages. Surely we were due a stop at Services sometime soon. I walked up to the front of the coach where Shauna was sitting on the pull-down seat between the driver and the doors.

"You ok, Dirk? We prefer you to stay in your seat while the coach is moving," she threw a look over to Jim, who was whimpering as traffic overtook him in the next lane, "Although it's difficult to actually call this 'moving.' Put your foot down tosser!"

"I was just wondering if we were going to be stopping at Services anytime soon," I said.

"Need to poke Percy at the porcelain do you?" Shauna looked at her watch, "Probably in the next ten minutes. Can you hold it until then? Apparently it helps if you squeeze the tip."

"I just want to get a coffee, actually."

She gave me a knowing look. "Yeah, ok Dirk."

I started walking back to my seat, nodding and smiling at my fellow travellers, trying to convey the message that I was only enquiring about getting a coffee and perhaps a snack at Services and not that I was desperate for the loo. I heard the click of the microphone again.

"Just to give you all a heads up," Shauna said, "We should be stopping at Services in about ten minutes for those of you that need a slash. Hope you can all wait until then."

Well, if the rest of the coach hadn't already worked out that I needed the toilet, they would have by now. I continued on to my seat, head down. I cast a quick glance at Angela but she was reading a book; a hint of a smile on her face.

I sat down and stared out of the window. I hadn't wet myself since I was six but it was certainly going to be a photo finish this time. I watched for the Motorway Services sign and prayed that we wouldn't go over too many bumps. Eventually the 'Welcome' sign appeared…and disappeared. I let out a little moan as we drove past the exit lane. From up the front I heard, "You bloody idiot." There was a small click as the microphone was switched on once again.

"Sorry Ladies and Gents, I'm afraid Joyride Jim has missed the Services turn off."

I'm sure I could hear him sobbing in the background.

"So the next stop we can do will be in…hang on, there's another sign. Jim, quick; there's another Services area. We can go there; it's coming up, get ready to pull in."

Jim's crying became more panicky.

"It's this next exit, turn off now, come on, we're here."

We weren't going to make it.

"Turn off here dickhead!"

Jim spun the steering wheel but managed to press down on the accelerator pedal rather than the brake. The coach skidded sideways across two lanes of the motorway. Cars tooted, we all screamed; Jim sang out, "Jesus wants me for a Sunbeam" but somehow he made the turning. We sped up into a small, unsurfaced car park area where he slammed on the brakes, sending us all crashing into the seat in front. There was a lot of heavy breathing and sighing as we tried to calm ourselves down again. Eventually Shauna switched on the microphone.

"Ok Ladies and Gentlemen, we seem to have come to a complete stop now. I think we should perhaps take a forty-five minute bog break here rather than thirty to give us some time to recover from that journey. I need to go and find a rifle so that I can put the little prick at the wheel out of his misery and I expect most of you oldies could do with some extra time in the toilets to get those support stockings rolled down and back up again. Dirk, I hope that scary little incident didn't make you soil yourself. I have the upholstery to consider."

Blimey I only needed a wee. Mind you I was surprised I hadn't wet myself. When the doors opened I threw coach etiquette aside and made sure I was first off.

I think Services was too grand a term to describe where we were. The far side of the parking area looked like it was being used for fly tipping with bin liners full of rubbish and old kitchen sinks and tyres piled in a heap. On the opposite side, in front of a row of poplar trees which screened the area from the motorway stood two rough-looking portacabins, joined together to form the toilet block. As I sprinted towards these I noticed a burger van was stationed right beside it, which appeared to be the only choice for any refreshments around here. Maybe I should have pissed myself on the coach. It looked more hygienic.

I raced up the steps to the Gents and the relief was immense. I even managed to ignore the little message the previous occupant had left for me in the bowl. I hoped Angela wasn't in the Ladies on the other side of the paper-thin wall when I let out a fart while having a wee. When I heard a louder fart in response I **really** hoped it wasn't Angela in the Ladies.

I emerged from the portacabin, wiping my hands on toilet paper as the hand dryer didn't work, and decided I had to get something to eat. I was starving. There wasn't a queue at the burger van as we were the only vehicle stupid enough to pull into this godforsaken place. I noticed the queasy guy from the coach munching away on a burger, while also holding a hot dog so the food couldn't be that bad. The van looked clean enough so I risked it and ordered a chicken burger. I felt a tap on my shoulder.

"Feeling better now?" Angela asked, smiling.

I laughed; too long and stupidly. "Yes, much better now; thank you."

"Do you want a drink with that?" the burger guy called out to me.

"No thanks," I said, then turning back to Angela, "Better not risk it. Not sure how long it is to the next stop."

She nodded. "The way Jim is driving we'll be lucky to arrive at all."

I gave my stupid laugh again. Why was I suddenly so

nervous in front of her? We'd been chatting away quite easily on the coach earlier on.

"Would you like something to eat?" I asked.

"No I'm fine thanks," she replied, "I have a sandwich on the coach."

I smiled. "You really have come prepared haven't you?"

The man behind the counter handed me my burger in a serviette. That seemed a bit quick. I really hoped it was cooked through properly.

"So where are you lot off to?" he asked.

Angela explained to him while I checked my food. It looked ok so I took a bite.

"You're quite a small group aren't you," he said, "But that's good for here really. It's manic when a large party arrives. Most of them can't be bothered to queue for the cubicles. I caught three blokes this morning weeing up the back of my van. I could only salvage half of my burger buns."

I didn't feel hungry anymore.

We stepped away from the van and I threw the rest of the burger into the nearest rubbish bin. The two ladies in matching rain hoods walked up to us. On closer inspection they didn't look as old as I'd initially thought they were; late fifties perhaps. They were both wearing floral patterned skirts and hand-knitted, round-necked cardigans under tweed jackets and it was this old-fashioned look that gave the impression of them being more elderly. I assumed they must be sisters.

"Hello," called the shorter of the two of them, and then to me, "Feeling better now?"

"Erm, yes, thank you."

"We haven't been introduced. I'm Susan; but everyone calls me Sooz, and this is my best friend, Josie. It's Angela and Dirk isn't it."

Angela sniggered.

"It's Derek actually," I said, shaking their hands, "I thought the two of you looked like sisters."

The two ladies laughed conspiratorially as they shook Angela's hand as well.

"People are often mistaking us for sisters," said Josie.

"It's quite funny really," added Sooz.

It wasn't that funny. Surely it must get on your nerves eventually.

"So what brings you two on this trip?" Angela asked.

"Oh Josie here has very kindly paid for the two of us to have a week away. She wanted to cheer me up after I lost my George."

"Oh, I'm sorry," I said, "Was it long ago?"

"End of last year," Sooz replied, "But you've got to go on haven't you and I've been looking forward to this. It's been a while since we last holidayed together hasn't it?"

"Yes," said Josie, "A few years."

The two ladies laughed again. I'm not sure what at. The queasy guy from the coach walked past us, throwing a screwed up paper napkin into the bin. It was probably best not to tell him about the burger buns.

"So how long have you known each other?" Angela asked.

"Ooh years now isn't it Josie?"

"Yes, just after you moved to the village."

Josie smiled at us.

"We got talking at the yearly church fete," she said, "After we both reached for the same phallus."

"I'm sorry?" It must be a very progressive sort of church.

Josie was laughing at the memory.

"It was the end of a long afternoon and we both wanted something satisfying inside of us."

I'd heard a few weird tales about village life before but this was an eye opener. A phallus at a church fete; what was it, some kind of raffle prize?

"I almost brought one with me today," Josie added, "I was going to slip it in this morning and surprise Sooz on the coach with it."

I think she would have succeeded.

"I noticed you'd had the same idea," Josie said to Angela, "I saw you struggling with yours earlier."

My mouth dropped open.

"Sometimes the top is a tight fit, isn't it?"

Bloody hell; was I on the same sort of holiday as Mrs Crabtree?

"I was going to ask if I could try it myself but we hadn't been introduced then," Josie continued, "But I could see you enjoyed it black when you gave it to Derek."

"Oh," Angela said, realisation dawning on her face, "You mean a thermos. You were talking about a thermos of coffee."

"Yes of course, dear. Didn't I say that?"

"Not exactly," Angela told her, "Are you alright, Derek?"

I was leaning over the rubbish bin, gulping in air to calm my heart rate down.

"I'm fine," I managed to say, before turning round to face them all again.

Sooz looked across to the burger van and wrinkled her nose.

"I don't think we should risk a drink here, do you, Josie?"

"No I agree with you," she replied, and leaned in towards me, "I must admit, Derek, this doesn't look the most hygienic of places does it. I don't know how often those lavatories are cleaned and that smell like used fireworks does tend to linger."

"Used fireworks? Do you mean it smelled like someone had just far…?"

19

"I'll be glad when we move on."

The four of us walked back towards the coach. The drizzle in the air was threatening to become a proper rain shower. I could see Shauna standing beside the door. She had a small tube of cream in one hand while the other was up her skirt rubbing it in.

"I take it she wasn't the courier on your last trip with this company," I said to Angela, "I suspect that would have been enough to make you not chance your luck again."

"The courier last year was short and stocky; had thinning hair, a little ginger moustache and needed the toilet every twenty minutes."

"That doesn't sound good," I said, "What was it; some kind of bladder infection?"

"No, she was pregnant."

Perhaps Shauna wasn't so bad after all. As we reached the side of the coach she extracted her hand.

"God that's a relief," she said, rearranging her skirt, "My Thrush is terrible at the moment. You feeling better now, Dirk?"

"Yes, thanks," I replied, "Glad you are too."

"How much further is it to the excursion this afternoon?" Sooz asked her.

"Not too far, although," Shauna indicated inside, "He's in a bit of a state still."

I looked into the coach where Jim was breathing into a brown paper bag.

"What's wrong with him?" I asked.

"He's superstitious and doesn't like the fact that there are thirteen passengers on the coach," Shauna said, "You were the thirteenth, Dirk. If you hadn't turned up today everything would have been okay."

I was beginning to think that way myself.

"Actually he wasn't meant to be our driver," she continued, "The regular one called in sick."

"And Jim was the next best thing?"

"Scary ain't it, Dirk?"

The rational side of my brain told me not to get back onto the coach. I could order a cab and still be home in time for dinner, but Angela boarded and I couldn't stop myself from following her. After all, my emotional side reasoned as I climbed up the steps, surely things could only get better.

Chapter 2

I managed to convince Jim to include Shauna in the passenger count to make the total fourteen and that seemed to perk him up a bit. Mind you it was his eyesight rather than his superstitious beliefs that was more of a concern for me. With the thickness of those lenses he could probably see into the future but I was more worried about the present and oncoming traffic. No one else appeared to be that alarmed. The youngsters seemed quite chilled, chatting away to one another up the front; the old lady opposite them had calmly nodded off again as soon as we'd left the Services area and Josie and Sooz just seemed happy to be here, no matter what. Even queasy guy was too busy groaning into his sick bag again to pay much attention to what was going on around him and nagging wife was only interested in berating her husband.

"I can't believe you didn't pack a spare vest. Didn't it cross your mind to pack a spare vest?"

Why was she still harping on about that? I felt like going up to her, shoving a tenner in her hand and saying, "Here, go buy some vests and for God's sake cheer up." I would have too, if she hadn't looked quite so frightening. Her hair was pulled back brutally into a bun. She was greying at the temples but otherwise it was still jet black, which contrasted severely with her very pale complexion. Her husband on the other hand was completely grey and his ruddy face made him look like he'd just finished laughing heartily about something. His appearance suggested a man that seemed kind and approachable. I guess opposites do attract.

The next leg of the journey was, thankfully, pretty

uneventful; apart from a few narrow misses on the motorway, resulting in beeping horns, shouting and rather a lot of swearing; mostly from Shauna. Eventually we took a slip road and were soon snaking our way through country lanes and picturesque villages, passing by patchwork fields of green grass and yellow rape.

We finally pulled up in one particularly beautiful village, right beside a striking, medieval pub covered in Tudor beams and with a very high, pitched roof. The village green opposite formed a large semi-circle with the local church at the apex and quaint thatched cottages surrounding the rest of the curve, each with a beautifully planted front garden that accessed onto a narrow, gravel pathway. The setting made even our ancient-looking coach appear modern.

"Right," said Shauna, over the microphone, "This is where we are stopping for a couple of hours."

In the pub, I hoped.

"We've arranged a short river cruise. We're going to leave the coach here with Jim (there's a blanket up the back and we give him an old shoe to chew on so he'll be quite happy) and walk the short distance across the green and past the church down to the river. There's a small tearoom there where you can have a snack before we embark on the cruise."

"It sounds lovely, doesn't it, Derek," Angela said, as we all got off the coach.

"Sounds, yes," I told her.

She laughed. "You're a very cynical man, aren't you?"

The drizzle that had been chasing us most of the day had stopped as soon as we pulled off the motorway. Although still overcast, the temperature was mild enough to make one feel that spring was finally going to put in an appearance this year. Maybe nagging wife's husband wouldn't need that spare vest after all. Shauna pulled a fold-down wheelchair out of the luggage hold.

"All yours Dora," she called.

The old lady from the front of the coach limped over and sat down in it. Her daughter began to push her across the road to join the rest of the group that were waiting on the green. There was quite a step up onto it from the road and I could see she was struggling to raise the chair.

"Would you like a hand?" I asked her, tentatively; not wanting to interfere or infer she couldn't do it on her own.

"She's fine," Dora called, "You're used to it aren't you, Margaret?"

"Yes mum," said Margaret, "But I'm not Charles Atlas. I can't lift you up this step. You're going to have to get out."

I could hear Dora grumbling under her breath. I stepped forward and offered her my arm to lean on. She smiled and grabbed hold, practically pulling it out of its socket as she rose. Once up and out of the chair I expected her to let go but she didn't.

"I might have trouble getting the chair across the grass," Margaret said.

"Don't worry," Dora told her, grinning at me, "I can probably make it across with a big, strong man to hold onto."

"Let me go and find you one," I said.

Dora gave me a 'playful' smack; that almost sent me face first into the grass.

"You're funny," she said, "Come on."

She pulled at my arm again and we set off across the green at quite a pace for someone who had just got out of a wheelchair. Fortunately the path beside the church was paved and as soon as we were off the green Dora plonked herself down into the chair again. After the pace set I wouldn't have minded a sit down in it myself.

The tearoom had a roofed, patio area beside the water's edge where the cushioned seats felt dry. It was warm enough for us all to sit down there and have our refreshments while Shauna disappeared off to sort out the final arrangements for the trip. An array of ducks swam around in circles in the middle of the river. They waited until one of us threw some bread and then a frenzy of flapping wings and a cacophony of quacking ensued as twenty birds chased one crumb of sliced white. Angela and I were sharing a table with Josie and Sooz.

"I thought it was going to be a bigger river," I said.

"Oh, but it's a beautiful setting," Sooz replied, buttering the last piece of her scone.

"It is beautiful," I agreed, "But when someone says you're going on a cruise, my imagination came up with a boat that just won't fit in this space."

"Come on Derek," said Angela, smiling, "After today's experiences so far what were you expecting, the QE2?"

I grinned. "Not quite that big, but I was hoping for something with maybe an outdoor deck and a separate indoor area; perhaps with a bar and some toilets."

"That was very naïve of you."

"It was really, wasn't it?"

"I've always loved the river," said Josie, pouring herself some more tea from the little silver pot, where the handle is the same temperature as the water inside (as I'd discovered the hard way), "My husband and I used to own a caravan and wherever we travelled to, we always made sure we stayed somewhere near a river. We'd hire a rowing boat and go out for little rows. The children enjoyed it too. Of course it was usually me that ended up rowing as Jeffrey always had trouble with his bollocks."

"Really," I said, a little startled, "I'm not sure why that would cause such a problem."

"Well he could never keep his oars in them you see," Josie replied, "I think his stroke was all wrong."

"Oh, you mean rowlocks."

"What did I say?"

"Never mind."

Shauna walked into the patio area with a young woman who was wearing a black, pin-striped trouser suit and carrying a briefcase. Her auburn hair was tied back in a ponytail and square, black-framed glasses were perched on the end of her nose. She looked like she should be sat behind a desk rather than taking a group of people on a river cruise. Alarm bells began to ring in my head.

"Right," said Shauna, "This is Caroline, one of the owners of the river cruise company. She's going to have a quick word with you before we take you down to the jetty."

Caroline beamed at everyone, displaying two rows of very white and even teeth.

"Hello," she said, "And a warm welcome from Malloy's River Cruise Company. Our pleasure crafts traverse many of the local waterways that surround this beautiful village. Our head office is still based here in Spreadbury where my father set up the business twenty years ago with one boat. Back then…"

Angela leaned in close to me and whispered, "It's all looking rather well planned so far, isn't it Derek."

"So far," I whispered back.

She grinned.

"And so," Caroline continued, "We've just introduced recorded audio tours across our entire fleet to give our customers a bit of information about the local places of interest as they sail majestically through them. Today will be the first time we use the equipment on this particular cruise and so we would welcome any feedback you may wish to give us at the end. I have some questionnaires here."

She opened her briefcase and a pasty fell out.

"Oh, I'm sorry about that," she said, scooping it up; her face reddening, "That's my lunch. Perhaps I'll pass the questionnaires out at the end. If you would like to follow me down the path behind us and onwards to the jetty; I'll introduce you to the skipper who will be taking you on the village cruise today."

We made our way to the jetty, the ducks still swimming alongside in the hope of more food. We didn't have any but perhaps they'd also spotted the pasty. The old, wooden boat waiting for us didn't really live up to the expectations that Caroline and her smart appearance had created. It was rather small, with a tiny cabin at the back and a larger deck area to the front that had gnarled bench seats built into the sides. This space would have been open to the elements except for a tatty-looking canopy loosely strung across the top. I had the feeling this was the one boat that Caroline's father had started the business with twenty years ago and it had probably been second-hand then.

"And so it starts to unravel," I said to Angela. She couldn't disagree.

Caroline was still beaming with obvious enthusiasm and pride. I'm not sure what she saw in front of her, bobbing about in the water, but it wasn't what the rest of us were seeing.

"Ladies and Gentlemen," she called, "If I can introduce you to your skipper."

She waved over at a figure standing inside the cabin.

"This is Jonah."

"Oh please, she's not serious," I said.

"I think she is," Angela replied.

Jonah climbed over the side of the boat and onto the jetty to greet us. He was a tall, beanpole of a man, wearing a crumpled, old, green t-shirt that had a picture of a fishing rod on it, with the slogan, 'Look at my Tackle' written underneath; and a pair of blue jeans that were rolled up at the bottom, displaying the thinnest ankles I'd ever seen. His long, bony feet were encased in a pair of faded sandals that I presumed he'd borrowed off of someone as his finger-like toes jutted out over the end and he kept flexing them to make the joints crack. He grinned at each of us in turn, his four teeth the colour of the sun.

"Jonah's one of our more experienced skippers," Caroline said.

I'd hate to see the inexperienced ones.

"If you'd now like to step aboard the vessel, I will hand you each a headset. Jonah, if you could help everyone?"

Jonah stared at Caroline, his grin never leaving his face which I found a little unnerving. Eventually he nodded and the two of them got onto the boat. He began to help people aboard while Caroline got the headsets out of her briefcase. I remained standing where I was, wondering if I could make a break for it. Only when I saw Angela climb on did I realise that I wasn't in the queue and I reluctantly walked to the back of it behind Dora. I hoped Angela would save me a seat next to her.

Dora's wheelchair was stowed in the cabin and Margaret got onto the boat first and then turned around to help her mother.

"Don't worry my lover," Jonah said, to Margaret, "I'm sure this gentleman here will help me get the dear, old lady on board."

Thanks for that, Jonah. I really needed my arm to be wrenched out of its socket again by Dora. When he took hold of her hands I was relieved; until I realised that left me with the back half.

"I'm not too fussy where you put your hands, Derek," Dora told me, "Just give me a good shove and I'll get my leg over."

That created an image in my head I wouldn't be able to erase in a hurry. Dora was definitely sprightlier than she made out. She got one foot onto the boat, with Jonah holding her hands for steadiness; and as I pushed so she swung the other over. The exertion of doing that caused her to fart and made me overbalance. I fell forwards into the boat, my face pressed right up against her backside. I heard a round of applause and presumed that was more for my fall than for Dora's output.

Margaret had sat herself down next to Angela on the boat, almost as if, now that I had helped her mother on board, I was responsible for her until we got off. The only space left was at the very front of the boat, beside the queasy man. Caroline gave us our headsets and while I shook the bits of flaky pastry off mine, Dora limped up to the front and plonked herself in the corner, meaning I had to sit between her and queasy.

"Hello," I said to him, as I sat down, "I'm Derek."

I was practically on his lap so it was only polite to introduce myself. He looked at my outstretched hand for a second before shaking it.

"I'm Colin," he said, without smiling.

Colin looked like he was probably around the same age as me or maybe a touch older. I reckoned he cut his mousy brown hair himself as the fringe was too high and not remotely straight. He was almost as thin as Jonah but as he sat there I could see a small pot belly bulging through his t-shirt. His sallow complexion actually made his brown eyes stand out. He wouldn't be bad looking if he could take the sour expression off of his face. After shaking my hand he reached into his bumbag, took out some antiseptic gel and wiped it over his hands.

29

"No offence," he said.

None taken, you bastard!

"I'm just very susceptible to germs," he continued, "Always have been. I probably shouldn't even be on this boat either. I get terrible seasickness."

"But this is a tiny river," I reasoned.

"Any kind of motion sets me off."

I assumed that meant he was single.

Colin sighed. "I can already feel the nausea coming on."

Nothing to do with the burger and hot dog he'd wolfed down at the service station then.

He replaced the antiseptic gel in his bumbag and pulled out his sick bag. Great; this was destined to be a fun trip, squashed in between Vomiting Vernon and Farting Frieda. As I looked over to the opposite side of the boat I noticed Angela glancing back at me. We both smiled. I felt a tap on my arm.

"Are you two together?" Dora asked, indicating Angela, who had now turned to talk to Margaret.

"No," I said, "No, we've only just met today."

"Oh right. It looked like you'd known each other for ages," she said, "What about those young ones up the other end of the boat? Do you know who's with who?"

Dora was still speaking rather loudly and I assumed that meant she was a little hard of hearing.

"Erm, I believe the pregnant girl is with that guy sitting on her left," I told her, raising my own voice for her benefit.

"The one who's had a face like a smacked arse all day?"

"Yes, that's him."

"Oh, I'd have put her with the other one; the good-looking, black chap. I can say black can't I, Derek?"

"Of course."

"Well I'm never too sure what is and isn't the right word to

30

use these days. I'm eighty-five and can't keep up."

"Right."

"I don't ever mean to cause offence or anything," Dora continued, "At least I know that we can no longer say…"

"Yes, well, anyway, he's with the other girl."

"That chunky one?"

"Yes, that's right, the chunky one," I said, just as 'chunky' glanced in our direction. I quickly took an interest in my lap.

Jonah started the engine.

"If you would like to place your headsets on," Caroline called, from the cabin, "We'll begin the audio tour. Any problems, I can speak to you via my microphone."

We all pulled our headsets on as Jonah gently steered us away from the jetty. After a bit of crackling, the audio began.

'Looking to the left you should now be able to spot the majestic elephants.'

"Sorry, my fault," Caroline's voice came through the headset, "That's the river cruise through the zoo. This should be right now."

'Spreadbury is one of the oldest villages in the area and was mentioned in the Domesday Book. As we start out on our journey you should be able to see, on the right; the spire of our local church, poking through amongst the thatched roofs of our many splendid local houses. This was built in…'

As the talk continued I had to admit to myself that I was enjoying this rather tranquil experience. It was the most relaxed I'd felt all day. The rich, baritone voice of the narrator had a soothing effect on me and was certainly a contrast to Shauna's microphone technique. We passed by many large residences with gardens that backed onto the river, most with their own moorings and the guide told us more about the history of the village and how the pub was now the oldest inhabited building.

'It is rumoured to be haunted by an eighteenth century landlord. Residents of the village have reported a number of strange sightings and weird experiences over the years. His name was Joseph and his sudden death was due to being crushed by a runaway...'

"Car fifteen, do you read me?"

Crushed by a runaway car fifteen? And it had all been going so well.

'He lingered for five days in the room that's now used as part of the kitchen.'

"Car fifteen, pick up at Penrose Gardens."

We all fidgeted in our seats, looking around at one another with puzzled expressions on our faces.

"I'm sorry Ladies and Gentlemen," Caroline said, "We're getting some interference, please bear with me."

I could see her in the cabin, frantically pressing different buttons on the electrical equipment.

'He was buried in the local cemetery but has never truly been at rest.'

"So anyway Sandra, he said he was going to take me out Saturday night."

Great, we now seemed to have picked up the local phone line as well as the cab service. Things went from bad to worse.

'After Joseph's death his widow ran the bar for another...'

"Fifteen minutes. I'll be back at base in fifteen minutes."

"Can you believe it Sandra; his idea of a romantic meal was at the local Indian of all places?"

'After her subsequent death the bar passed to the son who was named...'

"Dover Street. Pick up at number forty-seven. Do you need directions?"

"And I said to him, Sandra; for a romantic meal, you can

take me..."

"Up the old, Brown Avenue; then bear left onto the new road and first right onto Dover Street."

"I'm so sorry about this," Caroline said, "We've not had this problem with any of our other audio tours. Let me try one more thing."

She flicked another switch. A piercing screech made us all yell and then there was silence. I thought I might have gone deaf.

"I think that's sorted now," Caroline said, "Let's try and continue."

We all settled back into our seats.

'Hello Mrs Johnson. I'm from the washing machine repair shop. I'm here to give you a good servicing.'

I don't think she had it sorted.

'I'm in desperate need of a pump Mr Repairman. Well Mrs Johnson, I think I can help you with that.'

I looked around at the rest of the group. Margaret and Angela were both smiling. The youngsters were all laughing. Nagging wife had taken her headphones off and was in the process of ripping her husband's off of him as well. Josie and Sooz were listening intently, presumably believing that this was still the real guide. Either that or they were also having pump problems and were hoping for a few useful tips.

'Oh Mr Repairman, I don't think that tool will fit. I'll make it fit Mrs Johnson. Just bend over.'

"I'm so sorry," Caroline's panicked voice came through the speakers again.

The young, black guy shouted, "Put it back on," and the other youngsters laughed. Caroline was pressing everything she could on the electrical sound system. Suddenly, there was an almighty bang and the engine cut out. She and Jonah rushed out of the cabin in a cloud of smoke. No one was laughing now; well, Jonah still had that same grin on his face. He disappeared down behind the cabin. Caroline did her best to maintain the composure she'd had back on the riverbank.

"Please don't worry Ladies and Gentlemen," she said, her glasses all steamed up and her briefcase clung tightly to her chest, "Everything is under control. There's been a slight technical hitch with the audio equipment. I'm afraid we'll have to dispense with that for the rest of the journey."

What a surprise. I did feel a bit sorry for her though as she began to flounder under the number of questions raised.

"Was that tested thoroughly before today?"

"What's wrong with the engine?"

"Are we stuck here?"

"What's the name of that movie?"

She was saved from answering any more by Jonah's reappearance.

"Should be ok," Dora said, beside me, "Look, he's smiling."

Jonah whispered something to Caroline. Her face looked startled.

"Don't you have a spare?" I heard her ask.

Fortunately Jonah nodded. Relieved, she turned back to us again.

"I'm happy to tell you that we'll be on the move again shortly. There's a very small problem with the engine but Jonah can fix it, can't you Jonah?"

Jonah nodded, but remained standing where he was.

"Are you going to fix it now?" Caroline asked him.

He whispered into her ear again.

"Yes," she said, "You told me you had a spare part to fix it. Well; go and get it."

He stared blankly at her for a second before running past and

34

jumping off the boat.

"No," Caroline shouted.

We all turned around on my side and watched him half swim and half scramble to shore. He climbed out, waved at us and trotted off the way we had come.

"I thought he had the spare part with him," Caroline whimpered.

I couldn't believe she wasn't carrying a spare in her briefcase. Everything else seemed to be in there.

We didn't have much choice but to sit it out. Caroline gave up on maintaining her composure and had a little cry at the back of the boat while she ate her pasty. Shauna took over steering duty, not that there was much current to move us. I turned and looked at the view behind me. We were just outside of the village and the vista was of fields as far as the eye could see. It was so peaceful and I was quite glad the engine was off. I could only see one road from here and it was devoid of traffic, except for…

"Isn't that our coach?" I said.

Dora turned and squinted through her glasses.

"I think so. There's not many that age being driven around the country these days," she chuckled.

"Do you think Jim realises we're not on board?"

"Probably gone for diesel."

"Yeah, I suppose so," I said, "He drives it a lot better when no one's in it."

We both laughed.

"I don't know how you two can be so cheerful," said Colin, still holding his paper bag, "This is ridiculous; a complete and utter shambles. We've been marooned in the middle of a waterway and it's only day one. Once I get back ashore I'll be on the phone to the bosses of the coach company **and** this tin pot cruise one as well and I'll give them such a mouthful. They won't forget me in a hurry."

I thought abusing the companies down the phone seemed a little drastic. I certainly wasn't the advocate for this holiday so far but it could have been worse; as I pointed out to Colin.

"We're not exactly stranded in the middle of the Atlantic with no hope of rescue."

"If you don't complain, you don't get anything sorted," he informed me, "That's what dear mother always taught me. Oh God, now I'm getting heart palpitations."

Fortunately Jonah soon appeared again, out of breath but still grinning. He nonchalantly threw himself back into the water and swam out to the boat, somehow holding the spare part in a bag between his four teeth. A couple of us helped him aboard and he disappeared down behind the cabin.

"It's Mr Repairman with his pump," said the young, black guy, and we all laughed; bar Colin and nagging wife, who hadn't managed to crack a smile all day.

It didn't take long for the engine to be fixed and when it spluttered into life we cheered. Even Caroline managed a satisfied smile; although that could have been due to the pasty. We continued on with the cruise as the river wasn't quite wide enough yet to turn the boat around. We travelled through beautiful open countryside. The sun was trying to break through the clouds and, apart from Colin's dry retching; it was a very serene trip. There was a towpath one side of the river and a few people walking their dogs waved at us. We also passed some youngsters on bikes who gave us the finger, but even that seemed to be in a warm, friendly kind of way. A little further on, the river finally widened and Jonah turned the boat around to start the journey back to the jetty by the tearoom.

"This hasn't been so bad," I said, to Dora.

"I agree, Derek," she replied, "It's been nice for my Margaret. She's done nothing but smile sitting next to your lady friend."

I was going to correct her again but then decided not to. If she wanted to think of Angela as my lady friend, that was fine with me.

"She doesn't get out much," Dora continued, "Never been one to socialise really has Margaret. I've not often seen her with a boyfriend either. I told her I wouldn't have minded a girlfriend so long as she was getting some but apparently I'm barking up the wrong tree there."

Dora leaned in a little closer. "She could have fooled me," she said, not actually speaking any quieter.

I didn't know what to say so just smiled. Dora sighed.

"I'd definitely have preferred to see a happy lesbian rather than a straight mouse. Men like a strong woman don't they Derek?"

I was feeling embarrassed that the whole boat could probably hear this conversation. Dora was waiting for a response.

"Oh, er, well; I suppose; I mean; some do."

I couldn't help thinking about my own marriage. I guess Leanne could be described as a strong woman. She certainly knew where she wanted to be career wise, always had. I don't think it had been that part of her personality that had attracted me to her though. Dora was still talking.

"She's never really had any oomph, if you know what I mean. I was the complete opposite and my Billy loved that. No, she's a bit of a disappointment in that area really."

Margaret must have been able to hear what her mother was saying but she didn't look fazed by it when I risked glancing over at her. Perhaps she'd heard it all before.

"It would be nice if she got out more," Dora continued, "I'm always out. I go to bingo three times a week, I belong to a social group and always hit the shops a couple of times too. Margaret drives me to these places but never goes out herself."

I'm not surprised. When the hell is she meant to get the time?

"That's why I've paid for us to come on this trip; get her out more. I thought that was a nice gesture."

'It's the least you could do' is what I wanted to say, but I stuck with, "Oh yes, wonderful."

"Mind you, I did expect her to buy a few new clothes and get her hair done for the holiday," she said, "You know, make a bit of an effort; but she's done neither. I mean, look at that old cardigan. You can't be a vibrant, passionate woman wearing that much polyester can you."

"I'm sure she's comfortable," I replied; not really knowing if that was the right response.

Dora shook her head. "And don't even get me started on the hair," she said, "A new style would work wonders. I always feel better after I've been to the salon. I've told Margaret to come with me and get something similar but she always says no. I don't understand it."

"Well, not everyone can pull off a purple rinse like you can."

Dora smiled warmly at me. "I like you, Derek," she said, "I'm sure we'll get on famously this week."

Lucky me.

We'd reached the outskirts of the village by this time. As we passed the big houses so the ducks began swimming around the boat again, obviously used to passengers feeding them. None of us had any bread and the pasty was all gone but they continued to swim by us, quacking loudly.

"Oh that noise is giving me such a headache," moaned Colin, "And I can feel my prickly heat coming on."

He pulled a wet wipe out of his bag and dabbed at his face. As he patted the back of his neck so he lost his grip on the wipe and it fell into the water. The ducks made a beeline for it, expecting it to be food. They were pretty indignant when they found out it wasn't and the quacking got even louder.

"Oh why won't they shut up," he moaned, bringing down the cheerful atmosphere of the whole boat, "My headache's turning into a migraine."

At that point one of the ducks decided to see where we were hiding the real food and flew up onto the deck beside the cabin. He waddled towards the front of the boat and spotted Colin's bumbag. I suppose if I'd been a duck I would have thought it a reasonable assumption that the food would be in there too. He launched himself at it, landing on Colin's lap and quacking loudly. Colin screamed and threw his arms around my neck. He didn't appear to be too worried about his susceptibility to germs at that moment in time. The sound of the scream scared the duck into flight again and as it passed over it left Colin a message down the side of his head; a large and rather squelchy message at that. It probably wasn't the best moment for me to tell Colin that was meant to be lucky. Still, at least it gave him the chance to finally use his sick bag.

Chapter 3

While Colin cleaned himself up in the toilets at the tearoom we all stood outside, enjoying a good laugh at his expense. The mood lightened again and when he emerged, still grumbling about giving the travel firm a piece of his mind and how the boat owner deserved a right mouthful; his moaning fell on deaf ears. We made our way back across the village green. I walked with Angela, leaving Dora in the capable hands of the young, black guy. I don't think she minded as I could hear the two of them laughing and joking together. Mind you, his girlfriend didn't look entirely happy with the situation.

"Not quite the trip that was planned," Angela said, as we walked along together, "But enjoyable all the same."

"I don't think Colin would agree with you."

She smiled. "I guess things can only get better."

"I'm not so sure about that anymore," I told her, "I suspect we may have found the level for the rest of the week."

Angela laughed. I really liked the way her face lit up when she did.

We found Jim lying on a bench just on the edge of the green in front of the pub. He was wrapped in his tartan blanket and snoring away quite happily. Shauna gave him a hard shove.

"What? Eh? Where…where am I?" he said, sleep befuddled.

"You alright, Jimbo," Shauna asked, matter-of-factly.

"Oh, I must have dropped off," he said, sitting up.

He took off his glasses to rub the bridge of his nose. His eyes shrank to almost nothing without the lenses to magnify them and as he squinted up at us, enveloped in his blanket, he looked like some new species of Scottish mole. Shauna sat down on the bench beside him

"So," she said, "How are things with you; any problems?"

Jim looked puzzled. "No," he replied, "No problems."

Shauna smiled. "Good," she told him, "Good. I do have one question for you though. Where's the coach?"

Jim put his glasses back on and turned around to look behind him.

"Isn't it there?" he said.

I knew his eyesight was bad but surely he could spot if a thirty foot coach was there or not.

"They said they'd have it back by now," he added.

"What; who did?" Shauna's calm demeanour had vanished, "What the fuck have you done now, you nut job?"

"Boy scouts," Jim said, cowering under Shauna's gaze, "They told me they would wash the coach to get their 'clean a large vehicle' badge."

"There's no such thing," piped up nagging wife's husband.

"Of course there isn't," Shauna sighed, standing up. She gave Jim a smack around the back of the head, "Okay everybody; into the pub."

The interior was as beautiful as the outside with all of the original beams and timbers on show. Behind the bar wine casks had been built into the wall with taps hammered in at the front so the contents could be served by the glass. Both ends of the room had large inglenook fireplaces and the eclectic mix of wooden chairs that surrounded the tables complemented the rustic look and seemed in keeping with the age of the pub. It wasn't a bad place to wait while Shauna phoned through to the police.

"We saw the coach from the boat," I admitted, sitting at a table with Angela, Dora and Margaret.

"We'd assumed he'd gone for diesel, hadn't we Derek,"

41

Dora said.

I nodded. "I thought he was driving it better than he had all day. It didn't even cross my mind that it could be someone else manoeuvring it down the lanes."

"I can't believe it got stolen in the first place," added Angela, "I mean, who would want that old thing?"

"It was probably just boys having a laugh," Margaret said, "Hopefully they'll find it with all of our belongings intact."

Dora drained her large gin and tonic. "I don't think you have to worry about your stuff, love. I doubt whoever stole it wants to start dressing like a middle-aged virgin."

"Thanks for that, mum. Yes you're probably right. I'm sure they'd much rather get at your suitcase and dress like a geriatric lush instead; just so long as one of them takes a size twenty-two hip."

Shauna walked over to the group and all conversation stopped.

"Right," she said, "The coach has been found about a mile away with all the suitcases and bags still on board."

There were murmurings at this news but Shauna indicated she had more to say.

"Apparently the two boys who took it were just trying to wind up the driver. They didn't for one moment think he was dumb enough to fall for their prank and actually hand over the keys to them."

All eyes turned to Jim who was sitting on his own beside one of the fireplaces, still wrapped up in the blanket. He was staring down at his shoes but could obviously sense what was happening.

"Stop looking at me," he said, "I thought they were genuine. They were dressed as boy scouts."

"And you're dressed as a coach driver," Shauna shouted

over, "But you're not doing a very good impression of one are you? You know you're the only one who's meant to clean the coach, you lazy, little turd. Just be glad I've not reported you to Mr Scrimshaw."

She turned back to the group. "The boys pulled over up the road as they couldn't stop laughing. They put a call through to the police themselves as they really wanted to tell someone what had happened but neither had any credit left on their phones. They knew 999 was a free number. Evidently the operator was in stitches too. Anyway, if we don't press charges we can be on our way, if that is alright with the rest of you."

We all agreed, bar Colin; that we didn't want to prosecute as we just wanted to get to the hotel. Colin thought the boys could benefit from his wisdom, or as he put it; sit and listen while he gave them a right mouthful. Jim was sent off with the police to pick up the vehicle and soon we were on our way again. The rest of the journey passed in silence, apart from a bit of screaming around a few hairy corners on the narrow country lanes. I wondered if it would be possible to hire the kids who had stolen the coach to drive us for the rest of the week. After seeing their manoeuvring skills from the boat I knew I'd feel much safer.

We must have been staying in a hamlet outside of Cunden Lingus. Either that or the town was tiny with just a few houses and a church; the spa part being a quick dip in the old pig trough that stood beside the crossroads. We pulled into a sweep-in, sweep-out driveway at the hotel which, to be fair to Jim, wasn't very large although he did take it at a fair old pace. How he managed to swerve in time and miss hitting the rather impressive, two-seater sports car parked in front of the garage I'll never know. The result was that we were almost swept back out of the drive again and I only caught a quick glimpse of the hotel as we sped past. It was a large, double-fronted Victorian house and looked rather charming; a little gothic with turrets over the upstairs bays, but definitely charming. I ignored the sign saying, 'No hawkers, no food leaflets, no children, no hope.' (Ok, perhaps I just imagined the last one).

Jim had to reverse the coach back up the driveway, something else he was obviously nervous of doing; his yelps coming in perfect rhythm with the reversing beep noise the coach was making (beep, oh, beep, aargh, beep, ooh). Still, although he ended up parked diagonally across the driveway so that the driver of the sports car wouldn't be able to get out and no other visitor could get in, at least he managed to avoid crashing into the house. We all eagerly alighted from the vehicle, glad to finally reach our destination and anxious to see more of where we were going to be staying.

We collected our luggage and walked up the stone steps to the entrance. Inside, the hallway was wide but rather dark. It had retained its original features; beautiful cornicing, elegant ceiling roses and a black and white tiled floor; but it also looked like it hadn't been decorated in years. The paintwork, once white was now a dull yellow; the patterned wallpaper was peeling at the edges and the carpet on the impressive looking staircase which at one time must have looked rich and decorative was now balding and faded.

There was a small reception desk in front of the staircase with a bell to ring for service and a signing-in book. Still dreaming of the luxury offered by the Manor Park Spa establishment I couldn't help feeling that this place was being run more like a seaside boarding house rather than as an exclusive, country hotel. Still, after the day we'd had I was just grateful that we'd arrived safely. I was pressed right up against Colin and could tell he was enjoying the experience a lot more than I was.

I wouldn't have been surprised if the wizened, old lady sat behind the reception desk had been around to witness the property being built. She was hunched over and chewing toothlessly on a sweet of some description. She was making a loud sucking noise and didn't appear to have noticed the line of dribble down the left side of her mouth. She jumped when Shauna rang the bell.

"Party of fifteen from Scrimshaw Travel," Shauna said.

"Eh?" The woman stuck a finger in her ear and wiggled it about a bit. A loud, whistling noise resonated around the hallway, "Say it again dear, my battery's going."

Shauna repeated herself loudly.

"I'm afraid we're almost full, dear," the old lady said; peering at the register in front of her through glasses that gave Jim's a run for his money, "We've got a party arriving from, erm; Scrimshaw Travel."

"That's us," Shauna told her.

"Eh?"

"That's us!" she shouted.

Fortunately, just before Shauna leapt across the reception desk and decked her, another lady appeared through a door at the other end of the hallway. She looked late middle-aged and very business-like in a two piece, grey, skirt suit; her pink blouse done up to the neck with a cameo covering the top button. Her hair had obviously been recently set at the hairdressers and was dyed chestnut brown.

"Hello," she called, cheerfully, walking around behind the desk and standing in front of the old lady, "You must be from Scrimshaw Travel. I'm Barbara Goddard; owner and manager of The Grand. It's so lovely to meet you all."

I had a feeling that she could probably be sued under the

Trade Descriptions Act for the name of her hotel, but she seemed very nice. She turned around to the old lady.

"Louella," she called loudly, into her face, "I want you to go and check on dinner for me."

Barbara put out her hands and helped the old lady stand up. She passed her a walking frame and Louella slowly made her way through a door behind the desk as we all silently looked on. Surely she wasn't the chef.

"And please put your teeth in before you serve this evening," Barbara called after her.

My God, she was the waitress.

"Such a treasure," Barbara said, as she closed the door, "Been with us for years; since the war in fact."

The Boer War, I presumed.

"Right," Barbara continued, brightly, "Why don't I get the messy business of signing you all in done with your lovely courier here and you can all go and relax. Bar is through the door to your right, past the restaurant; and the lounge, where you can get coffee is through to the left."

We didn't need telling twice. It took me a while to get where I wanted, having to traverse the luggage and other members of the group in the confines of the hallway. I felt someone pinch my bum as I walked past. I turned, hoping to see Angela, but it was Dora who winked and smiled at me. I made my way to the bar. The four youngsters had got there before me and were already sitting at a table. The pregnant girl beckoned me over. After introductions I sat down with them as no one else had followed me in.

"Aren't you guys a little on the young side to be on this type of coach tour," I said, while trying to catch the barman's attention.

"It's our honeymoon," said the pregnant girl, Lauren; taking hold of her husband, Pete's, arm and grinning up at him. He didn't smile back.

"You've left it a little late, haven't you?" I indicated the bump.

Lauren laughed and stroked her stomach with the other hand.

"Yes," she said, "Two months to go."

She looked ready to drop to me but what did I know.

"We would have got married anyway but this little fella brought it forward. Bit of a surprise wasn't it, Pete?"

He managed a nod.

"I thought it was wind to begin with," Lauren said.

I laughed, until I realised she was being serious. I waved over at the barman again.

"He's not exactly cheerful," whispered the other girl, Karen, to me, "We came in and asked for four drinks and he groaned at us like we'd just asked him to do the impossible. I mean, it's not like he's busy is it, and it's his job after all. What would have happened if the whole group had come in?"

The description of Tenhamshire in the holiday brochure came back to me; '*Marvel at the stunning scenery, delight in the history of the local villages; experience the warmth and hospitality of the friendly community.*' Perhaps the barman was from out of town.

"So how come there are four of you on this honeymoon," I asked.

"It was Pete's nan's idea," the young black guy, Leroy, told me, "She thought it would be good for the four of us to get away and so booked this trip when she saw it advertised in the paper."

"That was nice of her."

"Yeah, we didn't know anything about it until after the wedding on Friday," Leroy grinned, "Pete's gran came over to

47

me at the reception and said, 'I've got a surprise for you in my pocket.' It was the holiday tickets. I told her I had a surprise for her in my pocket too, if you know what I mean."

I smiled politely but Leroy took this as a sign that I hadn't understood him.

"I meant my nob," he told me.

"Yes," I said, a little taken aback, "I knew what you meant."

"All our families were involved," Karen continued, obviously used to her boyfriend's sense of humour, "They arranged our time off from work and everything. It was a really nice surprise."

The glum barman came over with their drinks on a tray and slopped them down on the table, spilling beer onto the bowl of complimentary peanuts.

"Two beers, one vodka and tonic, and an orange juice."

"Oh," said Karen, staring at the tonic bottle, "Don't you have slimline?"

"Please, dear," he replied, placing one hand on the back of her chair and the other on his hip, "Look at the state of this shithole. You're lucky we've got ice."

I tapped him on the arm.

"Could I get a beer too, please?" I asked, "And maybe some more nuts?"

He mumbled something and walked back to the bar. I assumed that meant yes.

"I'll have to allow for this, Lee," Karen said, pouring the tonic water into her glass.

"Relax doll, you're on holiday now," Leroy replied, and then to me he said, "She's been dieting. Lost loads haven't you, babe?"

My God, how big must she have been to start with?

"I've still got a long way to go, though," Karen replied, "But it will be worth it in the end."

Leroy placed his arm around her and kissed her cheek. "I love you whatever," he told her.

He started nuzzling her neck. Karen laughed and pushed his head away.

"Get off," she said.

They seemed like good kids to me. I say kids, they were probably around twenty. My God when did I reach the age where I started referring to anyone under twenty-five as a kid? Glum barman returned with my beer and slammed it down on the table. The top third was froth.

"I see you give good head," I told him, before realising how wrong that sounded.

"Ooh, someone's read the graffiti in the village."

"I was talking about the beer," I said, "Could I get a top up."

The barman sighed and picked up the glass.

"I don't really enjoy froth in my mouth," I added.

"Yes dear, you've made that quite clear," glum barman replied.

"I was still talking about the beer," I called after him as he made his way back to the bar.

I had a quick glance around the room while I waited to get my drink. It wasn't a large space but there was room enough for a few tables and a small raised area over by the window at the back, which I assumed was used as some kind of stage. The bar itself was squashed into a corner beside the rather splendid, but unloved fireplace. It was a shame really, as the hotel, with a bit of money spent on it, could look amazing. Glum barman returned with my drink.

"One beer no froth," he said, as he put the glass down.

"Thank you," I replied, "Are my nuts still coming?"

"Really dear, I'm a barman; not a doctor."

He was gone before I realised what he meant.

"Are you all alone, Derek?"

Lauren was looking at me sympathetically and for a split second I thought she was talking about my life rather than the trip, but really it amounted to the same thing.

"Yes," I told her, "I'm travelling alone." I explained that I was recently divorced.

"My parents divorced when I was six," Lauren said, "But they get on okay now; well, apart from the arguing."

She started laughing. "It's quite funny really, mum calling dad a useless prick with a brain the size of a pea and him calling her a lazy slag who wears fur around her dress hem to keep her neck warm. It made the wedding day really didn't it?"

Lauren seemed like a lovely, young woman but she wasn't the sharpest knife in the drawer. I wondered how she and Pete had ever got together, he being the strong silent type. They seemed like chalk and cheese but then I wouldn't necessarily have put Leroy and Karen together as a couple either. Karen was an attractive looking girl but I imagined Leroy as more of a 'play the field' kind of guy; the type of bloke who would be out each night picking up a different girl, usually the thin blonde ones with big tits. I didn't see him as a long-term relationship man, especially with someone of Karen's size. But then what did I know about dating and attraction; here I was on holiday, alone.

We continued chatting and a short while later Shauna poked her head around the door and told us our rooms were ready. We finished our drinks, picked up our luggage in the hallway and followed her upstairs. She showed the young ones to two rooms on the first floor and then led me up another staircase. At the top, the stairs split two ways. Shauna took the left hand side.

"Here we are, Dirk; this is your room, number nine. Angie is across the stairs at number eight and you have the lezzas opposite you at number ten."

"Right, ok…sorry; who?"

"Flossie, Floozy; whatever those two old-fashioned birds are called."

"They're not lezzas," I whispered the last word, "They're widows, at least one of them is."

Shauna sighed at me, condescendingly. "Believe me, Dirk; I've been in this game a long time and I know what I'm talking about. I've seen it all; wife swapping during a coach tour of Norfolk churches, orgies at a pensioners' whist drive in Somerset; a mystery weekend where the real mystery turned out to be, what was Mr Preston doing hanging upside down in the wardrobe with an apple in his mouth."

I should have booked a flight to Spain.

"Your lives, your secrets; they'll all be revealed eventually," Shauna continued, "It always happens on a coach trip."

I couldn't believe our little group had any hidden secrets worth hearing about.

"I think you're wrong about those two anyway," I told her; "They're just a couple of innocents, living in a world where for them; it's still the nineteen fifties."

"We'll see," Shauna replied, as she turned and walked back down the staircase, "They're probably at it right now. See you at dinner, Dirk. Seven o'clock sharp."

I couldn't believe some of the stuff that was coming out of Shauna's mouth. Still, I did quickly listen in at their door; just to prove I was right.

"I can't get it in like that," I heard.

"Wait a minute; I'll try pulling the flaps further apart."

Oh God.

"No stop, that's not working. I need to get a better grip."

"Would it help if I tried to squeeze a bit more air out?"

I really shouldn't be listening to this.

"Hang on, how about if I lift this up and jiggle that?"

"Oh yes; that's got it. The suitcase is now safely under the bed."

Phew. I unlocked my door and went in.

I suspected that when the hotel was originally built it was as a house for the local landowner. My room was definitely one of those that had been set aside for the servants to sleep in. It was rather small and lacked the grandeur of the rooms downstairs. It was dark when I entered but heavy floor to ceiling curtains were pulled across the window. I walked over and pulled them back, only to discover one tiny, high window behind. If you stood tiptoe on a chair you had a lovely view across the front drive to the fields beyond but the room remained pretty dark.

To compensate it did look to have been decorated more recently than the other rooms I had seen so far. The wallpaper was mostly white with a delicate floral pattern on it. The bedspread and curtains matched the motif and it did feel rather cosy. There was only a single bed but this left space for the mahogany wardrobe and matching chest of drawers. The room also had a small, original fireplace with a black grate in it and beside that stood a washstand with mirror above. There was a narrow door next to this and upon opening I discovered the toilet. Glancing up I saw a shower head had been attached to the wall above it. Not so much a wet room as a wet cupboard. Still, I could shit and shower at the same time and if I stood on my head it could double as the bidet. Not ideal but seeing how today had panned out so far; at least it was my own 'en suite' and I didn't have to share it with anyone.

When I entered the dining room later on everybody else was

already seated at tables of four. The youngsters were all together, Josie & Sooz were sat with the nagging couple and Dora and Margaret had got Colin.

"Over here, Dirk," Shauna waved me over.

"You're with us," she said.

Fortunately that included Angela as well as Shauna and Jim. She beamed at me as I sat down beside her. Jim appeared to be in another world after the events of the day and was talking to himself under his breath.

"As we're only a small group, Dirk; it's best that we all eat together at the same time," Shauna said.

"Right," I replied, "Is there a menu?"

"No, it's a set meal apparently," Angela told me.

"Oh, what if I'm a vegetarian?"

"Are you?" asked Shauna.

"Well, no."

"So there's no problem then."

An overpowering smell of cheap aftershave entered the room. At least I hoped it was aftershave and not the first course. A figure appeared beside our table.

"Good evening. I am Chico and I will be your waiter for the week."

Chico was wearing black leather trousers and a white shirt opened to the navel. He wore a large, gold crucifix on a chain but there was a distinct lack of hair both on his pigeon chest and the top of his head to complete the look he was obviously going for; that of greasy, seventies, medallion man. The greying pony tail didn't really help either, nor the exaggerated Italian accent. His eyes were firmly fixed on Shauna as he spoke.

"Can I get a drink for the most beautiful woman in the room?" he asked, thrusting his groin in her direction.

"Do you have a wine list," she asked.

"Red or white?"

"Is that the whole selection?"

"Poterla raccomanda un buono vino rosso?" Angela said.

"Scusi?" Chico was taken aback.

"Can you recommend a good red wine?" she translated.

"But of course I know what you said, beautiful lady," it was Angela's turn to receive the Chico charm, "Please, allow me to select a bottle for you, cara mia. And for you," he added, looking back at Shauna again, "I have something long, full-bodied and tasty."

"I'd prefer an orange juice," she said.

"I'll make sure it's a large one."

Shauna rolled her eyes.

"That was very impressive Italian, Angela," I said, after Chico had left.

"Smooth Dirk," Shauna whispered, but I ignored her.

"Do you speak it fluently?"

"Oh, not at all," Angela smiled, "Just a little picked up on my travels. I only speak a very small amount."

"I have a feeling that goes for the waiter as well," I said, "I'm not sure I'd trust his knowledge on wine either. I hate to think what he's going to bring over; probably something in a plastic bottle that's labelled, 'Red.'"

The dining room was like all the other rooms in the hotel; lovely original features but needed a lot of updating. The room was at the front of the house and had a beautiful bay window with original shutters and expensive looking but dated curtains. The windowsills were starting to disintegrate from damp due to ill-fitting panes of glass. They needed replacing but I guess the owner didn't have the money to do it. No wonder she was so cheerful earlier on at having us as a late booking. Without us there were only three other people eating in the dining room.

"Who's that sitting with Margaret, Dora and Colin?" I asked Angela.

"Oh, that's Harry, Harry Towler. He's a very charming man. He's already taken the time to speak with everyone here."

I wasn't sure I liked the way Angela smiled as she spoke about him.

"Apparently he's having a barn converted into his dream home and is staying here while the final finishing touches are being put in place. It's his sports car outside."

Harry had obviously worked his charm on Dora as well who was positively glowing while holding court at her table although that could have been the gin. She was still talking loudly, something about selling her husband's business a few years ago; I didn't really pay too much attention. Margaret was smiling a lot too.

Chico returned with a bottle of red wine and Angela asked if I'd like to share it with her. I said yes, even though I hated red wine. The soup soon followed.

"This," said Chico, to Shauna, "Is like me."

"Lukewarm and past its best?" she asked, grimacing as she gave it a stir.

"It's hot and spicy." Cue another hip thrust.

It definitely was hot but not in a nice way. It tasted like someone had accidently dropped curry powder into a tin of mushroom soup. At the table opposite, nagging wife, who I found out was called Maeve, was still berating her husband; Gerald. I watched as she tugged the napkin out of the neck of his shirt where he'd placed it and tossed it into his lap instead. When he spilt some soup on his shirt (where his napkin had originally been) she moaned about that too. There was no need for it, or for her to wet her napkin in water and start trying to clean him up like he was a complete incompetent. It was embarrassing but he just sat there and took it. These were the only two people left that I hadn't officially met so far and I was certainly in no hurry to say hello to them.

Being served by Chico made us one of the more fortunate tables as the other side of the room was being looked after by Louella. She was still walking painfully slowly and the soup kept spilling over every time she moved her walking frame forwards. The result was that we were finished with the starters on our side a lot quicker than the others. Dora's table was also being served by Chico and Harry came over between courses and introduced himself to me. He looked to be a well preserved sixty-five. His white hair was short and neat and he wore a grey suit with a delicate blue shirt and tie and matching handkerchief.

"Derek, it's nice to meet you," he said, shaking my hand with both of his, "I've heard so much about you from our Angela here."

Angela smiled and blushed. What did he mean 'our' Angela; and what had she been telling him? He was a bit too, 'in your face' for my liking; acting as though he'd known me for years.

"Hope you enjoy your stay here," he said, "It's a little bit, shall we say, rustic; but Mrs Goddard does try her best; even though it appears her hotel is falling down around her ears. Anyway, must dash, have to phone New York; business meeting; very boring, but hope to catch up with you later."

With that, he was gone.

Once Louella had finally finished clearing the bowls on her side of the room, the main course (a stew) was brought in. Jim overturned the saltcellar which in his world was a calamity of epic proportions. He quickly threw some over his shoulder. It should have been a pinch rather than a handful and Colin wasn't best pleased at his shower. He took a piece of paper out of his bag and wrote something down. I heard him muttering under his breath about another item for the phone call and Mr Scrimshaw receiving a mouthful when he got home. Jim was too anxious to notice. He pulled a lucky rabbit's foot out of his pocket and placed it on the table beside him. It was rather off putting as that's what was in the stew.

Mrs Goddard came in while a dessert of ice cream was being served.

"Everyone happy; good, good," she said, "Now we do have some entertainment for you in the bar after dinner so please go in, relax and enjoy a very pleasant evening."

She bustled out again before anyone had a chance to say anything.

"I wonder what the entertainment will be," Angela mused.

"Probably the glum barman singing, 'I'm so glad to be me,'" I said. But as nobody at my table had met the barman yet I didn't get the laugher I was expecting.

For some reason we sat in the bar in the same groups that we'd sat in at dinner. I don't think glum barman had ever had this many people to serve before. He wasn't happy although he did have a bit of help from another member of staff. Louella really did work long hours in this place. All drink orders were added to a room's tab, to be paid off at the end of the week. This was a good idea on Mrs Goddard's part as, with no actual money being passed over at the bar, we probably all drank more than we normally would; especially as the singer was taking ages to set up his microphone and equipment.

"You know I'm worried about those four," Angela said to me, indicating the youngsters, "This can't be much of a trip for them."

"It's not been much of a trip for any of us," I replied, "Besides, they seem happy enough."

"Yes, but imagine having to spend a whole week with a load of pensioners."

"I'm not quite that old."

Angela grinned. "You know what I mean," she said, "I was thinking, how about one night you take the boys out to a pub and I'll have an evening here with the girls. What do you think?"

"I think that they wouldn't want to spend time with people of our…of my age either."

"Well, we're the best hope they've got," Angela said, "I thought it would be nice for them."

"If they're up for it, I'm happy to do it," I said.

"Great." She squeezed my hand again.

It looked like the singer was finally ready and a hush fell over the room. After greeting us all and apologising for the delay; he actually treated our group to an evening of bird impressions.

Chapter 4

It wasn't the most comfortable night I've ever spent in a hotel. I fell out of bed twice. The last time I'd had to sleep in a single was just before my wedding, back in my old room at my parents' house; shoved in beside the sewing machine, mannequin and all manner of other sewing implements and materials my mother had stuffed the room with after I'd left for university. Of course the amount of alcohol I'd consumed last night might also have played a part in why I woke up face down on the carpet.

I wasn't the only one to end up a little bit tipsy. Most of us were enjoying a good drink and we started doing our own bird impressions, much to the annoyance of the guy on stage. Angela and I quacked a lot around Colin to remind him of his boat trip. Dora's goose was more a hand gesture than a sound and the noise glum barman made when he passed too close to her table was very reminiscent of a peacock. It was a shame he was carrying a tray full of drinks at the time. Maeve's 'old crow' was uncanny and she managed to stay in character for the entire evening, just on orange juice. We called an end to the night when Leroy said he was going to climb the tree out front and shit on the windscreen of the coach.

Breakfast was a buffet affair. In the list of rules pasted on the back of the bedroom door it stated that it was served from seven until nine. What this actually meant was the food was cooked at seven and you then had two hours to eat it in. When I entered the dining room at eight o'clock the fried eggs were so cold and rubbery I dispensed with my plate and searched for a ping pong bat instead. I was going to complain to the chef but the only time he emerged from the kitchen he was wearing a blood-stained apron and carrying a meat cleaver. I didn't think it was the right time to approach him with any form of criticism.

"I'm off to get the chicken," he shouted, to someone through the swing doors, "Can you smell those meatballs for me."

Mmm, looking forward to dinner already.

I decided against the cooked breakfast and moved over to the cereal section. Just at that moment Louella shuffled into the dining room from the kitchen with a plate of toast balanced on her walking frame. Slices were falling off left and right as she made her way to the table.

"Cat's mistaken the muesli for the kitty litter again," she said, to no one in particular, before turning round and hobbling back through the swing doors.

I just had coffee. Looking about me I think everyone else had done the same thing; all except Colin, who was happily wolfing down a lukewarm Full English.

The most amazing thing at breakfast was Jim. He bounced into the room all smiling and happy; greeting everybody warmly by name. We were too startled to respond. Only Shauna seemed unfazed by the whole thing and she rolled her eyes when he sat down beside her with some coffee and the one piece of toast that Louella had managed to get onto the table.

We had a full day's excursion on the itinerary for today, a trip to a village called Baddlesbury. Apparently it was a well-preserved, medieval village full of old, timbered buildings dating back to the fourteenth and fifteenth centuries. I was hoping Angela and I would spend the day exploring it together.

We had half an hour after breakfast before the coach left but I only had to collect my jacket and camera and so was back downstairs in five minutes. I saw Harry talking with Margaret by the door to her room as I passed through the hallway. She and Dora had a room on the ground floor at the back of the hotel. Margaret was certainly looking livelier and more cheerful than I'd seen her so far. I guess anytime away from her constant drain of a mother was like a breath of fresh air. As I pulled on my jacket by the ornate mirror in the hallway so I heard Dora's voice from within their room.

"Margaret, come and help me take my medication."

Margaret shrugged her shoulders and smiled at Harry before disappearing back into her room. He saw me and walked over.

"Marvellous woman isn't she," he said, "So kind and generous, and actually very interesting once you get a chance to talk with her."

I smiled as a response. Harry patted me on the back.

"Have a good day, old boy," he barked, "Wish I was coming with you but work beckons. A barn doesn't just convert itself you know." He chuckled and disappeared back upstairs.

I really didn't like him. He was far too smug and sure of himself. The guy was able to collect his old age pension and yet Angela and Margaret were all smiley and giggly around him. I couldn't understand it. I bet his barn was some huge place set in acres of beautiful grounds. I wish we'd let Leroy shit on his sports car last night. I made my way outside to the coach.

"You're early, Dirk," Shauna said, "Only the lezzas have beaten you."

I ignored her and climbed on board where I found Jim shaking and sweating again. I turned back to Shauna.

"What's happened?"

She sighed. "Oh, he said he saw a black cat."

"I thought that was meant to be lucky." Although it hadn't been for the muesli, let's face it.

Shauna shrugged her shoulders. "It beats me, Dirk," she

said, "He mumbled something about witches. I had to drag the little prick out here."

Now there was a holiday photo opportunity missed. I made my way down the coach and sat in the same seat as yesterday. Gerald and Maeve were the next to get on.

"Have you got your camera?"

"Yes dear."

"Keep it over your shoulder; you don't want to lose it again do you."

"No dear."

"Are you sure that jacket is warm enough?"

"Yes dear."

"Are you wearing your vest?"

Oh please, not the vest again. Maeve was nothing if not consistent in her tirade against the poor man. When was he going to take his bollocks back off her and stand up for himself?

Angela got on next and came and sat beside me.

"I'm looking forward to today," she said, brimming with excitement, "I love old villages."

"Let's hope they have a decent coffee shop," I replied, "I think instant coffee around here is called that because that's how long the flavour lasts."

Angela laughed. "I'm sure we'll find you one when we get there," she told me, squeezing my hand again. She was a very tactile person.

"What's happened to Jim, by the way?"

"Black cat."

"Isn't that meant to be lucky?"

"That's what I thought," I said.

Angela sighed. "Well I hope we don't have another journey like yesterday."

"I know. There are so many winding, country lanes around

here and Jim doesn't seem to like driving on them."

"He doesn't seem to like driving, full stop."

I laughed. "You'd think it would be a lot easier now with Sat Nav."

"Apparently he left his behind on the coach that wouldn't start yesterday," Angela said, "When Shauna told me that she was the recorded voice all the drivers had to use I understood why."

We continued chatting while waiting for the rest of the party to arrive. Angela talked about her travels around the world and the various antiques and curios she'd picked up. I'd never actually asked what she did for a living but from what she was saying, I assumed it must be something to do with a museum or auction house. Her enthusiasm for history was infectious and I couldn't wait to explore the village now either; especially as it did seem we were going to be doing it together.

The youngsters were the last to board and then we set off. I heard the microphone switch on, although I don't think Shauna realised she'd pressed the button.

"Well if you think you're going to hyperventilate breathe into your paper bag; only for God's sake, this time will you remember to pull over first. Agnes told me all about the Folkestone trip. You bounced up the kerb and sent her flying face first into that poor bloke's lap. Apparently he's still got four of her teeth stuck in his…oh bugger. Erm, I have some info for you on the village we're going to today Ladies and Gents. It's all written down on this pamphlet. Well, there's no point in me learning all this shit; is there."

"She really gives a hundred per cent to her job, doesn't she," I whispered, to Angela.

"Right then; Baddlesbury is a fine example of an affluent, medieval village with its half-timbered cottages and impressive fifteenth century church. Its wealth came from the wool trade. No one is sure of the meaning of the word 'Baddle' but it's assumed it was originally 'Battle' and has just altered over the course of time; probably due to the generations of inbreeding that's rife around here."

"I don't think that last part's in the leaflet," Angela whispered back.

"The Dukes of Tenham once owned the land the village is built on and the eldest son always took the title, Lord Baddlesbury. During the Second World War there was an airbase nearby and a number of American servicemen from the U.S Air Force were billeted there. Due to their love of the local tavern with all of its draught beers, the name of the pub was changed from The Brewery Tap, to The Faucet Inn. Oh God, force it in; they're taking the piss! Anyway, the pub serves a decent enough lunch and there's the church and a museum that's apparently worth seeing. Not my thing really, old relics; no offence. We'll be there until five; mill around if you get bored."

Shauna sat back down in her seat.

"Well I'm sold after that glowing recommendation," I said.

"Me too," Angela replied, "Really looking forward to the milling around. Do you think we should do that first before going on to the museum?"

I laughed. "Sorry," I said, "First thing on the list is a coffee."

We drove through the village to get to the car park beside the pub. It really was beautiful. The road curved on the way in so that nothing could be seen until we drove over a small, arched bridge and then suddenly the whole of the main street was in front of us. Aside from the parked cars and telephone wires it was just like stepping back in time. The timbered houses leaned together at awkward angles, so old they needed the support of their neighbour to remain standing. I don't know what that did to the floors inside but I had a feeling you'd walk across them the same way I'd staggered across the one in my room last night after all the booze.

We were let off the coach before Jim attempted to back it into a parking space which must have given us an extra half an hour in the village by my calculation. Actually, to be fair, it had been a good drive really. Only Colin got off the coach, paper bag in hand saying, "Oh, what a journey;" but then he was the only one to have stuffed his face at breakfast time. Angela took my arm.

"Right," she said, "Coffee."

We walked back through the village the way we had driven in and found a charming, little café nestled between a private dwelling and a small newsagents-come-grocer. It was open but empty. In fact the whole street seemed deserted but then it was a not very touristy Tuesday and the local residents would all be out at work or going about their daily business like everybody else. The middle-aged man behind the counter leapt up as soon as we entered.

"I thought I saw a coach pass by," he said.

"Don't get too excited," I told him, "We're not exactly a big group."

We sat down at a table by the window which was covered in a light-blue, gingham tablecloth. There was a thin, glass vase in the centre with a real Gerbera in it. As I looked around I noticed all the tables were dressed the same with only the colour of the flower changing. We ordered coffee and a couple of homemade muffins. As we waited for the man to make our drinks on the beautiful, big, shiny coffee-making machine behind the counter, so the door opened and in walked Maeve and Gerald.

"See," I heard her say, "I said we'd find somewhere if we walked in this direction."

"Yes dear."

Gerald waved as soon as he saw us but there was no acknowledgement from Maeve.

"Don't be stupid Gerald; there'll be a draft by the window. Do you want a stiff neck? Come on; we'll sit over there at the back."

"Be with you in a minute," the owner called over pleasantly, to them.

"Take your coat off, Gerald. You won't feel the benefit when you go out again."

"I'm ok, dear."

"Take it off, Gerald."

He took it off.

The owner brought over our coffee and muffins and then went across to serve them. Gerald was perusing through the menu; Maeve was wiping the cutlery with a napkin.

"Do you fancy something to eat, dear?" Gerald asked.

"Pot of tea for two," Maeve said, to the owner; ignoring her husband.

"My God, how does he stand that woman?" I whispered to Angela.

"They've obviously been together a long time," she said, "I guess they must be used to each other's little ways."

I couldn't stop staring. The owner brought over the crockery and a china teapot he'd just filled. Maeve laid out the cups and saucers and poured the milk. She then poured a little tea into her cup, sighed, took the lid off the teapot and gave it a good stir before pouring again. Gerald helped himself to sugar.

"One spoon, Gerald," she said, "You don't need any more

than that."

"Maybe she's wild in the sack," I suggested, "There's got to be some reason he sticks with her."

"Derek, you're terrible," Angela replied, grinning, "I'm sure she has many hidden qualities. Of course sex may be one of them."

"I bet she tells him what to do in bed as well," I said, "No, don't grip me there; more to the left. You thrust when I tell you to. Don't you dare orgasm before me; you know I always go first."

We both started laughing, but stopped abruptly when Maeve looked over. She reached for her handbag.

"Now, where did I put my pills?" she said.

As she looked in her bag so Gerald took the opportunity to put another spoonful of sugar into his tea. He saw me watching and winked. I smiled back but it all just seemed so pathetic. Was he that scared of his wife?

The coffee and muffins were the nicest things I'd had since leaving home yesterday morning. I insisted on paying and then Angela and I walked further along up the high street. She took my arm again. There was a slight chill in the air this morning although the sun was trying to break through the cloud, its dappled light shimmering on the pavement where we walked.

We saw a sign that advertised a Farmers' Market in the square on Tuesday, Thursday and Saturday afternoons. We followed the arrow pointing us up a side street to the right and came out into the square itself. This area had more people strolling about. There were shops, mostly selling antiques and touristy gifts; and the skeletal structures for the stalls had already been assembled, awaiting their striped covers which were piled up neatly nearby. A market cross stood in the middle of the square but unfortunately it was surrounded by a number of parking spaces, each of which was being used by a car or van and this did detract from the medieval character. Angela pointed to the far side where the museum was and we made our way over to it.

We spent a very pleasant couple of hours there on our own away from the rest of the group. The museum was set out as a history tour of the village from its earliest settlers up to the present day. I enjoyed learning about the years of prosperity, its nineteenth century decline and later restoration. The museum itself had been both a prison and a workhouse in its time, although I couldn't really see any difference between the two. There were photos of the building before it had been restored forty years ago and it was amazing to think that at one time, someone could have covered those stunning beams behind plaster and stone cladding and also for the next owner to have realised its potential and complete the pain-staking restoration back to its former glory. I emerged from the museum on a high.

We made our way back to the pub for lunch. I'd so enjoyed my morning with Angela that I felt a little disappointed when I found the rest of the group already there.

"Where do you want to sit?" Angela asked.

"Hmm, what a choice," I said, "The nagging wife, the blind driver or the lezzas."

"The who?"

"Shit; sorry. That's not what I meant to say; it was Shauna who…I'll explain later."

I felt so guilty about what I'd said that we did go and sit with Josie and Sooz. The table was beside the four youngsters. We ordered drinks and some lunch and began chatting; all of us talking about what we'd done that morning. Most of the group had gone over to the church first. Apparently you were able to climb the tower and the views from the top were spectacular.

"That part's not always open," Sooz said, "They say that if it gets too windy it's possible to get sucked off."

"I prayed for a gale while I was up there," Leroy nudged me in the ribs, "If you know what I mean."

I smiled politely.

"I'm talking about blow jobs."

"Yes." I said, "I know what you meant."

Josie tapped me on the arm and leaned in towards me.

"Derek, I thought I knew what he meant but I'm sure I ask for a cut and blow job at the hairdressers."

"You ask for a cut and blow dry," I told her.

"Do I?"

"God I hope so."

The conversation moved on. Karen informed me about the amount of calories and fat I was consuming in my lunch, which I could well have done without, and this brought up the subject of Lauren's pregnancy cravings. We then heard all about her job.

"I'm so going to miss it when I go on maternity leave," she said, "I like all of it really, but my favourite bit is the waxing."

"So you're a sadist," I said.

"No Derek; I told you, I'm a beauty therapist," she started laughing; "Do you remember when I first started out and practised on you, Pete?"

Pete looked like he wanted the ground to open up and swallow him.

"I did his legs first, that went okay didn't it."

"Stop it, Lauren," Pete whispered, but she was in full flow.

"And then I tried the back, sack and crack, didn't I. It took ages to do. Pete is rather hairy down there."

We were all feeling a little uncomfortable now.

"I caught your foreskin at one point."

Oh dear God.

Lauren chuckled. "Well it just popped out of the towel as I ripped. We often laugh about that now don't we?"

"I've certainly got a tear in my eye," I said, as I picked up a spoonful of chilli.

"I waxed you shut, didn't I Karen."

My spoon clattered back into the bowl. Karen looked mortified.

"She didn't know until she needed to wee and couldn't."

Lauren was shaking her head and smiling; a faraway look in her eye as she recalled these stories; thinking of them as happy memories of long ago that one didn't want to forget. I picked up my spoon again.

"Do you know; it's really interesting how different women's vaginas can be?"

I wasn't going to finish my lunch.

"There are so many different shapes and sizes. They change as you age too. Some hang really low…"

"Alright, Lauren," said Pete, in a harsh whisper, "For God's sake, enough fanny talk."

The table fell silent. It's the most I'd heard Pete say. I was glad he'd stopped the conversation but Lauren looked crestfallen, not really understanding the reason for his outburst. I tried to lighten the mood.

"Still," I said, "Pete's just come up with an idea for the baby's name if it's a girl."

I got a few polite smiles and a couple of chuckles but Lauren looked puzzled.

"I don't think Vagina's a good name for a baby, Derek."

"No I didn't mean that, you see Pete said…"

"I've not heard of that before."

"Bless you, you've got the wrong end of the stick; what I

meant was…"

"I guess you could shorten it to Gina. That's quite nice actually."

"No," I said, my voice rising, "I was talking about Fanny." A hush fell across the entire room.

"Geez, Dirk," Shauna called over, "That's hardly a lunchtime conversation, is it. Most people just stick to the weather."

I was glad when lunch was over. Angela and I left the pub and walked across to the church. She'd mentioned to the youngsters her thoughts about a night out and they'd all said it was a great idea. So in the next couple of days I would be out pubbing it with a couple of twenty year old lads. I wasn't sure what sort of evening that would prove to be but I guessed there'd be no fanny talk; although now I came to think about it…

The church was large for a village this size owing to the rich locals in the wool trade wanting to get to heaven and donating heavily to the building works. A Yew hedge led the way through the churchyard to the entrance. It was mostly one large open area, a cavernous space interspersed with tall, theatrical columns climbing skyward towards heaven. The feeling of calm serenity hit us as soon as we entered and every time Angela or I spoke, it was in barely a whisper. Standing in the nave we looked up towards the majestic stained-glass window at the back of the chancel, even at this distance the colours so full and striking it enticed us forwards to take a closer look.

Afterwards we walked over to the stone staircase leading up to the top of the tower, passing the eagle shaped lectern and gifts area selling postcards, pens and books about the church. It was a hundred and ten feet up and a long climb. I hadn't been to the gym for over six months and I felt every step; although I

71

put some of my heavy panting down to having Angela's bum in my face the whole time.

The views were as spectacular as they'd been described to us. From the high vantage point we could see for miles across rolling hills. The wind whipped at my face and stung my eyes but I didn't care. The sun had burnt off most of the cloud now, leaving only delicate white wisps in an endless sky of blue. Fields of meadow flowers and crops carpeted the landscape, divided only by leafy hedgerows; giving the vista a checker board effect. In one field sheep were being herded by a Border collie, while in the next, young foals were prancing and cavorting around; only stopping to get a drink from their mothers.

It was a peaceful, pastoral scene I was watching and yet, in the country lanes that meandered between the villages in the distance, I couldn't help noticing a number of lorries transporting their cargo to distant places; spoiling the sereneness of the areas as they thundered down placid high streets. In some areas red roof cottages nestled between an abundance of trees while in others lone trees stood enclosed by an abundance of red roofs. New housing developments on the outskirts were casting their arms out wide, eager to join others and swallow up the identities of the individual villages forever.

Angela and I moved around the top of the tower. As we reached the opposite side from the staircase so we saw Gerald gazing out at the view. He jumped at the sound of footsteps and spun round, quickly pulling a cigarette out of his mouth.

"Oh, it's you two," he said, relieved, and took another drag, "I thought Maeve had changed her mind and come up the stairs."

"I take it your wife doesn't know you smoke," I said.

Gerald shook his head as he took a final puff.

"No," he told us, dropping the butt and treading on it, before picking it up and placing it inside a tissue, "She thought I'd stopped years ago."

He reached into his rucksack and pulled out a container of fabric freshener.

"It was a lot easier to get away with it when you could still smoke inside pubs," he said, giving us all a quick spray, "It didn't matter if I smelled a little of smoke then. I could blame it on someone else; but now…" He shrugged his shoulders.

"I'm surprised Maeve allows you to go out to the pub on your own," I said.

Angela shot me a look but I couldn't help it. Gerald laughed.

"Yes," he replied, "Maeve likes to keep me on the straight and narrow where she can. But I do prefer a quiet beer at home these days anyway."

I bet you do, I thought.

Gerald placed the freshener back inside the rucksack and produced a packet of mints. After offering to us first, he unwrapped one and popped it into his mouth.

"Maeve and I both gave up the cigarettes together," he said, between chews, "She has more willpower than me. I don't want to disappoint her by letting her know I started again."

Too scared to tell her more like.

We all looked out at the view in silence while Gerald finished his mint. This side of the tower looked across Baddlesbury itself, the roofs of the houses as crooked as the buildings they covered. From up here I could see the river that skirted around the edge of the village before heading out through the fields beyond. The Square was a lot busier now that the stalls had finished being set up for the Farmers' Market.

Gerald sighed. "It's so beautiful up here," he said, "But I

suppose I should be getting back to Maeve."

"I'm sure she's fine where she is," I told him, "Stay up here for longer if you want to."

"No," he said, "No I really should get back to her."

"What will she do, smack your bum if you're late?"

"Derek," Angela quietly admonished, but I couldn't help it. The woman was running this poor man ragged.

"Nothing like that," Gerald said to me, "It's just…it's just…I just worry about her."

Just talking about her was making him all flustered.

"Of course you do," Angela said, "It's natural. We all worry about our loved ones."

Gerald smiled gratefully at her.

"Yes," he said, "Yes, I suppose we all do."

"I don't think you need to worry about your wife though," I was off again, "She gives the impression she can take care of herself."

Gerald smiled broadly, as if I'd just paid him a huge compliment.

"Oh yes, definitely," he said, "Maeve has always been the strong one."

The grin disappeared as quickly as it had emerged and his face crumpled.

"Oh dear," he said, "So stupid of me."

He reached back into his rucksack again for a tissue and dabbed at his eyes. It was the same tissue he'd wrapped the cigarette butt in and I watched as it fell out and got caught on the breeze, sailing gently away over the top of the tower. Angela and I stood there in silence, not really understanding what was going on.

"Maeve's sick," he said, wiping his nose, "She has cancer. Thought she'd beaten it five years ago but it came back on our

Golden Wedding last year. Afraid it's beaten her this time."

"I'm so sorry," said Angela, moving closer to him and rubbing his arm. I was rooted to the spot.

"She only has months left at best," Gerald said, "I don't know what I'm going to do without her. Maeve's my life. She's always been there for me and our two sons. She's continuously pushed and encouraged me. Without her help I'd never have opened our Stationery business. She worked tirelessly in the office but still somehow made sure there was a home cooked meal on the table for the family every night. I don't know how she did it. Even now, all she's thinking about is me; making sure I can cope with the everyday things when she's…when she's no longer here to look after me."

Gerald turned back to look out at the view again. We waited patiently while he composed himself.

"Please don't let on you know," he said, turning back to face us again, "Maeve doesn't want to spoil anyone's holiday with this."

"We won't say a word," Angela told him.

I was too dumbstruck to speak.

"This is our last little trip together," Gerald whispered.

Jesus Christ, I hope Maeve hadn't been hoping for the Orient Express and got this.

"I'd best get back to her now," Gerald said, pulling his rucksack onto his shoulder.

As he passed by us Angela silently stopped him and gave him a hug. He smiled at us both and then disappeared down the stairs. The wind was still blowing into my eyes but that was no longer the reason why they were stinging.

Chapter 5

It's always sad to hear news about someone who's dying but when it's a person you've taken an instant dislike to and whom you've ridiculed behind their back; there's an overpowering feeling of guilt. Angela and I remained at the top of the tower, standing where Gerald had stood, not saying anything to each other; both lost in our own thoughts. Eventually a young family emerged from the staircase, chatting and laughing loudly and this broke the silence.

"Let's go shall we?" I said.

Angela nodded.

We made our way out of the church and walked back down the high street, past the café and straight on out of the village to where I'd seen the river from the top of the tower. A short way along the bank there was a rustic-looking wooden footbridge and we walked onto it and stood in the middle. Only then did we speak.

"Oh God," I said, leaning on the handrail, my head in my hands, "That was so awful. I feel terrible."

"You weren't to know, Derek," Angela said, rubbing my back, "Neither of us did. I thought she was just a nagging, miserable, old woman the same as you."

"But the ribbing about their sex life, in the coffee shop, this morning. Oh my God!"

"Don't beat yourself up like this, Derek. You can't change what has been done and it's not like you said anything to her face. You haven't actually hurt her."

I looked up into Angela's eyes. "I just feel so guilty."

"I know," she told me, "I do too, but it's not our fault that she's ill. It's tragic but we can't do anything about it. How about we dwell on the number of years they've had together. There aren't many people that reach their golden wedding these days. That's pretty special, however sad that their time together is coming to an end."

"You're right," I said, standing up again, "I know you're right. I'm still going to feel guilty, but you're right."

"Are you trying to tell me, albeit subtly; that I'm right?" Angela asked.

I couldn't help smiling. "Yes; and I bet you're never wrong are you."

"Never."

We took a quiet walk along the riverbank, chatting sporadically; but it was only idle small talk; neither of us able to forget the news we'd just heard. I couldn't help remembering Shauna's words from yesterday, "Your life, your secrets; they'll all be revealed eventually." In the space of two minutes up on the tower Gerald had indeed spoken of his life with Maeve and revealed her secret. What else was I destined to discover this week; Colin worked as a gym instructor; Dora was Miss Home Counties 1945; Lauren was a member of MENSA?

It was better to dwell on the fifty years Maeve and Gerald had been together as Angela had said. It was something I wouldn't experience. I felt a pang of jealousy for this couple that I'd been ridiculing. I'd fully expected to grow old with Leanne and had thought us settled. We'd been married for fourteen years after all and had lived together for six before that. We'd discussed having children earlier on, but in the last few years I hadn't even brought the subject up. Why was that? Too afraid of her answer I suppose. Didn't that make me the husband scared of his wife rather than Gerald? I pictured Leanne and me on our Golden Wedding. My God; I **was**

Gerald.

The sun remained with us and in the sheltered spots along the riverbank it now felt quite warm; warm enough to sit down for a while and enjoy the countryside. I made the gallant gesture of placing my jacket on the ground for Angela to sit on. It would have been more romantic if she hadn't sat right on my keys but I think the action was appreciated.

The setting was beautiful and the only sounds around us were birdsong and the gentle rustling of leaves in the breeze. It should have been a pleasant experience but the news about Maeve had cast a long shadow and the conversation dried up completely as we sat there. We really needed to be around other people.

"Shall we head back to the Farmers' Market," I said.

Angela readily agreed.

There was a steady throng of people in the market square now and a distinct buzz in the air with the sound of excited chatter alongside the clamour of heels on cobbles and the raised voices of the stallholders advertising their wares. Upon entering we bumped straight into Josie.

"All on your own?" Angela asked her.

"I've left Sooz looking round the antiques shops," Josie said, "I went in the first one with her but that was enough for me. I'm not into knick-knacks like she is. I much prefer a good book."

"Something classical," I suggested.

"Oh yes, definitely," Josie replied, "I love the classics. I did have a look at the ones on sale in the shop."

"But nothing took your fancy?"

"Not really. I was fingering 'Howard's End' for a while."

"I bet that brought the colour back to his cheeks," I told her, "We'll see you at the coach later on."

I grabbed Angela's arm and we walked off before Josie could ask me what I meant.

The stalls were set up around the outside of the square and faced inwards; which left enough space for people to walk behind them to get to the various shops. The cars that had been parked by the market cross had been moved leaving much more room in the centre to manoeuvre. Although busier there still weren't too many people, making it pleasant to wander around. I spotted Dora and Margaret over by a stall selling English Wines. Dora was enjoying a free sample while Margaret stood behind her, looking bored. From the look on the face of the stallholder I didn't think it was Dora's first taste.

"I wonder why there are so many people at that cheese stall over there," Angela said, "The one with all the bunting hanging up."

We wandered over and saw Lauren and Karen at the front of the queue. Karen appeared to be arguing with the stallholder.

"But why can't you make it with skimmed milk?" she asked.

"Because it will lose its creaminess," said the stallholder, wearily.

"It's people like you who are responsible for all the fat people in the world."

"Look love," the stallholder said, "I make cheese for its flavour and texture. You're meant to savour the taste and enjoy the experience with a small piece. It's not my fault if you can't stop shovelling it in by the kilo."

Karen turned away angrily and spotted Angela and myself.

"Oh, hello you two," she mumbled.

"Enjoying yourself?" I asked.

"Oh, this market," said Karen, "The cheeses are full of fat, the jams are full of sugar, all the breads have gluten; I think I'll just stick with the gift shops. At least I don't have to worry about the calories in a souvenir tea towel."

"No, but think of the fibre content," I told her. She didn't look impressed.

I didn't like to mention that I agreed with the stallholder. People just don't seem to like taking responsibility for their own actions these days. We live in a blame society. 'It's fast food establishments that have made me fat; it's cheap alcohol that's made me a drinker.' No one is forcing anyone to eat or drink unhealthily. We all know what is bad and what is good for us and we choose what we put into our bodies. If you're eating more calories than you're burning off you're going to gain weight. Crash diets don't work as no one can stay on them indefinitely. We're all different shapes and sizes and all we can do is eat a well-balanced diet, limit the treats and get a little exercise. I don't think Karen was really in the mood right now to hear me tell her that.

"What's the bunting for?" I asked instead.

"It's National Organic Soft Cheese Week," said Lauren; "Isn't that good?"

"Oh please, it's always National something week," I pushed Karen off the soap box and climbed on myself, "Does anyone ever actually do anything during these weeks? There's always a big announcement on the radio at the start of the week, saying 'it's National Cheese Week, it's National Doughnut Week or it's National Stick a Toe up your Arse Week' but after Monday you never hear anything more about it. What's the point?"

"When is that?" Lauren asked.

"When is what?"

"National Stick a Toe up your Arse week? When is it? Does it have to be your own toe?"

"You don't have to worry," I told her, "It doesn't apply to pregnant women."

"Phew, that's a relief."

It was definitely time to move on. Angela and I made our excuses and walked away; quickly.

There were all manner of stalls in the market selling local produce such as breads, jams and organic vegetables. I spotted Colin over by a meat stall that was also cooking its food on a barbecue. The aroma was intoxicating and my stomach started to rumble. He was tucking into a large sausage in a baguette, eating it like he was sword swallowing.

"Ooh, look at all these organic creams and yoghurts," Angela said, as we walked up to another stall.

The lady behind the counter handed her a tiny pot with a free sample inside.

"Mmm, this is delicious," Angela said, tasting a spoonful, "Do you want to try some, Derek?"

She held out the pot for me but it was full of the runny sort of yoghurt which I wasn't keen on. I shook my head and told her,

"I prefer having it Greek style."

"Oi, oi, Dirk; don't tell everybody," Shauna always managed to show up at the wrong moment, "Greek style eh? Careful Angie, you know what that means. This horny whippet will have you stripped down if you're not careful, licking taramasalata off that perky bosom of yours."

She gave me a smack on the back before moving off; leaving Angela blushing and me with an image that I was going to treasure for the rest of my life.

We continued perusing the stalls and then I heard someone call out my name. I turned round and was alarmed to see Maeve beckoning me over to her.

"Oh my God, what does she want?" I said, "You don't suppose she heard us this morning in the café do you?"

"Maybe Gerald told her that we know about her illness," Angela suggested.

There was only one way to find out. We walked over to where Maeve was standing by the market cross. Gerald remained just behind her, looking rather sheepish.

"I wanted to give you some advice, Derek," she said, eyebrows knitted.

Here it comes, I thought, she's about to tell me to stop acting the fool, to grow up and behave myself. I'd heard the same words from Miss Savage, my junior school headmistress; although I think I felt more frightened now than I did back then. I certainly had the same urge to wet my pants.

"You really should give up the cigarettes," Maeve told me, "It's not worth putting your life at risk like this."

I hadn't expected that.

"I'm sorry?" I said.

"Gerald told me he caught you smoking at the top of the tower. I could smell it on him when he came down."

"Did he really?"

I glanced behind her. Gerald was looking at the floor.

"Believe me, Derek," Maeve continued, "You'll feel better if you give them up. We did, didn't we Gerald? It's all a question of willpower."

What could I say?

"I'll definitely try," I said, "Thank you."

Gerald visibly relaxed. Maeve nodded her approval.

"Good," she said, "Good. Come on Gerald, I need to go and sit down for a while."

Gerald patted my arm as they walked passed us. I turned to Angela.

"I really need a drink," I said.

We weren't the only members of the group to have

gravitated back to the pub. Pete and Leroy were having a drink together at the bar, standing beside a wall-mounted display of black and white photographs of the world war two airfield, Dora and Margaret were at a table at the back of the room, sitting by the large picture window that overlooked the garden and Colin was sat at another table right beside them, eating a bag of crisps. Margaret was still looking fed up but when she saw us she smiled and waved us over.

"Come in for a rest have you?" she asked, "I don't blame you. It's getting quite warm out there now."

"What would you like to drink?" I asked Angela.

"That's very kind of you," Margaret said, "I'll have another orange juice; mum?"

"Gin and Tonic, cheers Derek," said Dora, raising her half-filled glass to me and downing it in one.

"How about you?" I asked Colin. I had to include everyone now.

"I'll have a vodka and peppermint, please," Colin replied, "It helps settle my stomach. It's been such a trying day."

He leant back against the cushioned headrest of his bench seat and closed his eyes.

"Haven't you enjoyed any of it," Angela questioned.

"Not really."

"Did you visit the museum?" I asked.

"I did, but the stuffiness brought on my heart palpitations."

"What about the church?" Angela said, "There were wonderful views from the top of the tower."

"With my vertigo?" Colin opened his eyes and shook his head.

"Well, you looked like you were enjoying the market just now," I told him, remembering the image of the rapidly disappearing sausage baguette.

"It was okay, I suppose," he sighed, "But the crowds made me feel claustrophobic and I could sense a panic attack coming on."

I went to the bar and ordered the drinks.

"Had a good afternoon, Derek?" Leroy asked.

"Yes thanks, how about you? I saw the girls in the market."

"Oh God, was Karen still being militant dieter?"

"Well, yes."

Leroy sniggered. "She takes this dieting way too seriously at times. At every stall she was asking about sugar and fat content. Pete and I escaped and came in here."

"To down a few liquid calories in peace," I said.

Leroy laughed. "Yeah. She knows the calories in everything. It's got to where I daren't ask for a blow job."

Fortunately the barmaid finished my order at that point so I didn't have to come up with a response. I returned to the table with the tray of drinks. Angela had sat down opposite Dora and Margaret and so I took the chair opposite Colin.

"Dora was just telling me about her upcoming hip replacement surgery," Angela said.

"Oh, don't talk to me about hips," Colin interrupted, "I get terrible rheumatics in mine, especially in this damp weather."

"It's my second one," Dora said, taking a healthy swig from her drink, "So I know what to expect. I'll be glad to get the bugger out, if I'm honest. They know me down the hospital anyway, don't they Margaret?"

"Yes, mum; they all know you."

"I was in there a year ago with my gallbladder."

"Oh, gallstones," Colin winced, "I had suspected gallstones once; never known pain like it."

"And was it?" I asked.

"No; actually it was trapped wind."

"And before that," Dora continued, "I had a…well, let's just call it a gynaecological scraping."

I looked back at Colin. "Don't tell me, you've had one of those as well."

"Well, something very similar," he said, taking a sip of his drink.

I had an overwhelming urge to drown Colin in his vodka and peppermint. His whining was getting on my nerves, especially after seeing how Maeve was coping in silence with a genuine illness. Still, I tried to maintain my composure. I didn't really know anything about Colin after all, and just maybe he actually was ill. He screwed up his empty crisp packet and pulled a chocolate bar out of his pocket. There was nothing wrong with his appetite; that was for sure.

I turned back to the other table to join in their conversation. Unfortunately they hadn't moved off of gynaecology and there was more talk of scrapings, an exploratory and something about a speculum; which I thought was the brand name of a computer I had back in the eighties.

"Enough now mum," Margaret said, "I think we're embarrassing Derek."

"I'm ok," I lied, as three sets of eyes turned on me, "In fact a gay friend of mine is a gynaecologist. He's rather a lonely man, really. He told me he's been looking for love in all the wrong places."

All three women nodded sadly. I'm not sure whether it was at this fictitious man or at the level of my sense of humour.

We had another round of drinks, which Angela bought, before getting back onto the coach to return to the hotel. I'm not sure how many drinks Dora had had that day but I'm guessing quite a few. She was becoming rather adept at pinching my bum and for an eighty-five year old woman, had a pretty decent grip on her. Maeve and Gerald were the last to board.

"I don't know why you bought that book."

"It's a history of the village, dear; thought it would be a nice keepsake."

"You've spent the day in the village taking photographs. It will just remain unread on the shelf, collecting dust."

The nagging didn't seem so bad now.

"Don't know how you're going to get that book home anyway. There's no room for it in the suitcase. It's far too heavy to carry in a plastic bag. You'll just have to leave it behind and it will be another example of you wasting all of our money."

Well it was still a bit annoying.

I don't know what Jim had done all day but at least he hadn't lost the coach to boy scouts. The journey back to the hotel was as uneventful as the morning, until we pulled into the driveway and he had to swerve to miss hitting a white van. As we all lurched inside the coach so several workmen outside threw themselves into bushes to avoid getting run over. We left Jim breathing into his paper bag and Colin throwing up into his and got off the coach. Mrs Goddard was standing on the steps waiting to greet us.

"Hello everyone," she said, "Nothing to worry about but I'm afraid the lounge will be out of action today. We had a slight mishap when a few boards from the floor above fell through the ceiling into the lounge. I'm afraid one of them caught the window and caused a little crack."

The scaffolding and big gaping hole suggested more than just 'a little crack.' Mrs Goddard was still smiling but I noticed that a curl from her shampoo and set had broken loose and was now hanging awkwardly over her twitching right eye.

"I've got it on good authority that the rest of the house is absolutely fine; absolutely fine; very stable, so please don't worry. I'm sure your stay here will be as good as it has been so far."

Bugger; I was hoping for some improvement.

"No one was hurt, were they?" Angela asked.

"Hmm? Oh, no; no one at all, not really," Barbara said, "Louella was clearing some tea things away and managed to dive for cover but she's fine; really she is. See, here she is now."

Louella appeared on the front steps, a large bandage wrapped around the top left side of her head. She was carrying a long plank of wood on her walking frame, which was now buckled down the right side so that only three of the four feet touched the floor. One of the workmen took the plank off of her at the top of the steps.

"A treasure," said Mrs Goddard, beaming, "Always eager to help aren't you, dear?"

We made our way inside. From where I stood in the hallway I could see right into the lounge. A few boards; it looked like the whole ceiling had caved in. I don't know how long the workmen had been there but the floor was still covered in bits of wood and glass and something that looked like a metal bedstead. Mrs Goddard saw my gaze and swiftly closed the door.

"Hello Harry," I heard Margaret say, behind me. I turned and saw Harry walking down the stairs.

"Good evening," he said to all of us, but walking over to Margaret and Dora and taking their hands in his, "Heard about our little drama today?"

"Mr Towler," Mrs Goddard said, pushing past me, "Please let me say once again how sorry I am about the floor in your room."

"It's quite alright my dear lady," he said, now taking Mrs Goddard's hand instead, "I didn't lose anything and nobody was hurt."

Well apart from poor Louella, who seemed to count as nobody around here.

"My new room is wonderful, please don't fret. It was very kind of you to let me have yours."

Mrs Goddard smiled and giggled up at Harry. "Oh it's nothing, really," she told him.

I saw Margaret pull at her mother's arm and they walked off, rather quickly, to their room. We all followed suit and made our way up the stairs.

"He's getting special treatment," I said to Angela, as we reached our floor, "First that big bedroom with the bay window at the front of the house and now Mrs Goddard's room."

"Do you think Mrs Goddard has moved out?" Angela said, and winked.

"I think Margaret hopes she has," I replied.

By the time I came downstairs for dinner the lounge had been taped off. I say taped, Mrs Goddard had improvised with what she had available and so the room was actually red ribboned off. There was a big bow right across the door, making it look like a gift.

The chicken the chef had gone off for this morning was definitely fresh as my piece still had most of the feathers attached. I guess the meatballs had smelled good enough to go another day. Chico was still hanging around our table.

"How did you enjoy my meat?" he asked Shauna, while clearing away the dinner plates, "Was it (hip thrust) moist, tender and mouth-wateringly juicy?"

She looked him up and down, pityingly. "It was dry,

tasteless and very unsatisfying."

Chico just smiled. "I like a woman who plays hard to get," he said, "You feisty fox."

He took the plates away and quickly returned with dessert, a fruit pie.

"This comes with the same warning I have written on my underpants," he said.

Shauna sighed.

"It says, 'Warning, contents may be hot.'" There was another hip thrust on 'hot.'

"Yeah," sniffed Shauna, picking up her spoon, "But unfortunately that slogan is on the back of your underpants."

"He's a trier," I said, once he'd left again.

"He's a lot of things," she replied.

Mrs Goddard breezed in.

"Good evening everyone," she said, "Hope you're enjoying tonight's sumptuous meal; good, good. Now, there is some entertainment for you in the bar after dinner. I'm not saying what it is; it'll be a lovely surprise for you; but do enjoy. I'm sure you will. You don't get this at other hotels."

You don't get collapsing floors at other hotels.

After dinner we all traipsed into the bar. We found board games had been placed on all of the tables. Mrs Goddard must have had them for years as they were all worn and tatty. The four youngsters made straight for the 'Frustration' table; the game with the dice in the middle of the board under a plastic dome that you pressed to make it bounce. Josie and Sooz headed for the Chess table while Maeve and Gerald settled down to a game of Scrabble. Dora and Margaret decided on Monopoly and Colin followed them. That left Shauna, Jim, Angela and I. If it was just me and Angela I would have happily played a long game of Monopoly or Cluedo or strip poker, but if it was the four of us, I wanted something that was done with quickly. Shauna grabbed my arm.

"Come on," she said, leading me to the table where 'Operation' sat, "Let's get it over with."

Glum barman came over to our table with a pad and paper as we unpacked the game.

"Right, what do you want?" he asked.

"A battery for this by the looks of it," I said, "Ah, don't worry; found one."

"To drink, I mean."

"Oh," I said, "Are you waitress tonight as well?"

He gave me a sarcastic smile. "Mrs Goddard gave Louella the night off. Can you believe that; just for a little concussion?"

"She was hit by a floor," I reasoned.

"Don't think about me and my workload," he said, "So, what do you want; I can't promise a speedy response."

"I bet you say that to all the boys."

The evening actually started out ok. We ordered two rounds of drinks at a time so that we wouldn't have to keep on interrupting the game. Plus it really pissed the barman off having to get so many drinks at once, but as always happens; we just drank them twice as fast. We laughed every time the buzzer went off and the red nose on the patient lit up. I heard laughter from the other tables as well, except for Josie and Sooz who were concentrating hard on their chess game, but then, the mood somehow changed. I couldn't really pinpoint a time but I heard it first from the youngsters' table.

"That's a four Lauren, not a six," said Karen.

"Is it? Are you sure? Ok."

She moved one of her pieces backwards.

"Why do you keep landing on my pieces and sending them back to the start?" Karen said.

"That's the point of the game."

"You're not landing on the boys' bits. Well, not in the game anyway."

"What's that supposed to mean?"

There was also a disagreement at the Scrabble table.

"That isn't a word, Gerald."

"Yes it is. I've used it many times before."

"To cheat with maybe. Fetch the dictionary."

"There isn't one," Gerald told her.

"Well you're not having Nobchood. It sounds filthy."

"It's a word."

"Use it in a sentence."

"You like your ears nibbled while I like my…"

"Gerald!"

I thought our table was fine but Jim's ability to keep winning was becoming bloody annoying.

"Hey, that was a buzz," I said.

"Wasn't."

"Are you deaf as well as blind? Yes it was."

"We all heard it, Jimbo," said Shauna, "So it's my turn to have a go."

"With me, baby?"

"You wish; you wrinkled little toss pot."

There wasn't much harmony with Monopoly either.

"I own Mayfair, Dora," Colin whined, "You've got to give me rent."

"I wouldn't give you the drippings off my nose."

Once this angry mood had begun, the evening started to deteriorate pretty quickly. Things went from bad to worse back on the Frustration table. Lauren was crying.

"You'd rather I'd have had an abortion," she wailed.

"I only said I want you to roll the fucking dice."

"Alright, calm down Pete."

"Stay out of it, Leroy. You're always poking your nose in somewhere; and not just your nose."

"What's he mean, Lee?"

"Nothing, Karen."

"Gerald," Maeve admonished, over on the scrabble table, "You can't have fart face; especially on a triple word score."

"Why not, it's what I call you?"

"That's heart face and you know it!"

Colin was screaming in pain over at Monopoly.

"Dora; get off my waterworks!"

"Erm, hello," Sooz called out, "Would you mind keeping it down a little, we're trying to concentrate over here."

There was a brief second of silence before everything exploded.

"What do you mean, keep it down? This ain't a fucking library."

"Well there's no need to be like that."

"Chess isn't even fun."

"Well, we're enjoying it; and managing to keep some dignity."

"Oh, shut up and go back to your prawns."

"They're pawns you ignorant, little child."

And so it went on. Mrs Goddard poked her head around the door to see how her fun evening was progressing.

"Oh dear," she said, "Please, everyone; they're only games. No need to get wound up. It's not the winning. Dear me, we've never had this trouble before. How about a game of cards? Anyone?"

"Shove your cards up your arse."

"Do something," she called to glum barman.

"Do what, dear," he said, leaning nonchalantly on the bar

watching everyone, "All join hands and sing a few hymns?"

Things only died down when the chef entered the room.

"What's going on in here?" he shouted out, in his deep, booming voice.

We all stopped what we were doing. Pete let go of the front of Leroy's shirt and Dora loosened her headlock on Colin. The chef was a hefty sort of chap and his six foot, stocky frame filled the doorway. He was wearing an old-fashioned nightshirt and for some reason was still carrying the meat cleaver around with him. Mind you that wasn't the reason we were lulled into silence. Standing in the doorway with the light of the dining room behind, his body was silhouetted beneath his clothing. To put it into culinary terms, meat and two veg was the chef's special of the day and he wasn't being stingy on the portion size.

We began to quietly pack up the games. Only when he was satisfied everything was under control did the chef turn round and walk back through to the dining room.

"You know, I'd like to get my hands on a chopper like that," Colin said, as he looked wistfully at the retreating figure, "I just don't have the strength for dicing vegetables with a knife anymore."

Chapter 6

I woke up the next morning with a thumping head, a dry mouth and a feeling of shame. How had last night descended into such chaos, just over a few board games? How could our quiet, gentle group of people have become so rowdy? How on earth did the chef find pants to fit him?

I could have quite happily turned over and gone back to sleep, putting the entire evening out of my mind but we had another full day excursion lined up. Today we were going to a working farm come nature reserve. At least that sounded quite restful. Surely there was little chance of anyone getting over emotional there.

I got up and pulled the curtains back to see what weather was waiting for me. As I squinted up at the tiny window I saw a face staring down at me. The window cleaners certainly started early around here. I noticed him looking me up and down and became aware that I was stark, bollock naked. When he looked me in the eye again he smiled and winked. I suppose I wasn't fully awake yet and, not wanting to appear rude, I smiled and winked back before closing the curtains again.

Breakfast was a rather quiet affair with sore heads and a general feeling of embarrassment. Mrs Goddard was obviously still shocked by our conduct as well. When she poked her head into the dining room I could see that the top button of her blouse had come off and the collar was turned up on one side. The shampoo and set had collapsed with the chestnut curls falling forwards over her face. She kept tipping her head back and blowing at them so that she could see. I didn't think this was the image of a woman in control.

"We've had to cancel Quiz Night tonight," she said, sharply, before disappearing again.

No reason was given, but I think we all knew why. I suppose yesterday hadn't been one of her best days in the hotel business. Not only had a ceiling caved in, breaking a large window; but her planned evening of entertainment, meant to be a fun, easy night enjoyed by all had descended into a drunken farce with a group of people who really should have known better.

Only Jim was upbeat and as perky again today as he had been yesterday morning. He bounded into the dining room, greeting everybody individually and generally acting as if he was the host at a big dinner party. He practically flirted with Angela when he sat down before turning around and having a laugh and joke with Harry at the next table. I didn't pay too much attention as I was busy testing my gag reflex on breakfast.

"I gave up on mine," Josie said to me, as she passed by my table. She indicated the rubber egg and cardboard-looking bacon I had on a plate in front of me that I was staring at with a look of revulsion.

"I can't say I blame you," I replied, picking up my coffee, "I don't think I can face eating this either."

"I managed a few bites of toast," she continued, "But I just couldn't get my mouth around the chef's sausage."

I spat my coffee across the plate.

The fight between sun and cloud for supremacy was today won by the cloud. It was overcast and pretty dull but fortunately rain wasn't forecast, seeing as we would be spending the whole day outside. When I got onto the coach half an hour later Jim was again breathing into his paper bag and rubbing his rabbit's foot (not a euphemism). Shauna looked ready to kill him.

"Walked under the window cleaner's ladder," she said, seeing my puzzled expression.

"It was right outside the front door," Jim moaned, between breaths, "I didn't see it until it was too late."

It was going to be another interesting journey. I sighed and walked down to my seat.

"What's wrong with him now?" Angela asked, as she sat down beside me a couple of minutes later.

I explained. I was expecting her to roll her eyes and laugh but she just tutted and said, "Stupid little creep."

I think Jim's flirting earlier on had pissed her off but Angela had been very quiet in the dining room even before that. She remained silent now while the rest of the group boarded but I put it down to the hangover most of us were experiencing. She only spoke again as we were about to depart.

"Who's that waving at you?"

"Oh, that's the window cleaner," I told her, waving back; still trying to be polite.

"I must say, the locals are very friendly around here."

"Yes," I agreed, as the window cleaner did something suggestive with his tongue, "But perhaps just a little too friendly."

We pulled out of the driveway and Shauna switched on the microphone.

"Morning everyone," she said, and then burped loudly through the speakers, "Oh God I needed that. Thought I was going to puke my guts up earlier. Anyway, Tyler's Green Farm and Nature Reserve is about forty-five minutes away from here with a regular driver. With this superstitious, little shit at the wheel we're probably talking an hour and a half. The day will pretty much be your own to do whatever you want but please remember; bestiality is against the law in this county."

I'm sure that's true for every other one as well; isn't it?

"There are guided tours of the farm and the nature reserve and lots of other activities including horse riding, tractor driving and cow milking. A word of warning for all you townies; don't squeeze or pull it if there's only one teat. That's a bull."

Words of wisdom indeed.

"The leaflet here says that for younger members of the group, there's also a petting zoo. I should stress for the benefit of **our** younger members, that's a petting zoo; not a heavy petting zoo."

Shauna's prediction of journey time turned out to be optimistic. After getting lost twice, with Jim squinting at a road map of Wales, we eventually had to ask for directions. I think we passed the same dead badger in the road three times. After that we had a near miss with a tractor and then had to contend with a breakdown. Not the coach; Jim. By the time we arrived I was so glad to get off I almost bent down and kissed the ground.

The place was vast and to begin with we just stuck together as we wandered around, getting our bearings. Pete and Leroy were both keen to have a go at tractor driving and we all went down to watch them. There were two tractors set up for training and a short course had been roped off in the field. A member of staff stood inside each cab to guide the driver. Both started off well and then competitiveness took over. Pete moved ahead and so Leroy put his foot down, caught up and passed him. Pete then did the same and a race began. The instructors were frantically waving their hands around and shouting out advice but it didn't help. Neither did the rest of us taking sides and cheering them both on. As the tractors hurtled around the final bend, near to where we were standing, we could hear the screams over the noise of the engines.

It was a dead heat finish. Pete and Leroy climbed out and high-fived each other. The poor instructors crawled down from the cabs, both looking rather pale. One of them walked over to where I was standing and bent over to catch his breath.

"Jesus Christ," he said, "It's usually a gentle run around the course. I'm stressed out already. How many of you are there?"

"Don't worry," I told him, "I don't think you'll have too much custom from us today."

"Thank God for that," he said, looking up, "Ah, that's more like it, someone experienced. Your coach driver is going to have a go."

I looked over and saw the second instructor helping Jim up into the cab. Several of our group were already walking away. Angela turned around and looked at me.

"Time to go," she said. I nodded my head, frantically.

I hadn't thought the screams of the instructors could get any louder, but they could.

We now started to split up and go off to different areas. Margaret wheeled Dora over to the petting zoo, Maeve and Gerald followed a sign for a nature ramble and Colin made his way to the café, complaining of hay fever.

"Derek, do you fancy coming horse riding?" Angela asked. Hell no!

"Erm, I've never done it before," I said.

"It's marvellous fun, Derek," I hadn't heard Sooz come up behind me, "We love it, don't we Josie."

"Ooh yes. I don't think there's anything more thrilling than getting your legs astride a wild beast and enjoying a good, long romp in the fresh air."

"I don't doubt that for a second," I told her.

"Can I come too?" Karen asked me, as if I was team leader and had made the initial suggestion, "I've not done it before either, but I've always wanted to."

I guess I was going horse riding. I was the only man in the group but had a feeling it would be me screaming like a little girl. Lauren, Pete and Leroy decided they would look around the farm instead. I'd rather have gone off with them but felt I'd lose face in Angela's eyes if I did. She'd been so quiet this morning and I was glad that she now seemed her normal self again.

We queued up at the riding school to be asked about our level of experience and to get our riding hats. The woman took one look at me and called out, "Give him Freddie."

Having been given our hats we all stood in the yard, four excited women and one petrified man. Angela's horse was already tied up outside and she mounted it perfectly. Josie and Sooz's horses were brought out to them and again, they mounted like they had been doing it from birth. A shire horse was brought out next, at least that's what it looked like to me.

"Jesus," I said, to Karen, "What poor bastard has got to ride that?"

"Ok," called the woman, leading it, "Who's on Freddie?"
Oh shit!

I reluctantly raised my hand. The lady beckoned me over and explained how to get on. I didn't realise I needed to be a contortionist to go horse riding. I'm still not sure how I managed to lift my foot above my head to get it into the stirrup but I did it. I guess the threat of the kiddie steps being brought out for me helped; that would have been embarrassing. I sat astride the horse and the woman adjusted the stirrups.

I took a look around me. My God, it was high up. I expected a nosebleed to start any minute.

"Right," she said, handing me the reins, "Now hold these like this. That's right. The horse can feel any tension you have through these so be gentle and relaxed."

Easier said than done.

"Now I just have to get a horse for your friend. Don't worry, Freddie's a sweetie. He won't move."

As soon as she left, Freddie moved. It may not have been far or fast but he moved and I let out my first scream. As he bent his head down to feed on a patch of grass so the reins I'd been asked to keep loose slid through my fingers. I was now perched high up in the air with nothing to hold onto except a furry neck. I wasn't surprised to see Shauna standing by the fence as she always seemed to show up at the most inopportune moment. She was leaning on the rail looking at me, a big grin on her face.

"You know Dirk," she called over, "I heard that men select horses like they do their cars. The bigger it is the "smaller" the driver is, so to speak. That's one big fucker you're on there."

I opened my mouth to tell her where to go but Freddie decided to move across to another patch of grass and all I managed was another startled scream.

The lady reappeared with Karen's horse. Karen was pretty light on her feet for her size and she deftly swung up into the saddle, beaming. Hers didn't move when the lady left her and came over to me.

"Now then, what's going on here?"

"He moved."

She handed me back the reins. I looked over at Angela. Someone had just untied her horse (why couldn't Freddie have been tied up while I got on?) and she expertly manoeuvred it around and brought it over to me, smiling all the time.

"Ok?" she said.

I tried to smile back but I think it was more of a grimace.

"Fine," I lied.

We were led away from the stables (and fortunately from Shauna as well) into a small field that had a circular path cut into the grass. A trainer stood in the middle and gave us instructions. Sooz was up the front, followed by Josie, then me, then Karen and finally Angela. To begin with we walked gently around the circle. Freddie moved with no instruction from me and I was just thinking that I could get used to this when he decided to take a detour over to some hay he had spotted tied to the fence. Did he ever stop eating? No wonder he was the size he was.

"Just bring him back," was the helpful advice the trainer gave me.

"And how do I do that?" I called out to her.

The list of instructions for how to turn the horse using the reins and my feet seemed mind boggling. Eventually another member of the team came over and led Freddie back into the group; who had all stopped to look at me. We started walking again. After another circle I started to relax but then Josie's horse stopped dead in front of me and Freddie decided to take advantage of the situation and eat some more grass. As his head bent down so the reins once again slipped through my fingers. I was left balancing, what felt like, seven feet from the ground and all I could think was that Karen was probably making a note of all the calories the horse was consuming.

"Just bring his head back up again," the instructor called.

Still aware that the horse could feel tension through the reins, I gingerly grabbed at them and tugged upwards as gently as I could but Freddie was too engrossed in the grass to move.

"Bring his head up or the horse in front could kick him."

Oh great, Freddie was about to get a blow to the head which would probably send him shooting off out of the paddock, right past Shauna; with me clinging on for dear life; wailing like a banshee and soiling myself like a baby. The trainer came over and pulled Freddie's head up sharply.

"Tut, tut," she said, condescendingly, "You need to grip the reins tighter."

"I was told not to grip them tightly because of tension," I snapped back, "Although I'm feeling more of that with each passing moment."

I so wanted the lesson to end.

"Oh, er, well; you need to grip them a little tighter," the instructor said, quietly; probably more used to horses baring their teeth at her than students.

I didn't think much of this lesson. I felt there was a lot of information I should have been told before I even got onto a horse. They also shouldn't have lied about Freddie not moving off when they left him alone with me. Maybe then I would have had more trust in the animal. We began walking again.

"Right," said the instructor, "We'll now move around the circle at a trot. You need to kick the horse with both legs to make this happen. We'll go one at a time so that the first horse joins the back of the group."

Great, one at a time so everyone else can watch.

Sooz kicked and her horse broke into a trot. I watched; impressed at how she moved in time with the motion of the animal. Josie followed and then it was my turn. I kicked the horse with both my feet. Nothing. I hadn't done it too hard as I didn't want to hurt Freddie; the instructor maybe; but not Freddie. I tried again, a little harder. Nothing. I could feel myself blushing, all eyes on me.

The instructor came over.

"You need to do it harder than that," she told me, and promptly grabbed my leg and slapped it against Freddie's side.

This time he set off. I let out another yelp and bounced

about while he ran around the circle. I don't know how I kept my balance but I was just glad I did. My buttocks were clenched together so tightly I think I'd sucked up half the saddle. It was a relief to reach the back of the group. The whole trot had probably lasted about five seconds at most but I was sweating and out of breath. I hoped I could get a sponging down alongside the horses at the end of the lesson. I doubted I'd looked quite as professional as Josie and Sooz had; or Karen as it turned out, who got her horse to trot straight away and happily bounced up and down in her saddle as she made her way to the back of the line.

Once Angela had re-joined the back of the group I hoped that would be an end to the lesson. No such luck. A side gate was opened and we were lead out into a much larger field. The instructor had now mounted her own horse.

"Right," she called, "We'll have a ride up to the top of the field and back to finish the lesson. Those of you that have ridden before, please feel free to have a canter. Those of you that haven't," And she shot me a pitying glance, "Remain with me and just enjoy a gentle walk."

Angela held back to begin with but I told her to go off ahead. I ignored the instructor and walked beside Karen across the field.

"Are you sure you haven't had any lessons before?" I asked her.

"None; honestly," she said.

"Well, you're definitely a natural."

"Thanks Derek. I wish I could say the same."

I laughed, throwing my head back before realising I was still on a horse and in danger of toppling off.

The field sloped gently upwards and contained scrub and a few trees, rather than being just grass. I hadn't particularly enjoyed the first part of the lesson but it was peaceful out here, sitting up on a horse, enjoying the scenery. I realised that my headache had cleared.

"So how long have you and Leroy been together?" I asked Karen.

"About a year," she said, "I met him through Pete. They work together as mechanics at a car dealership. I'd originally set him and Lauren up and he returned the favour."

"I'd wondered how Pete had managed to chat up Lauren."

Karen sniggered. "I was at school with him. He's a nice guy once you get to know him and he opens up, but he's really shy. All I had to do was get them together and then Lauren did all of the talking."

"It worked," I said, "Ever thought of taking matchmaking up as a profession?"

"I think I'll stick with insurance," she replied, smiling.

Josie, Sooz and Angela came flying past us again, having reached the other end of the field and turned back. Karen and I fell silent as we approached it. How on earth was I going to turn the horse around? I couldn't manage it earlier and I was damn sure I wouldn't be able to do it now either. The wooden fence was getting nearer and nearer. Karen did something and her horse turned. How did she do that? I was hoping Freddie would follow her but he didn't. He continued walking until we came right up to the fence and then he stopped. It was a lovely view across fields to the estuary but there was only so long I could get away with saying this is what I intended to do. Embarrassingly I had to be rescued by the instructor. Karen was waiting for me as I turned.

"So, has Lauren and Pete's wedding made you think of getting hitched?" I asked quickly, not wanting the conversation to dwell on my inadequacies as a horse rider.

"No," Karen said, "Not yet anyway. I started dieting after meeting Leroy and I still have a long way to go before I'm happy."

"But Leroy doesn't mind," I said, "He told me as much the day we arrived."

She smiled again. "Oh no, he's great like that. He's said, if I want to lose weight he'll back me all the way; but if I don't want to then he loves me anyway. He's a great guy. I wonder at times what he's doing with me. But still sometimes…"

I remained silent while Karen worked out what she was going to say.

"He is a bit of a flirt with women," she finally said, "I know it's just part of his character; the life and soul of a party, but I'm not sure I like it. I do trust him, but at times I feel…"

"Insecure?"

"Unsettled, I guess."

"So do I; on this horse."

Karen laughed.

"But I think everyone feels like you do at some point in their relationship," I said.

"Did you?"

"Oh yes, definitely. If I was at one of my wife's work functions and she was standing in a group of male colleagues who were each hanging on her every word I would feel insecure and wonder if she found any of them funnier or more interesting than me. Of course, as it turned out, she did find someone funnier, and more interesting, and attractive..." I became aware I probably wasn't helping Karen feel settled, "But that was just me. You and Leroy make a nice couple; so do Lauren and Pete."

Karen grinned. "Thanks," she said.

I found that getting on the horse was a lot easier than getting off once we were in the barn. I was leaning forwards, right up against Freddie's neck but I still couldn't swing my leg over his back to get down. In the end I kind of half fell onto the poor girl who was trying to help me and we both ended up on the floor. It was a shame it wasn't the instructor, I would quite happily have fallen onto her from a great height.

"How was that, Derek," Sooz asked, as I stood up and brushed the straw off of my jacket, "Going to take it up as a hobby?"

"Who knows?" I said.

I bloody knew. I was never going to get onto a sodding horse ever again.

The whole group congregated in the café around the same time and everyone appeared to have enjoyed their morning. Angela raved about the horse riding, Gerald said the guided nature ramble was very informative and Lauren told us how she was fascinated watching a piglet get neutered. I'm afraid that part did put me off my sweet and sour pork balls. Only Colin still looked miserable.

"Come on," I said, "Make an effort and you'll probably enjoy yourself more."

He took this as an invitation to spend the afternoon with me.

*

I say me; I made sure Angela didn't go off with anyone else. After the horse riding she owed me. We decided to walk through the petting zoo and then into the farming area before going on the guided nature walk which was scheduled for three o'clock.

I bought three paper cups filled with animal feed and handed one to Angela. I held one out for Colin but he looked at it like I'd just shown him the contents of my tissue after a sneeze. He shook his head, pulled a handkerchief from his pocket and held it over his nose.

"You don't have to come in the Petting Zoo if you don't want to," I said.

"No, I'll come," he replied, "I'll make the effort to be sociable."

I opened the gate and let Angela in first. Colin was fiddling with his bumbag so I walked in next and told him to shut the gate behind him. Once he'd done that we opened the second one into the animal compound. As he closed this he yelped.

"I just put my hand on bird poo," he said, looking on the brink of tears.

"It's dried. Any germs will have died," I said, rather credibly I felt.

"Really? Ok."

He opened his bumbag and got out the antibacterial wipes.

"Here, hold this, will you?" he said, tossing the bag at me while he wiped his hands.

I almost dropped the two cups of food I was clutching. Angela took the bag off of me. It was still unzipped.

"Hold it open," I whispered.

Angela looked at me quizzically, but did it anyway. The bag was full of tissues and pills and potions of varying kinds. I tipped in half a cup of the animal feed and pulled a couple of tissues over the top.

"Derek," Angela giggled, "You shouldn't." But she didn't actually stop me.

"Thanks," Colin said, walking over and holding out his hand.

I gave him back the bag. Without looking he threw the bacterial wipes in, zipped it up and fastened it around his middle.

The zoo was made up of chickens, sheep, goats and a small pony. They all raced over to us as we walked in. Colin let out a whimper and cowered behind us.

"Come out Colin, they're really cute," Angela said, "You don't have to be afraid of them. It's a petting zoo after all."

"That's what I'm afraid of," Colin said, "How many other people have petted these? What germs do they have living on them? I'm sure I'm allergic to horses; probably all livestock really."

Colin watched me as I held out my hand and let a goat feed from it.

"Euugh," he said, "That's goat saliva you've got on your fingers now."

"Are you sure?" I said, turning around and holding my hand right in front of his face.

He yelled and ran out from behind me. The pony got a whiff of the bumbag and gently tugged at it. Colin screamed and took a few steps backwards but the pony had the scent now.

"Why's he following me?" His eyes were wide open in fear.

"He likes you," I called over.

Angela was making a brave effort not to laugh, I didn't bother trying to stop; especially when Colin turned and ran. Rather than running back to the gate we'd just come through, he instead, ran past us down the path into the main area of the zoo; the pony and two sheep in hot pursuit.

"And as they take the farmhouse bend in the menagerie stakes, it's Colin in the lead followed by the pony, two sheep and a chicken…"

"Derek, stop," Angela said, laughing out loud, "We've got to go and get him; make sure he's alright."

"He'll be fine," I replied, "A little exercise is good for you."

We made our way along the path, handing out the food as we went. There were a couple of hutches with rabbits and guinea pigs but we didn't really have time to stop and look. As we turned the final corner so we saw Colin outside the exit gates, leaning against a wall; breathing heavily. As we reached the first gate so a member of staff walked over to him.

"Are you ok?" he asked.

"Those...those monsters; are freaks," he said, between gasps.

Puzzled, the staff member looked at us.

"They look like two normal people to me," he said.

"Not them, the animals."

"Oh right. Did you run through the area?"

Colin nodded. "Had to; had to escape."

"I'd best go check on them then," the man said, "We don't want the animals upset."

We let him pass us and then Angela and I walked out of the final gate.

"The animals?" Colin said to us, incredulously, "Why's he worried about them? My God it's not safe for a human to walk through that safari park of terror. The owner of this place is going to get such a mouthful off of me when I get hold of him."

"Didn't you enjoy that then?" I asked, tongue in cheek.

He ignored me and unzipped his bum bag.

"I need my smelling salts."

He moved something aside and stared, a puzzled look on his face. Colin shook the bag up and down.

"What's this? How did the feed get in here?" He looked accusingly at Angela and me.

"Oh no," I said, "Did it really? Must have fallen in when you threw the bag at me earlier on."

I could tell he was thinking over what I'd just said in his mind; wondering if I was telling the truth. I thought I sounded pretty convincing and eventually, so did Colin. He emptied out the bag and repacked it.

"Shall we move on?"

We walked into the farmyard, Colin once again with his handkerchief held over his nose.

"There are lots of germs in the air on a farmyard," he told us, "Not to mention stenches."

I agreed with him on the latter. As we walked past the end of a high wall we saw a huge, steaming pile of horse manure and it wasn't exactly an aroma you'd want in a scented candle. From where we stood in the yard we could see green fields, gently sloping upwards towards a ridge, most of them filled with sheep.

"It's such a beautiful setting," Angela enthused, "So tranquil."

"Best place for that livestock is far away from me," Colin moaned.

I didn't think he was going to become an animal lover any time soon.

"You know, you can have a go at milking," I said to him, "That sounds fun doesn't it?"

"Ooh no," he replied, turning his head away in disgust, "Haven't you ever heard of udder rash? It's terrible."

"For the cow, surely?"

"Diseases have a habit of spreading between species."

I suspected Colin didn't have udders to get a rash on, but if he did I didn't want to see them.

"Ok, how about a browse around the farm shop?" I suggested, "No diseases there."

"Are you kidding me?" he said, as if I was an ignorant child, "They have food unwrapped; they weigh different things on the same set of scales; people tread all the farm muck inside."

"This isn't really your sort of trip is it?"

"Hello," called a voice, from inside the barn beside us, "Can I be of any help?"

Angela and I walked in the door and found a vet examining a cow; reaching parts of it no one else could. At least I hoped he was the vet and not some weirdo with an unusual fetish. He had a bag with medical equipment in, so I assumed he was qualified.

"Are you waiting for the next tour?" he asked, "Or were you looking for the cow milking demonstration?"

"Actually we were just having a look around this bit on our own," I said, "Is that ok?"

"I'm sure it is," the vet replied, "I'm just checking on a breached calf," he added by way of explanation.

I heard a dry retch beside me. Colin had wandered into the barn and was just surveying the scene; his face screwed up in disgust. He mopped his sweating forehead before quickly returning the hankie to his nose.

"Ah, Colin," I said, "Just in time. It's your turn to have a go."

His eyes widened in horror and his mouth dropped open. The vet slowly pulled his hand out of the cow's bottom, the long, yellow glove suitably stained. Colin let out another yelp, turned and bolted again.

"Don't run," I called after him, "I meant your turn to be the vet, not the cow."

We heard another yell and then a loud splat. As we ran outside we found Colin face down in the manure pile. It was fortunate that the vet was on hand to pull him out as I certainly wasn't going anywhere near that heap. There might have been less screaming from Colin if the vet had remembered to remove the long glove first before grabbing at him.

Seeing the despondent look on poor Colin's face was quite moving but once a couple of the staff members began hosing him down in the yard to get the worst of the manure off I'm afraid the laughter flowed. Even they had trouble keeping the hose steady and their faces straight.

Afterwards, as he complained and talked again about giving the owner a mouthful, we bid Colin farewell as he was taken away to be properly showered and changed and be as good as new; albeit with probable pneumonia and some kind of equine infection. Another member of staff re-stacked the manure pile so that no one would know anything had happened…unless of course they happened to see the series of photographs on my camera.

Chapter 7

On the plus side, Colin's mishap meant that Angela and I could go on the guided nature ramble without him. When Gerald had spoken about this during lunch it had sounded like he and Maeve had been alone on the tour. I liked the sound of that, me and Angela being alone together on a gentle stroll through the countryside. However, when we reached the meeting point we found that Josie, Sooz, Dora and Margaret would be joining us.

"I've been told it's a gentle route," Margaret said, "So it's ok for wheelchairs."

"I'm sure Derek wouldn't mind pushing your mum for you for a while," Angela offered, "Give you a bit of a break."

Wasn't that kind of her?

"Sure," I said, "That's so long as Dora doesn't mind."

"Not at all, Derek," Dora said, giving me a wink, "I don't usually let men push me around, but in your case I'll make an exception."

Well at least she couldn't pinch my bum if I was pushing her.

At three o'clock sharp a short, dumpy, young woman bounded over to us, wearing the green t-shirt and black trouser uniform of the nature reserve's staff. She was carrying a large telescope on her shoulder that was practically the same size as she was.

"Hello," she said, brightly, "My name's Emma. I'll be showing you around this afternoon."

She heaved the telescope from one shoulder to the other, almost losing her balance in the process.

"Actually, I'm quite new and this is my first tour where I'm not chaperoned by another member of staff," she confided, "I'm so glad you're a small group."

I'd been hoping for smaller still.

"Of course, if you would rather have a more experienced tour guide I can easily run back and get someone for you."

We said it was fine.

"It's no trouble. Ken's good. He's over the other side of the reserve but I can go and get him; it's only a couple of miles. I could be back in ten minutes if I run."

I doubted that. We told her again it was fine and she beamed. Emma was obviously eager to impress. She began by asking each of us our names but then promptly forgot them.

"Is Eric your grandson, Norah?" she asked, patting Dora's hand and leaning in a little too close to her than was comfortable.

"No he bloody isn't," Dora said, pulling her hand away, "He's my lover, actually. It's strictly physical, isn't it Eric? In fact we might have to stop somewhere quiet on the way round."

"She's joking," I added, quickly.

"Don't deny it, Eric," Dora continued, "You know you want me."

"Isn't it time for your nap, Norah?" I asked.

Dora laughed. Emma looked totally bewildered and decided the best course of action was to continue on with the tour.

"We'll be walking by hedgerows and woods and then along a path by the estuary before stopping at a bird hide which overlooks the salt marsh," she said, "I'll set up the telescope there so we can get a good look at some of our wonderful wading birds. Please feel free to ask any questions en route. The going's very smooth so the wheelchair should be fine Eric."

Maybe I should have told her my name was Dirk. She might have remembered that.

"Right, if you'd all like to follow me."

Emma walked away followed by the others but I was having a bit of trouble trying to move the wheelchair.

"Is it stuck on something, Derek?" Dora asked, "Should I get up and pull you off?"

There wasn't a response to that. Eventually Margaret walked back and informed me the brake was still on. Great, couldn't she have mentioned that earlier? I was knackered before I'd even started walking. We all set off again.

"As you can see," Emma said, "We've encouraged the farmers to separate their fields of crops using hedgerows rather than fencing. At this time of year they're bright with spring blossom and provide a valuable nest and feeding sight for many birds, including Willow Warblers, Greenfinches and Chaffchiffs…I mean Chiffchaffs. We also get many species of butterfly here including Large White, Red Admiral and erm…oh it's on the tip of my tongue. What is it now? It's like a doorman; or a locksmith. Not locksmith, lock keeper."

"Oh you mean a Gatekeeper," Sooz interjected.

"That's it," Emma said, "Oh, stupid of me to forget." And she hit herself rather hard on the side of her head.

We were all a bit too startled to say anything. Emma carried on walking but was mumbling to herself under her breath. I kept hearing the words 'stupid' and 'idiot.'

"That's pretty," Angela said, pointing out a white flower in the hedgerow.

"Oh, that's…" Emma screwed her eyes up, trying to remember.

"It's Bladder Campion," I said, leaving the wheelchair and walking across to stand beside Angela.

"Bladder?"

"Yes," I said, "The name comes from the bladder-shaped

calyx, see; just behind the bloom."

"Oh yes," said Angela, gazing first at the flower and then at me.

She appeared impressed and I felt rather proud of myself; until I caught Emma's eye. She looked mortified and her bottom lip was trembling as if about to cry.

"Sorry," I said, "I'm sure you were about to say the same thing."

I returned to the wheelchair where Dora had nodded off and we walked on. Emma's commentary seemed to have stalled but she was still berating herself under her breath. We continued along the path with hedgerows either side of us and then the one to our right stopped, enabling us to look out across open fields.

"Oh look," said Josie, pointing into the sky, "A Kestrel, hovering."

"Great," said Emma, pulling the telescope off of her shoulder, "Hang on a minute."

She set the tripod stand on the floor, puffing as she struggled to get the three legs straight. She pulled the scope around so that the eyepiece was facing the right way. In her haste to get the bird in focus she managed to bang her left eye quite hard as she leaned forward to look through the lens. Both Angela and I gasped but Emma carried on, holding one hand against her hurt eye and frantically trying to focus on the bird with the other.

"Oh, it's gone," said Josie, "Shame."

Shame? I thought Emma was going to throw herself down on the grass and cry her eyes out. I was really feeling sorry for the poor mite; she was so keen to please us. I helped her get the telescope back onto her shoulder.

"I should have been quicker," she said, more to herself than to me, and then banged her head violently against the telescope.

"Stop that!" I said, sounding exactly like my father, and then a little more gently, "Don't worry. We're all enjoying ourselves."

"Oh Eric," she whispered, tears seeping out of her red, swelling eye, "I so wanted this to go well."

"It is," I lied.

"But I'm forgetting everything."

"Tell you what," I said, "I know a bit about wildflowers, how about I remind you of a few as we pass them and then you can tell the rest of the group."

Emma smiled. "Oh that would be great Eric, thank you," she replied, wiping her nose on her bare arm.

Of course doing this meant I had to keep pace with Emma up at the front of the group while still pushing Dora who was talking in her sleep. I didn't want to imagine what she was dreaming about.

"You're a dirty boy, Derek," she murmured, "Fancy you dipping it in my jar of lemon curd like that."

"Here, look at this," I said, to Emma, catching sight of a flower I knew in the hedgerow. It was a relief to step away from the wheelchair, "This is Pignut. It's a member of the carrot family. It has these umbrella-like clusters of white flowers and is attractive to a range of insects. Have you got that?"

"Yes," replied Emma; "Thanks."

She turned around to the rest of the group.

"Everybody," she called, "If you'd all like to stroll over here I can show you some pig's nuts."

No one came over.

As the fields on our right gave way to woodland I attempted a few more flowers but Emma became more and more flustered and quickly forgot what I told her. Cow Parsley she called Bull Tarragon, Hogsweed became Pigspiss and when we passed by a small, blue flower she couldn't remember the name of, I had to remind her that it was Wood Forget-me-not.

The route we were taking veered to the left through the hedgerow and then climbed gently upwards until we came out onto a wider path that overlooked the estuary and mud flats to the left and the fields and wood we'd just walked by, down to our right. Just as the path levelled out again, Emma's foot caught in a hole. She yelled as she twisted on the spot and went down, the telescope flying away from her. She'd already dragged herself across to it before we could reach her.

"Oh it's fine, thank goodness."

"Forget that, are you ok?" Angela asked her.

"Yes," she replied, wincing as she tried to stand and get the telescope back onto her shoulder again; staring at us all through one eye, "I'm fine. Let's move on."

"Here," I said, "Let me carry that."

"No Eric, I couldn't do that," Emma said, "I'm meant to do it. It's part of my job."

"I insist."

"But I'm meant to do it all," Emma pleaded, "I should be able to take you on a walk, answer all of your questions and basically give you all a pleasant experience; just like all the other wardens do."

"It will make me happy to carry the scope for you," I told her, "I think you're trying a little too hard and that's why you're having a few slight problems."

Slight, like Niagara Falls is a slight trickle of water. But still, what I said seemed to do the trick and Emma handed me the telescope. Really, she should have given up on the tour altogether and gone back to rest her foot but I couldn't convince her to do that. We set off again; rather slowly due to the limping. Carrying the telescope was a lot easier than pushing

Dora along and Margaret was so much better at it anyway.

Eventually we reached the hide and I hoped the rest would do all of us some good. We opened the shutters and found ourselves overlooking the salt marsh to the left and in front of us, just beyond a bushy, overgrown area; a small lake that had what looked like concrete islands built into it. Nests had been erected on the top and the whole area was covered with a vast array of birds. Emma arranged the telescope in the middle of the hide; fortunately without incident this time.

"Right then," she said, "The Lagoon that you can see out the front was created by the Trust here at Tyler's Green Farm about ten years ago. Although man-made, the habitat has established itself and we now have breeding pairs of several species of gull and tern. Please feel free to each take a look through the telescope. Eric, perhaps you'd like to look first."

I wasn't much into birds but the telescope really brought them up close, enabling me to see that those birds that appeared drab to the naked eye actually had a lot more detail and colour in their plumage.

"On the left there you'll see a variety of our waders," I heard Emma say, "Ooh, and if you quickly bring the scope around to the right, I can show you my Chough."

My head whipped back.

"Whoa," I said, "I'm happy to carry the telescope without that level of thanks."

"There he is," Emma continued, ignoring what I'd said and pointing to a black bird outside, "He's not mine really but he's such a funny little thing; a real character."

"And that's a Chough?" I questioned.

"Oh God, not Chough," Emma said, "Jackdaw. Sorry; both are members of the Crow family."

"Perhaps someone else would like a turn," I suggested.

I could see Angela in the corner with a tissue over her eyes, shaking with silent laughter. Josie got up.

"Oh this is interesting," she said, "Sooz, come and have a look at this."

While Sooz stood up, Emma had a look down the eyepiece.

"Ah," she said, "Looking at the Grey Heron, fishing."

"No dear," Josie told her, "It's an Egret."

Emma's face fell. Sooz had a look and then moved the scope more to the left.

"What's that?" she asked, stepping back.

Emma took another look.

"That's a Grey Plover."

"No dear," said Josie, her eye back on the scope, "It's an Oyster Catcher."

"Is it?" Emma checked again, "Oh yes; so it is."

I wished Josie would sit down but birds were obviously her thing. She started giving us a running commentary of all the different species she could see and Emma was becoming more and more dejected.

"Shouldn't we be moving on?" I suggested.

"Oh not yet, Derek," Josie said, "Here Sooz, have another look. I've found an Avocet."

"I don't know my Avocet from my Egret," Emma wailed.

"What's that over there?" Sooz asked.

Josie looked through the scope.

"I'm not sure," she said, "Emma, dear; do you know what this is?"

Emma reluctantly looked through the scope. I really hoped she knew what she was looking at this time. She studied the bird for what felt like ages before she stood up again, frowning. Then she bent down once more for another look.

"That's odd," she said, "It looks like a Water rail. We do

have them here but not usually at the Lagoon. They like to stay in the reed beds over at the lake. They're common but often difficult to spot; especially now during the breeding season."

Josie had another look through the scope.

"I do believe you're right."

I was so pleased for Emma, who began grinning again.

"This is great," she whispered to us, "Now then everybody, we should all remain very quiet but each of us should take a look through the scope because this is a rare occurrence."

She beckoned to Margaret and Dora to come over first. Margaret helped her mother get out of her chair and Dora limped silently over to the telescope. As she bent down to look through the eyepiece she farted rather loudly. Startled, the Water rail and several other birds took flight.

"You can share that one amongst you," Dora said.

What a giving woman she was. We decided to leave as quickly as the birds had.

The next part of the tour took us back down away from the mudflats. As we walked along so Emma's limp became worse. It didn't help that Josie, totally oblivious of the situation, kept stopping to look at birds in the sky or plants in the undergrowth and asking questions. Eventually Emma allowed Angela and I to help her walk along.

"It's not too far now back to the meeting point," she said, "Let's keep going."

Dora had nodded off in her chair again otherwise I would have suggested she and Emma swapped places for a little while, although I doubt either of them would have been keen on that.

By the time the path came up beside the river bank Angela had the telescope and I was giving Emma a piggyback. She was still attempting to give her talk, although the story about the Water Mole was factually incorrect. I spotted a pale pink flower by the riverbank and thought I'd try one last time to help her out.

"Look at that," I said, "It's Cuckoo Flower. Now, this is also known as Lady's Smock but it's called Cuckoo Flower because it starts flowering in April and coincides with the arrival of the first Cuckoo. It's a sure sign that spring is on its way."

"Thanks Eric."

"Now, you've got that; Cuckoo Flower, also known as Lady's Smock."

"Yes," she said, "Everyone; if you could come over here and look at this. Now then, this is called Fuck you Flower. It's also known as Lady's Cock…"

I gave up. Suddenly, Emma let out a little moan. She grabbed her arm and slipped down off my back.

"What's wrong?" I asked.

"It's nothing," she said, wincing, "Let's move on."

"Have you been stung?" Angela asked.

"Yes, but don't worry," Emma said, "Let's move on."

"Hang on, I've got something for stings," Angela rooted around in her bag. She found the spray and looked up, "Jesus Christ."

We'd all been looking at Angela but in the meantime Emma had started to swell up. Her entire face had ballooned; the red mark around her eye where she had hit it on the telescope had stretched across the whole of the left side.

"I'm allergic," she said, sounding muffled as her lips continued to swell, "But I'b fine. Leb's moobe on."

It was difficult to get Emma to admit defeat and call it a day. In fact she was still apologising for not finishing the tour as she was stretchered onto the ambulance.

An eventful day I was actually looking forward to getting on the coach and getting back to the hotel. Colin was already on board when we arrived. He'd sat himself right at the back out of the way but I could see he was now wearing an oversized pair of dungarees and carrying his other clothes in a carrier bag. I wanted to tell him, "shit happens" but he looked far too distraught for me to make any comment.

I flopped down into my seat. I could quite happily have dozed off but Angela wanted to talk.

"Derek," she said, "I was chatting a lot with Margaret this afternoon. She's really taken with Harry."

"Right," I said, not listening too closely.

She continued to speak but my eyelids were so heavy and I felt myself dropping off.

"And so I thought it would be nice to spend some time together tomorrow."

"Tomorrow; yeah, that sounds good," I said.

"Great," Angela replied, "So you're happy to go on the optional wine tasting excursion?"

"Sure," I said. Another day out with Angela; what could be better.

"Terrific, I'll let Shauna know."

Jim managed to get lost again on the way home but it was nice to catch up with the same rotting badger we'd seen this morning and see how his day had been. A bit flat, as it turned out. When we got back to the hotel we found Mrs Goddard waiting for us on the steps. Her suit was looking more crumpled than this morning and she'd back-combed her hair and sprayed it into place, making her appear about a foot taller. Alarmingly her face was spattered with, what looked like, blood.

"Hello everyone," she said, still trying to sound as bright as a button, "Hope you've all had a lovely day. A slight change to this evening, I'm afraid. Our wonderful Chef has left us quite suddenly."

That sounded like a plus to me.

"There was a little disagreement when I questioned him about the freshness of his meatballs."

I guess any man would react to that.

"Are you ok?" Angela asked her, "You've got a…erm, little something on your face."

"Oh it's nothing," Mrs Goddard said, wiping her cheek, which just smeared the blood across it even more, "It's not mine." And she laughed, a little too hysterically.

She turned to go back in before any of us could ask whose blood it was, but then quickly turned back and said,

"Oh, by the way, Louella has stepped in and will be preparing dinner for you this evening," And with that, she was gone.

"Oh great," I said, to Angela, as we all traipsed inside, "So that will be dinner served at midnight then."

"A midnight feast can be romantic you know," Angela replied, and she squeezed my hand.

I wanted to say something romantic back to her, but the phrase, "I've got something for you to get your lips around and feast on darling" was the first thing that came to mind and I didn't feel that was quite appropriate, so I just smiled instead.

We all ventured down to dinner at the usual time but as suspected, we sat there waiting. Only Colin was missing. Eventually a soup was brought around. Chico, who had to serve all the tables, only had time for a quick pelvic thrust in Shauna's direction as he passed by, carrying three bowls.

"I wonder whose blood that was on Mrs Goddard's face," I said.

Shauna froze; her spoon halfway to her mouth.

"Jesus Dirk, this is tomato soup."

124

"Oh yeah; sorry."

She put the spoon back into the bowl.

"Well I've gone right off that now."

"I'm sorry."

"Oi, arsewipe," Shauna called over to Chico.

He obviously thought this a term of endearment and beamed as he ran over.

"What can Chico do for the sexiest woman in Tenhamshire?" he asked.

"You can grab these for me," she said.

Chico's eyes widened, lustfully.

"Oh Dio la mia bellezza."

"I meant the bowls, you sex-starved aardvark," Shauna told him, "Take them away. I can't eat this soup."

Chico went off with the crockery, none too steadily.

"I wonder if he's half Italian," Angela asked.

Shauna grunted. "Half Italian, half Prick."

The main course arrived and Louella had obviously sided with the chef and served us the meatballs, which begged the question, 'Why the fight in the first place?' The hotel must have bought a job lot of tomato soup tins as she'd also appeared to use it for the sauce, but it was really rather tasty, although Shauna didn't look too keen still. Dessert was bananas with ice cream. When it arrived the ice cream was pink and I did wonder if it was going to taste of tomato as well. Fortunately it was raspberry.

Afterwards we all retired to the bar where we found Colin, still in his dungarees, sitting on a bar stool and knocking back what appeared to be large brandies. I guess no one could blame him really after the day he'd had; chased by a menagerie followed by a horseshit bath. I probably hadn't helped matters when I passed my camera around on the coach on the way back to the hotel to show everyone the photographs.

We seemed to have got into the routine now of sitting in the bar in the same groups that we'd sat in at dinner, so I was surprised when Angela said she wanted to go and sit with Margaret to talk to her. I thought she'd been doing that all afternoon. That left me with Shauna and Jim.

"I wonder whose blood that was on Mrs Goddard," I said again, sipping another frothy beer.

"Oh you're not still on about that are you, Dirk?"

"Isn't anyone else worried?" I asked, "Mrs Goddard didn't mention the chef resigning, all she said was he'd left suddenly. They'd obviously had a big argument."

"About meatballs, Dirk," Shauna said, "It doesn't exactly sound like a reason for murder."

"We've only got Mrs Goddard's word for it that the fight was about that. She was acting very strangely when we got back," I reasoned, "After the last few days here I wouldn't be surprised if the chef was dead and buried under the rubble in the lounge. Maybe the floor caving in was all just a ruse. A way to hide the body before it was taken off and buried somewhere else."

"You've got an overactive imagination haven't you, Dirk."

"That would mean Harry was also in on it," I continued, warming to my theme, "It was his room after all. And it's odd that Mrs Goddard gave him her room rather than an empty one."

"Harry? Don't be ridiculous. He's as straight as they come. He's been given Barbara Goddard's room because she fancies him, that's obvious. Besides, she could have just made sure he was out of the way before the room caved in so that he didn't get hurt."

"Louella was though."

"We don't know that for sure," Shauna said, "We'd need to get a look under that bandage she's wearing, it might just be a prop…Jesus, what the hell am I saying? Christ Dirk, you've got me at it. The chef had a temper tantrum and stormed off and the blood was probably chicken's blood off of that meat cleaver he always seems to carry around with him."

"Oh," I said, a little disappointed, "I guess that would make sense."

Colin got clumsily off of his stool and downed another large brandy before picking up another and making his way over to the raised stage area. After a couple of failed attempts he managed to climb up, the baggy dungarees dropping as he bent over which gave everyone the chance to see a different side to Colin. He stared at the back wall for a few seconds until he got his bearings and then turned around to face us.

"This place is a disgrace," he told the group, swinging his arm in a wide gesture and spilling most of his drink, "The food's crap, the staff are ancient and the floors are falling down. I've seen more luxury in a Brazilian prison."

"When was he in a Brazilian prison?" I said, to Shauna.

"And you," Colin turned his attention onto me, "I'm never spending an afternoon with you again. A wild animal, chasing me, biting at my arse; sticking a fist up, bent over; in shit."

I felt Colin had missed out quite a few key words and his description really wasn't painting me in a good light.

"And as for you," he pointed at Shauna this time. I quietly moved my chair aside, "You and your little driver friend; shit, that's what you are. This trip…complete shit. I'm going to give so many people a mouthful when I get home. Oh yes I am. A piece of my mind. People are going to notice me. Not like her."

I think he'd forgotten we were all still there listening to him.

"Never noticed me; did you. Not until my hands were on you and you screamed, bitch. Now you're dead, mother; you and him. Hope you're happy!"

He fell silent and looked down at his feet; swaying a little on the spot. I couldn't speak for anyone else but I was feeling a little uncomfortable after that speech. I thought Colin had loved his mother. Surely he hadn't put his hands on her and...No stop it, Derek. You had the chef as a murder victim twenty seconds ago. It was just drunken ramblings; leave it at that. Colin looked up and seemed to realise we were all still sitting there in the room staring up at him.

"I want to sing," he said, throwing his arms wide, the brandy glass flying out of his hand and smashing against the wall. Luckily glum barman ducked just in time.

Colin proceeded to give us a medley of songs from the musicals. Apart from being a little slurry, he wasn't half bad; a lot more entertaining than the bird impressionist at any rate. We had 'Hey Big Spender', 'I Dreamed a Dream' and 'I'm Just a Girl Who Can't Say No." At the end he got a round of applause. He made a dramatic bow, overbalanced and tumbled off the stage. Colin fell heavily onto Josie and the two of them flew backwards over her chair. He was asleep before they hit the floor. She shrieked and called out, "Get him off me." Colin, in his sleep, placed a hand over her mouth.

"Ssh, mummy," he said, "Screaming won't do you any good now."

Chapter 8

The wine tasting was an optional, half-day excursion so it wouldn't necessarily be the whole group going. Hopefully that meant Angela and I would finally get some time alone together. Not since the trip to Baddlesbury had we been on our own and that felt like so long ago now. Plus that afternoon by the riverbank had been marred by the news about Maeve.

"I'm so pleased you agreed to do this," Angela whispered, over breakfast, squeezing my hand under the table and grinning at me.

"It's my pleasure," I replied.

She seemed to be as happy and excited at the prospect of spending some quality time together as I was.

"Off to the wine tasting, old boy," Harry patted me on the shoulder, "Very decent of you."

That seemed an odd expression to use. Why was Harry so glad that I was taking Angela to the wine tasting? It wasn't just him. Margaret kept smiling warmly at me every time we made eye contact and even Jim kept winking across the table at Angela and me, although maybe that was just conjunctivitis, or some other kind of eye infection.

Only Colin wasn't looking very cheery, which after last night wasn't very surprising. We'd left him in the capable hands of glum barman who'd informed us he was used to picking up drunken men in his line of work. When Colin walked into the dining room he was met by a spontaneous round of applause. He took a step backwards and winced.

"Please keep it down," he said, holding his head, "I have a terrible migraine."

"Are you going to be this evening's entertainment as well, Sunshine?" Shauna asked him, as he walked by our table.

"That stage is a death trap," he told us, "Look at this."

Colin pulled his sleeve back to reveal a tiny bruise on his wrist.

"I'll have to give Mrs Goddard another mouthful later. I'm not putting up with this."

I definitely preferred him drunk, although his little speech last night still left me cold if I thought about it. Shauna had said everyone's lives and secrets would be discovered. Maeve's terminal illness was one thing but a confession to murdering your own mother; surely that was way beyond even what Shauna had thought would be revealed. Colin had admitted that, hadn't he? What was it he'd said; something like she only screamed once his hands were on her and now she's dead? No wait, he said two were dead. I shivered. Why did no one else seem to be concerned by this? Had they forgotten his rantings once he'd started singing? I looked over at the cereal table where the man in question was sighing as he struggled to pick up the half-filled milk jug with two hands. He didn't exactly convey the image of a mighty, cold-blooded killer. Drunken ramblings; last night had to have been drunken ramblings; why couldn't I just accept that and move on?

After breakfast I arranged to meet Angela back down in reception and went upstairs to fetch my jacket. I was really looking forward to the trip, even though I don't drink a lot of wine myself. I much prefer a beer, although a decent one of those was hard to come by in this hotel. It felt great that Angela was obviously feeling the same way about me as I felt about her. I fairly skipped back down the stairs, whistling. I realised it was the tune of, 'Hey Big Spender' and stopped.

She was waiting for me in the hallway, looking radiant in her clingy red top and blue jeans.

"There you are," she said, grinning at me, "Ready?"

For anything, baby.

"I'm ready," I said.

"Great. I'll go and fetch Dora."

"Right. Sorry, what; fetch Dora?"

"Of course," Angela said, "Margaret and Harry can hardly spend some time alone together with Dora hanging around. That's why I suggested we take her on the wine tasting excursion."

"Margaret and Harry are spending some time alone together," I said, realising what I had actually agreed to and why I had been flavour of the month at breakfast.

"Yes," Angela looked a little puzzled, "Derek, you did realise what I meant didn't you?"

"Of course," I smiled, "Of course. We're taking Dora to the wine tasting. Terrific; marvellous. Let's go and get her."

We both walked up the hallway to Dora's room, Angela still with a perplexed expression on her face. Margaret opened the door. She'd changed outfits since breakfast and was now wearing a blue dress and cardigan. She had a decorative clip in her hair, a hint of blusher on her cheeks and a great big grin across her face.

"Thanks so much for doing this both of you."

"It's our pleasure, isn't it Derek?" Angela said.

I was miles away, still trying to work out how I'd misconstrued the conversation on the coach yesterday.

"Isn't it Derek?" she repeated.

"Hmm? Oh yes, sure; our pleasure."

"Mum, I'm just popping out," Margaret called, "Have a lovely day."

"Day?" I said to Angela, as Margaret rushed past us, "I

thought it was just a morning excursion."

I didn't want to be saddled with Dora for the whole day.

"Well technically it's a half-day excursion, rather than a morning one. I'm guessing ten 'til two would count as a half day, time wise," Angela was still looking at me oddly, "I'm not sure a wine tasting trip would usually start too early in the morning, Derek. Are you sure you're okay with this; you don't have to come."

"No, I'm fine," I said, trying to sound happier than I felt. Any time shared with Angela was better than no time at all.

We walked into the bedroom. It was quite dark, like the rest of the ground floor but it was a decent size. It contained both a double and a single bed.

"Margaret, are you still there?" Dora opened the door from the bathroom. I could see that it was a proper en suite, unlike my cupboard upstairs. She looked like she was all ready to go; dressed in a pink blouse and brown, pleated skirt.

"Oh hello you two," she said, "Has Margaret gone out already?"

"Only just. Shall I see if I can catch her?" Angela asked.

"If you wouldn't mind, dear," Dora replied.

"I can go if you…," but Angela was already gone.

So that left me alone with Dora the pincher; in her bedroom. I felt very uncomfortable.

"I haven't taken my medication yet," Dora explained, limping into the room, "Margaret always helps me with it."

"Can I get it for you?" I asked; glad to have something to do.

Dora sat down on the double bed. "If you wouldn't mind getting it ready for me," she said, "It's in that packet over there on the dressing table."

I walked over and opened the packet. There was a strip of capsules inside.

"Is it just one?" I called.

"Yes, thank God."

I tore one off the strip and split it open. It was rather a large, long pill to take.

"I'm glad I don't have to swallow this," I said, turning round.

"Me too," Dora replied, crouching face down on the bed, her knickers caught over one of her ankles.

"Jesus Christ!"

"Come on Derek," said Dora, "It's not much fun for me either. Hitch up the old skirt and pop it in. Be brave now."

An image entered my head of the vet from the farm yesterday.

"No, sorry," I said; shaking my head, "I can't."

Dora started laughing, her whole body rocking; making the bed creak.

"Don't worry Derek, I'm only joking," she told me, getting up and rearranging herself, "I wouldn't make you do that. If Margaret's gone I can leave it until later."

It so wasn't going to be the day I'd hoped for.

Margaret had already left with Harry in his two-seater sports car. She hadn't wanted Dora to know where she was going or who with and so had raced out before we set off. Angela and I walked Dora out to the coach.

"It's good of the two of you to do this," she said, "Margaret isn't much of a drinker so this would have been boring for her. I think she said she was going to take a walk around the village this morning. I'd much rather be out getting sloshed on wine."

"It's no problem," Angela told her, "We're looking forward to it, aren't we Derek."

I wished Angela would stop including me in her conversations.

"Oh yes," I said, "We are."

Jim was muttering under his breath and clutching onto his rabbit's foot for dear life as we boarded.

"He stood on a crack," Shauna told us. She saw our confused expressions, "Step on a crack, break your mother's back."

"Is that possible?" I asked.

"Well, apparently she does have osteoporosis."

Jim started hyperventilating.

"Oh pull yourself together and phone her," Shauna shouted at him, "I'm sure she's fine. Your mother suffered all her bad luck the day you were born."

Jim hopped off the coach while we sat down. Angela kindly let me sit next to Dora up the front and she took the seat behind. Not only was I squashed up against the window I was right behind Jim's seat for a good view of his driving technique. I also had a view of Shauna's cleavage when she sat down so it wasn't all bad. Mind you, when she picked her nose and smeared it on her left breast while looking for a tissue in her handbag, I felt pretty disgusted.

"There's only two more coming today," she called out, wiping the tissue across her tit.

With my luck Angela had probably invited Maeve and Louella along for me to look after as well. I was so relieved when Karen and Leroy got on. I grinned broadly and waved over at them as best I could now that Dora had nodded off on my shoulder and was dribbling down my jacket.

Jim got back on and started the engine. He still looked close to tears but at least he'd put his rabbit's foot away. Shauna dispensed with the mike as there were only the five of us and we were all sitting up the front.

"Right," she said, "Langton's Vineyard. It's only an hour's

journey so we hopefully won't need to stop for a bog break on the way."

She glanced over in my direction but I decided to pretend she was referring to Dora.

"There'll be a short tour of the vineyard and the winery and then some wine tasting and a ploughman's lunch. We should be back by two."

Great, we were going to spend as much time getting to and from the vineyard as actually being there. I realised how much I was moaning but I'd expected a quiet morning with Angela; laughing together and sipping different wines; enjoying each other's company over a nice meal. Now I was going to be stuck pushing an old woman around all day, doubtless drinking stuff I wouldn't even sprinkle on my chips and eating a lunch that was destined to be a stale hunk of bread with some whiffy cheese; probably eaten while Dora told us all about her feet.

From my new vantage point I could see how hard Jim gripped the steering wheel whilst driving, his knuckles white from the tension. More scarily, he was leaning so far forward to look out of the windscreen his bum had actually left his cushioned booster seat. He was standing up while driving a coach. I couldn't look. I turned to my left. Shauna was scratching her left tit. I guess if she stopped leaving bogeys there she might not get an itch. Suddenly she pulled it out of her top and began studying the whole breast; twisting it around and staring at the nipple. I couldn't believe she'd done that, right there on the coach for anyone to see.

"They're real, Dirk," she said, without looking up.

I whipped my head back and stared out of the window for the rest of the journey.

The vineyard was a beautiful place. We drove up a long drive, past fields with rows of vines growing in them and emerged into what must have once been a farmyard, with a large Victorian-looking farmhouse to the left and a stunning thatched barn on the right.

The sun came out as we got off the coach and it was warm enough to leave jackets off. Mrs Goddard, on one of her fleeting visits into the dining room this morning, had mentioned the weather was meant to be getting warmer, which might lead to a storm or two at the end of the week. Dora was wide awake now after sleeping for most of the journey.

"When do we start tasting?" she asked, as she got into her wheelchair.

"At the end of the tour," I said, giving my neck a good stretch.

"Damn, there's always a catch."

A man came rushing out from the farmhouse, pulling on his suit jacket as he ran over.

"Hello," he called, "Sorry I wasn't here to greet you as you drove up."

He stopped by the coach and his face fell.

"Oh," he said, looking down his nose, "Have you booked; we've got a large coach tour arriving any moment."

"We've booked," said Shauna, showing him a receipt.

The man's eyes opened wide as he looked at the ticket.

"But, this must be some kind of mistake," he said, "We thought you were a coach booking."

"We are," Shauna told him, "What do you think this is?" She indicated the coach.

"I wouldn't like to say," the man muttered, under his breath.

"Look," said Shauna, "We booked this up months ago. Your company said it was no problem to let you know a final headcount the day before and that's what I did yesterday. It's not my problem if you have the numbers written down wrong. I spoke to someone called Nigel. I take it he does work for you?"

"Not for much longer," the man whispered. He sighed and then forced a smile onto his face, "Anyway; not to worry. This is Langton's Vineyard. You are most welcome."

I didn't feel we were.

"I'll get one of our guides to come and meet you and then you can begin the tour."

He took one last look at our small group, shook his head and returned to the farmhouse.

"Not a happy person," I said.

"Truth is, Dirk," whispered Shauna, "I did pretend we were a larger group so that they'd lay on a guided tour for us."

That was unusually nice of her.

"Otherwise I would have had to do it."

That sounded more like Shauna.

The lady that came over to the coach was a lot friendlier. She smiled warmly at us as she introduced herself. She was wearing a long, blue apron, which I assumed amounted to a uniform around here. Carole was probably about fifty and had none of the snobbery I associated with wine.

"Now I know you're most interested in the tasting," she told us, "But I'm afraid I have to take you around the vineyard and winery first."

"Boo," Dora called out.

"Don't worry, I won't linger or waffle on," Carole continued, "But do please feel free to ask any questions on the way."

"Yeah, I have a question," said Leroy, raising his hand, "How many wines do we get to taste?"

Carole laughed. "Actually," she whispered, conspiratorially, "I shouldn't mention this but, because you're a smaller group than we anticipated, there are a lot of bottles already opened for tasting."

"Sounds good to me," Leroy said, rubbing his hands.

"And me," Dora agreed.

Leroy bent down beside her wheelchair.

"I bet you can't wait to get your lips around something tasty, can you," he said, "If you know what I mean?"

"She knows what you mean," I said, pushing Dora away, "Shall we get on?"

Carole led us over to the vines. She told us all about the different types of grape that they grew and how they blended certain ones together but to be honest I wasn't listening that closely. This part of the tour wasn't designed for wheelchairs and I was having trouble pushing Dora. It didn't help that every so often she kept calling out, "A bit faster Derek. Let's get to the tasting." It was much easier once we moved on to the winery, which was housed inside the barn.

"And so once we've picked the grapes at the optimum time, remember a good wine can never be produced from a bad grape; they're brought here," The barn was vast and Carole's voice echoed around the space, "The grapes are taken by conveyor belt to a tank where the fermentation process begins."

"Now we're getting to the good bit," Dora said, wringing her hands in anticipation.

Leroy laughed.

"This is the point where the process changes for red and white wines," Carole told us, "It's assumed by some that white wine is produced using white grapes and red wines using red grapes, but this isn't true."

I saw Angela nodding, knowingly. I hadn't a clue. I was at the level where I thought grapes were red or green; where did white come from?

Carole continued, "For red wines, the grapes are fermented

with their skins on; whereas for white wine, the grapes are first pressed; thereby separating the juice from the skins before fermentation begins. As well as wine, we also make ciders, liqueurs and fruit juices; all are organic."

"What's the cider made from?" Karen asked, "I didn't see any apple trees."

"We have orchards behind the farmhouse," Carole told her, "We make cider from our apples and Perry from our pears."

"I like a nice pear, if you know what I mean," said Leroy.

I rolled my eyes.

"I'm talking about tits," he said.

Dora chuckled.

"Yes, we know what you meant," I sighed.

Carole, not used to Leroy's ways, seemed a little startled but she managed to maintain her composure.

"We ferment the apples once to make a cider. We then ferment them a second time, which turns it into a cider vinegar."

"Damn waste of time that," said Dora, "You really shouldn't bother with the second one, love."

Leroy laughed. "A woman after my own heart," he said, throwing his arms around Dora's shoulders and giving her a squeeze.

I saw Karen shake her head and walk on a few yards. I followed her.

"Honestly, if it's in a skirt he flirts with it," she said to me.

"I really don't think you have anything to be jealous about," I replied, "Dora is eighty-five years old."

I couldn't believe Karen felt so insecure. What did she think; Leroy was about to trade her in for an older woman? Besides, it was my bottom that Dora liked to pinch, not his.

"Hey Derek," Dora called over, still laughing with Leroy, "You've got some younger competition."

"Bloody cheek," I said, to Karen, "Who am I, Old Father Time? Let him push her around for a while, see if he's still laughing later on." She smiled knowingly at me.

Carole's tour continued on and I did find it interesting. Eventually we found ourselves in the storage area which was filled with barrels. Dora's eyes lit up and her mouth dropped open. No sound emerged; the sight of all that wine had rendered her speechless.

"After fermentation has finished most red wines are moved to barrels to complete their maturation," Carole said, "These ones are all made of oak. Where they come from, and if they've been used before, affect the character of the developing wines."

As we moved through the area we came across another member of staff in his blue apron who appeared to be filling up a random barrel with red wine through a tube. Carole stopped by his side.

"Winemakers need to check the maturing red wine at regular intervals," she said, "What Philip here is doing is topping this one up as some of it will have evaporated during the maturing process."

"Isn't it fascinating, Derek?" Angela whispered.

I turned and smiled at her. "It is," I replied, "I didn't know half of what went on in wine making."

When I turned back I found Philip had gone off and Dora now had the tube in her mouth, sucking away quite happily.

"What are you doing?" I hissed, moving the tube out of her reach.

"I'm gasping, Derek," she said, "How long until the tasting?"

"I'm sure it won't be long now." I felt like I was talking to a child on a lengthy car journey.

"At the end of the maturing process the wine is ready to be

bottled. It's first filtered to make it clearer and remove any risk of microbial spoilage, but once that's done it's into the bottles," Carole smiled, "And that completes our tour. If you would now like to follow me, I'll take you across to the tasting area."

So excited was she, Dora had started wheeling herself across the room before I had a chance to push. We were led across to the farmhouse. As we entered a room to the right so I saw that the ones to the left had been knocked through and adapted into a restaurant, where two waitresses were collecting up crockery and glasses, leaving only one small table set up for lunch for our party.

The tasting room consisted of a large table at the far end, behind which stood the man who had greeted us upon arrival, and to the sides, two trestle tables were filled with trays of wine samples. Several other members of staff in their blue aprons were ready to hand around the glasses.

"Wahey," said Dora, "Let's get started then."

The man from earlier cleared his throat.

"If you'd all be so kind as to move over here, I'll be taking you through the tasting process."

We all moved closer; some of us a little more reluctantly than others. There were a number of different bottles of wine on the table in front of him.

"My name is Edward and I have been a taster here for five years. I'd like to take you through the way wine should be enjoyed."

"I've been enjoying it for over sixty years, darling," Dora called, "There's nothing you can teach me. Let's get at it."

Edward ignored her.

"First of all," he said, lifting up a glass of white, "You should look at it."

"Look schmook."

"Then you gently swirl the wine around the glass before using your next sense; smell."

Edward put his nose in the top of the glass and took a big sniff.

"Some wines," he said, "You can only smell the bouquet at the top of the glass. Others still have an aroma when smelled from three inches away, but there are examples where even six inches will still give you pleasure."

"I've got nine inches that gives pleasure, if you know what I mean," said Leroy.

Karen's smack across his arm told all of us, she knew what he meant.

"And finally," said Edward, concentrating on the wine glass, "We take a sip."

"About bloody time," Dora called out.

"Move it across the tongue," Edward mumbled, with the wine still in his mouth, "Get all of the flavours."

He then spat the wine out into a pot beside him.

"You should be thoroughly ashamed of yourself," Dora scolded.

It was now our turn to taste. We started with the wine Edward had just tried. The other staff members picked up the trays and brought them over to us. One of them, a man with very black, dyed hair sidled up to Shauna.

"Buen dia Senorita, I am Carlos. Can I offer you something strong and fragrant with a little kick?"

Shauna sighed. "Unless you want to feel 'a little kick' right where you keep your corkscrew, I suggest you piss off and bother someone else."

The guy that served Dora, Angela and I looked very young. I wasn't even sure he was old enough to drink the stuff himself. I took a sip and tried not to grimace. Angela followed the same steps that Edward had done; bar the spitting out. Dora downed hers in one gulp. The guy turned to replace the tray on the trestle table.

"Where do you think you're going?" she called.

He turned back and Dora took another glass off the tray, downed that and had one more. She smacked her lips.

"That's better," she said, "Alright; you can go now and get the next one ready."

Each round was the same. Edward would try the wine first, informing us that we could purchase all of them after the tasting. Sometimes he told us what to expect and other times he would ask us what we could taste. He did his best to ignore the less helpful comments.

"This has an intense, crisp flavour. What can you taste?"

"A crisp flavour; I'm getting smoky bacon," said Dora.

"This one has a hint of spice, a smooth texture and a long finish."

"I like a long finish, if you know what I mean."

"This robust blackcurrant palate will enhance any beef or game meal."

"And it would go great with a savaloy and chips as well. Oi pipsqueak, where are you going with that tray? I told you to stay here."

"This one has a delicate bouquet but the taste is ripe, smooth and full-bodied."

"I like a full body, if you know what I mean."

Edward was obviously used to a better behaved group; and a bigger one. At least he had Angela as a willing pupil.

"What fruits can you detect in the flavour?" he asked.

Angela sniffed and then tasted.

"Cherry?"

"Very good. And what else?"

143

All I was getting was grape. Angela took another sip.

"Is it damson?"

"Excellent."

I think Dora had three glasses to everyone else's one. She was pretty merry by the fifth bottle and told us all a limerick about a loose girl from Buckingham.

"That's all of the wines tasted," said Edward, finally; sounding very relieved, "The ploughman's lunch is ready to be served across in the dining room, unless you would like to try the organic fruit juices?"

"Are they alcoholic?" Dora asked.

"No."

"Wheel me to lunch, Derek."

Before we went in we were asked if we wished to purchase any of the wines. Angela spent rather a lot of money on several cases. No one else offered to buy any and I felt guilty. I found myself forking out two hundred and fifty pound on eight bottles of wine I didn't want to drink and which I really couldn't afford. At least Angela looked impressed.

The ploughman's was surprisingly delicious. Homemade bread, a large chunk of cheese with pickles, chutneys and a fresh green salad were great at soaking up the wine. We all chatted amiably, enjoying a dessert of lemon meringue pie and then coffee. Dora nodded off after the main course and I moved her over to the far corner when she started snoring.

Once the coffee was finished and mine and Angela's wine purchases were brought out, it was time to go. Shauna arranged for the wine to be loaded onto the coach where she said it could stay until we returned home at the end of the week. Angela was worried about what the movement of the coach over the next few days would do to the wines but when told the alternative was for her to carry all of the purchases to her room and store them there she decided the coolness of the coach's storage area was perfect.

I walked over to where I'd parked Dora. She'd slumped over to one side in the chair, her head hanging loosely. How could someone sleep like that, unless…? I walked back over to the table where Angela was putting her wine receipt into her purse.

"I think Dora's sick," I whispered.

"I'm not surprised after what she drank," Angela replied.

"Turn round and have a look."

She did.

"Oh," Angela said, "I see what you mean. Maybe she's just passed out."

"Or worse."

"What, you think she's dead?"

I nodded. "I only said sick to soften the blow."

I took another look over at her myself.

"I'm being silly aren't I? She can't be dead; not on the day we're looking after her. How can we go back and face Margaret?"

"She isn't dead, Derek. Go over and wake her up."

I couldn't move. If she had died and I tapped her hand to try and wake her, wouldn't it be icy cold already? The thought made me shiver.

"Are you two ready?" Karen had just returned from the Ladies.

"Ah, Karen," I said, "Can you go and wake Dora for me."

"Derek!" Angela admonished.

It was worth a try.

"Is she ok?" Karen asked, looking over at Dora with the same concerned expression as Angela and I, "I mean, how can someone sleep all slumped over like that?"

"That's what I thought," I admitted, "I moved her there when she started snoring. Why didn't I hear the noise stop?"

Leroy walked in from the Gents.

"Ready guys. Hasn't this been great?"

"Lee," Karen whispered, matter-of-factly, "We think Dora's dead."

My mouth dropped open.

"My God, there's no soft soaping with you, is there?" I told her, "You're not a Samaritan in your spare time are you?"

"Derek, will you just go and wake her," Angela said, "I'm sure she's fine, just plastered."

"Then you go and wake her," I replied, "Today was all your idea, remember?"

"Why don't we all go," said Karen.

It seemed the best solution. The four of us gingerly walked over to the old woman and stood there in front of her.

"Well, what do we do now?" Leroy asked.

"Someone should take her pulse," Karen suggested.

"Not me," I said, "I'm not touching a dead body."

"Has anyone got a mirror?"

"This isn't the time to check your appearance, Lee."

"No, they do it in the movies don't they. Hold a mirror under someone's mouth and if it fogs up, they're still breathing."

"Why don't we all lean in and see if we can hear her breathing," Angela suggested.

That sounded like a plan. We each leaned forward. As we did so, Dora let out the loudest fart I think I've ever heard. It ricocheted off the walls and startled one of the young waitresses who overturned her tray of glasses. We all reeled backwards. Dora opened her eyes.

"Think that one scorched the cheeks of my arse," she said.

Chapter 9

I felt both relieved and repulsed as we made our way outside. We'd all left a lasting impression on the vineyard but Dora had certainly given them a little something extra they weren't going to forget in a hurry. While we were on the tour Jim had taken the coach off for refuelling. Amazingly he'd managed to find his way back to the vineyard again. What with this and his mother still being in one piece after the crack incident it was turning into a red-letter day for him. He was sat up on his cushion in the driver's seat, grinning away like a myopic Cheshire cat.

Shauna was having a bit of trouble folding down the wheelchair; until a bottle of red wine from the tasting fell out of it. Dora sprang forwards with the grace of a panther, snatching up the bottle from the floor and holding it to her chest in a vice like grip.

"I wondered where that had gone," she muttered, under her breath.

She pushed passed us all, not making eye contact and for the first time that week; climbed onto the coach unassisted.

We spaced ourselves out on the return journey. Leroy had a lie down on the back seat while Karen remained up front. Dora had disappeared down into a seat in the middle row, hopefully to continue her sleep and Angela and I sat together in our usual place. She put her hand over mine.

"Thanks for coming today," she said, and then kissed me on the cheek, "I realise I enjoyed it a lot more than you."

"It's just become worth it," I said.

Angela smiled, ignoring the cheesiness of the line and rested her head on my shoulder. She was asleep within a minute but unlike Dora; she didn't dribble down my jacket.

I eventually dozed off too. I awoke when Dora began loudly singing a song about Mary from the Diner, who had a big...well; you get the gist. Fortunately we were just pulling into the driveway of the hotel so I didn't hear what happened after she met Rod from the Dock in the second verse; but I could guess. I walked up the coach to get her.

"Hello Derek," Dora sang. The wine bottle lay empty beside her on the seat. So it wasn't a sleep she'd been enjoying.

"We're back," I said to her, slowly, my face right in front of hers, "We've got to get off now. Do you understand?"

She stared at me intensely. "You know; if I were thirty years younger, Derek, I'd shag the arse off you; with my teeth in and my tits out."

What a lovely image that conveyed.

"Come on," I said, taking hold of her arm, "I need to get you into bed."

I could have phrased that better.

"Derek, you dirty boy," Dora trilled, before pulling me down onto her lap and spanking my arse.

"A little help needed here," I called out, desperately, through the pleats of her skirt.

Together we eventually managed to get Dora safely down the steps of the coach. She said she didn't want to go inside but wanted to dance. After a couple of dangerous pirouettes that sent Jim flying into the hedge, the only way we finally got Dora into the hotel was by forming a conga and directing her up the steps. The effort of that seemed to tire her out so she was much easier to handle once inside.

"Don't worry," I said, to Angela, "I'll take her to her room. I can manage."

148

"Ok Derek, but come and give me a knock in twenty minutes and we'll go for a walk; just the two of us." She smiled and disappeared upstairs.

I practically dragged Dora across the hallway to her room.

"Right you," I said, "In here."

I opened the door, pulled her inside and dropped her onto the bed; where she began snoring away quite happily. I checked my watch. Oh, that had taken less than a minute; still over nineteen to go.

When I came out of the room I bumped into Margaret. She was grinning from ear to ear.

"Had a good day?" I asked.

"Wonderful," she replied. I noticed her cardigan was on inside out, "We went to see Harry's barn. Oh, it's a beautiful place and in the most stunning location. I took a picture of it on my phone. How's mum?"

"She's sleeping it off."

Margaret sniggered. "I bet she is. I can't thank you enough." And for the second time that day, I received a kiss on the cheek.

"I'll go and see how she is," Margaret said, "And then I must buy you and Angela a drink."

"We're going out for a walk first," I told her, "But we'll be around later on."

I didn't want anything getting in the way of Angela and me spending some time alone together.

I wandered back down the hallway and saw that the ribbon on the lounge door had been split open. I'd noticed the scaffolding had been removed and the glass replaced while Dora was performing Swan Lake out on the driveway. I wondered what state the room was in now. There was no one about. A quick look wouldn't hurt, surely. I opened the door.

It was still a mess. Everything that had fallen through the floor appeared to have just been swept away from the window area so that the glaziers could do their job. There was a huge pile against the opposite wall. Bits of broken chair and table were mixed in with pieces of smashed glass and the debris was entirely covered in a fresh layer of dust. Why on earth Mrs Goddard hadn't yet hired a skip to get rid of all this rubbish I didn't know. There was still a gaping hole in the ceiling and I realised I probably shouldn't even be in here without a hard hat. I wondered if the room above had been cordoned off with a ribbon; or perhaps with some tinsel and a few decorative baubles.

I turned to leave but as I did, something caught my eye. It was just poking out from the edge of the rubble. A shoe; well a trainer actually with the laces tied. I still wasn't convinced by Mrs Goddard's story about the chef leaving the hotel and my theory of him being under the rubble returned to my mind. It would explain why the mess hadn't yet been cleared away. I walked over and bent down beside the footwear. I didn't want to pick it up in case it turned out to be evidence.

"What are you doing in here Mr Noble?"

I leapt up and span round. Barbara Goddard was standing in the doorway, blocking my only means of escape. Her hair was still back-combed into a tall, menacing shape and the twitching eye that I'd noticed yesterday had developed into a full blown tic. I realised how stupid I'd been to come in here without any back-up. If she'd managed to kill that big brute of a chef in a fit of anger during an argument, she'd have no trouble dealing with me.

"This room is off limits as you well know," Barbara continued, "Are you from a hotel guide or something; come here to spy on me?"

150

"I, I, I…no; no I'm not; I'm not."

I was gibbering.

"I erm, thought the room was open again," that's it Derek, play the innocent, "The scaffolding is down and the ribbon on the door has been split open."

"Well you obviously must have realised it wasn't safe as soon as you walked in. What are you still doing here?"

Bugger, she had me there. Oh sod it, go for broke Derek, the best form of defence is attack. I picked up the shoe.

"Can you tell me what this is doing here under the rubble?" I asked.

Barbara frowned. "It's a shoe," she said, walking over to me.

"Yes; and whose shoe is it?"

"Louella's probably," she replied, taking it off of me for a closer look, "The poor woman was in the room when the ceiling fell in."

"And what about the chef?" I asked, "Doesn't he wear trainers?"

That's it Derek, keep the attack going.

"Not mauve striped ones in a size four," Barbara said.

"What?"

I looked at the shoe in her hand. Oh, I hadn't really noticed the style or size.

"Why did you think it was the chef's?" Barbara asked.

She looked questioningly at me but I couldn't speak. Suddenly, realisation dawned on her face and she smiled.

"You don't think he's buried under there do you?"

She began to chuckle and I felt like a complete pillock.

"Oh Mr Noble," Barbara said, "That's a good one. Did you think I'd done him in because I thought his meatballs were off?"

Her chuckling turned into a big, hearty laugh. All I could do was stand there, going redder and redder in the face while she got louder and louder. In the end, Mrs Goddard was practically bent double, one hand grabbing onto my arm to stop her toppling forwards and the other clutching her side, she was laughing that hard. Eventually, through probable exhaustion, she began to compose herself.

"Oh dear me," she said, pulling a tissue out of her sleeve, "That felt good. I've not laughed like that in years. To think, little me, battering a big man like the chef to death; just because of his…of his meatballs."

And off she went again. At no point did I feel like joining in. After what felt like an eternity, she finally managed to calm herself down.

"The chef's emptying his room as we speak. His brother's got him some work over at a hotel in Cunden Lingus," she said, wiping her eyes and then blowing her nose, "You can pop out the back and see him if you want proof."

I didn't want to barge into his room and risk a glimpse of those enormous knackers again, but as I was escorted out of the lounge, I did spare a thought for this other hotel's takings; they were bound to fall.

Barbara left me in the hallway and continued to giggle as she disappeared through the door behind the reception area. I wandered into the dining room, still feeling embarrassed. Josie was sitting at one of the tables with a pack of cards.

"Hello," she said, brightly, shuffling them, "How was the wine tasting?"

I'd almost forgotten I'd been on that. Shit, I'd forgotten I was meeting Angela.

"It was good," I replied, checking my watch, "Quite enjoyable really."

I still had a few minutes to spare.

"Where's Sooz?" I asked.

"She went out for a walk," Josie said, "I think up to the church."

Note to self, avoid church on walk with Angela. I wondered if I should freshen up first.

"I don't know when she'll be back," Josie continued, laying out the cards, "But I don't mind sitting here playing with myself."

"It can help to pass the time," I told her, absently; my mind concentrating on what I should do next. Maybe just a quick change of clothes. Angela would be wearing something different, I was sure of that.

"Would you like to play with me, Derek?"

"What?" My God, where had that come from?

Josie was smiling sweetly up at me.

"Oh, well," I said, "That's a bit out of the blue. Erm it's a lovely thought, and another time I'd be flattered, but I'm…oh, you mean the cards. Sorry, I already have plans with Angela."

I headed upstairs to meet her. I could probably change my top quickly first. As I reached the set of stairs that split off between our rooms I heard her door open. As I looked up I was shocked to see Jim emerge from the room, zipping up his trousers. Angela was right behind him.

"I'm sorry," I heard him say, "I'm so sorry."

"That's alright," Angela said, "It's over now, isn't it."

Jim nodded miserably and walked off in the other direction. She looked down the stairs; saw me and jumped.

"Oh God, Derek; I didn't see you there," she indicated Jim, "The blind, old sod got the wrong room. I came out of the shower just now and found him lying on my bed in just his pants. That'll teach me for leaving my door unlocked."

I relaxed. "I guess it must have been quite a shock for both

153

of you."

"You're telling me. I'm still not sure who screamed the loudest."

I laughed. "Are you ready to go?" I asked, "I was going to change first but I don't have to."

"Actually Derek, would you mind if we make it another day? I think that wine has finally kicked in. I've got a splitting headache."

"Oh," I said, trying not to sound utterly devastated, "Okay; sure. I hope you feel better soon."

"I'm sure after a sleep and a couple of aspirin I'll be fine."

I turned and walked back down the stairs.

"I'll see you at dinner," she called after me.

"Yep."

It was silly, I know, to feel so downhearted. Angela and I had only met four days ago after all. I was very attracted to her but could I really be sure those feelings were reciprocated? So she'd squeezed my hand a few times, she'd done that with lots of other people too, it was part of who she was. Perhaps her friendliness towards me was due purely to what I had told her on the coach on day one about my recent troubles. What if she didn't want to see me again after we all returned home on Sunday? That thought really chilled me to the bone. I couldn't imagine my world now without Angela in it.

I walked out of the hotel and up towards the crossroads where the old pig trough was. There weren't any touristy sights or pubs or shops in the village, just a few houses placed sporadically along the main road. I wondered why Mrs Goddard had her hotel out here in the middle of nowhere. There wasn't any traffic to speak of, so no passing trade and I'd looked on the map to see how far away the spa town of Cunden Lingus was and it was miles. I guess that explained why the hotel was so deserted and in such a poor state of repair.

The church was opposite me and I walked over to it. No point avoiding the place now. It was tiny and as I got a little closer, I noticed that most of it was made of wood. Intrigued I walked in through the gate.

On closer inspection the church appeared to be made up of three separate sections. The tower was clad in white weatherboard with a shingle roof. The middle section next to this, behind the front porch, was covered in black, worn, wooden timbers, which gave it the look of a barn. The final part was made of what seemed to be two different sizes of brick. Both this and the wooden section were topped with a tiled roof that had several dormer windows placed in it. The building as a whole had a real old-world charm to it. It was beautiful, and the setting so tranquil.

I walked around the outside of the church first, passing grave stones and a stone tomb surrounded by railings, presumably containing the remains of some local dignitary. On the opposite side of the building I noticed three small holes and one larger one about a metre off the ground in the wooden section. I had no idea what they were for. As I made my way around to the front again I spotted a grave stone on the ground, right next to the porch. It was for a crusader. This church really was ancient. Perhaps there had been a larger village here at some point? If so, what had happened to it?

I entered the church through the porch. Just inside on the left stood a large shelving unit that was full of pens and guidebooks and badges. I picked up a guidebook and placed a couple of pound in the honesty box. Inside, the space felt more like one whole building rather than three separate areas as the outside had seemed. It still looked small but the sensation I got was just the same as I'd felt in the vastly larger church at Baddlesbury.

I wasn't alone in there. Sooz was sitting in the front pew. I walked quietly up the aisle, looking at the rest of the interior as I went. At first she didn't notice me. She appeared deep in contemplation, staring towards the altar, a guidebook lying open beside her. I could see the moment she sensed she wasn't on her own. She jumped when she saw me, but then smiled.

"Derek, I was miles away."

"Sorry, I didn't mean to startle you."

"Isn't this a beautiful, little church," she said, picking up her guide book, "I've been reading all about it."

"It's certainly old," I replied, sitting down in the pew on the opposite side of the aisle, "I wanted to find out what those holes at the back were."

"Arseholes."

"Pardon?"

"They're eye-holes," Sooz repeated.

"Oh, right. Sorry, I completely misheard you the first time."

"Did you notice that larger one?" Sooz said, "It says in here that a lot of people believe it's a Leper Squint; a place where lepers could receive alms without coming into contact with anyone. Isn't that fascinating? Apparently most archaeologists disagree with this theory and suspect it was either just another eye-hole or possibly a ledge that held a holy water stoup back in the middle-ages. I rather prefer the leper squint theory."

"I think I do too," I said.

Whether it was the beauty of the church or Sooz's informal guided tour of it I wasn't sure, but my mood had begun to lighten again.

"Of course, those eye-holes would have been the only source of natural light in here for hundreds of years," she continued.

"What about the dormer windows?" I asked, looking up above me.

"A later edition. They were Tudor to begin with but restored in Victorian times."

"Oh, so the windows are quite modern for a church this age then."

Sooz chuckled. "I suppose they are," she said, "Every generation adds something."

She sighed, happily. "I do like coming into a church. They're always so beautiful and peaceful. I love being able to come in and just sit down and contemplate things."

"Would you rather be on your own?" I asked, half getting up.

"Not at all. I've been sat here for far too long already, to be honest with you. I was thinking about my George so I do tend to lose myself in thought."

An image entered my head of me and Shauna standing outside my room back on day one when she referred to Sooz and Josie as lesbians; although not quite in those terms. Well, she was wrong about them both. Josie had already mentioned her family boating holidays and now Sooz was telling me about George; although I guess that could be short for Georgina.

"George wasn't much for the Church," Sooz admitted, "Thought it too corrupt and wealthy. I always enjoyed the Sunday service but George said too many bible stories were twisted into meanings to suit the bigoted view of the teller."

I noticed she always said George; never 'he' or 'my husband.' That could be significant. Oh, stop it Derek.

"So eventually I stopped going too," Sooz continued, "I wasn't made to, but it was easier to go along with the man of the relationship."

Well that could mean anything.

She smiled, lost in her thoughts. "When I think about it now, I realise we were such opposites really. I liked to dress up in my best when we went out but George was always happiest in a pair of dungarees."

Wow; perhaps there was something in what Shauna had said after all.

"I was always the little homemaker and George took care of all the big DIY jobs."

I'd heard there were often male/female roles in a same sex relationship.

"I was so coy and George was so butch."

There was the clincher.

"But we did have plenty of things in common as well. We both loved to play tennis."

"You must miss her very much," I said.

Sooz whipped around and looked at me.

"What did you say?" she asked, "George was my husband. Did you just say 'her?' Whatever made you say that, Derek?"

"Oh sorry, did I say that?" I said, blushing and feeling like a complete pillock for the second time that day. Where the hell had that nineteen seventies stereotypical view suddenly come from? So much for me being a modern man. Forty-five and turning into my father.

"A slip of the tongue," I said, adding, "You must miss **him** very much."

Sooz nodded but still with a questioning look on her face. I wanted to shout out, 'It was all Shauna's fault' but I couldn't blame her for my own idiocy.

"So, you said he wasn't very religious." I wanted to move the conversation on; and quickly.

"On the contrary Derek, George was a great believer in God; just not the Church. We used to take a walk through the countryside around our cottage every Sunday. We'd go down to the river and sit and contemplate. I believe that's where my George liked to do his praying; in God's own, natural church so to speak."

"I see." I was only half listening, still berating myself. What an attitude. All I'd missed out were a pair of Doc Martin boots and a shaved head for God's sake!

"No, George stopped going to church after his son from his first marriage came out as gay," Sooz continued.

I was listening now. At least someone was gay.

"He absolutely adored his son, so did I. Well, I wasn't much older than him really, George being twenty years my senior. I'm afraid in the eyes of the particular church that George attended; this lovely, young man was no longer welcome and destined to an eternity in hell. Not a very Christian attitude in my mind. George couldn't believe that was right. His beautiful, kind, generous son was, in his opinion, created by God, and if God loved him, so should everyone else."

"That's very true," I said.

Sooz's smile faltered.

"His rather pious mother didn't share her ex-husband's opinion and threw him out of the family home when she found out. She'd never granted George a divorce and so we were forced to live together while she was still alive. She didn't like that either. Anyway, Michael came and stayed with us but he wasn't the same person he once was. The light in him had died and no matter what we did, we just couldn't seem to help him."

Sooz pulled a tissue out of her cardigan pocket.

"He eventually took his own life," she said, "It was the early eighties and he was one of the unfortunate men to contract the Aids virus. After what his mother had called him (and I won't repeat that in here, Derek) I think he felt God was punishing him. Stupid, stupid reason for doing it! Of course he wasn't being punished. George found him hanging in the barn at the back of our previous home. The poor man was devastated."

159

I flicked through the guidebook I'd purchased and pretended to read, while Sooz wiped her eyes. Eventually she said,

"I'm sorry about that."

"You've nothing to apologise for," I told her.

"Well, you didn't really need to hear about my woes."

I felt I was meant to. It was Shauna's line again, 'Your life, your secrets; they'll all be revealed eventually.' She was right. Moaning Maeve was dying, Colin was somehow mixed up in two suspicious deaths as far as I was concerned and now simple, old-fashioned, ever cheerful Sooz had just told me a terribly sad story and revealed what a modern attitude to life she actually had. I'd had her down as an out-dated prude. How wrong was I? Had I misjudged everyone on this trip?

"Did you and George have any children of your own?" I asked.

Sooz shook her head.

"No," she said, "We tried but it just didn't seem to happen for us. But we had each other and made the best of our years together. One can't ask for more than that. Josie has been a good friend and George and I are God Parents to her youngest."

"That's nice."

"Mind you, she's started having children of her own now. But Josie's been very good to me over the years. George had Alzheimer's disease for the last eight years of his life and I nursed him at home. Josie was always there for me, either with a home cooked meal or if I just wanted to shout or cry. Yes, she's been very good."

"That must have been a terrible time for you," I said.

"It's not easy to watch the man you love disappear by inches," Sooz told me, "The body is still there, but the person is missing. I won't lie to you Derek, I could handle the cleaning up when George was too late for the toilet; I could deal with the anger tantrums that developed; I coped the times he went missing, sometimes for hours before the police found him again; but when your husband no longer recognises you; it's heart breaking."

I would never have thought happy-go-lucky Sooz had been through such heartache. It often seems to be the happiest people one meets are the ones that have suffered so much. They have such strength and inner reserve while those of us whose lives haven't turned out too badly are the ones who constantly moan about everything. My God, just today I'd moaned because Angela and I weren't alone on the wine tasting trip and I'd been feeling sorry for myself this afternoon because she hadn't come on this walk with me either. It wasn't exactly a major problem was it? I'd be seeing her at dinner and perhaps I could tell her then that I wanted us to continue seeing each other after Sunday.

"People keep telling me George's death must be a happy release," Sooz continued, "And I know what they mean, but I still miss him, dreadfully. He wasn't the man he used to be at the end, but he was still there somewhere. Just very occasionally I got a brief glimpse of him, in a smile or a gesture; before he was gone again."

"I understand what you mean," I said, closing the guidebook on my lap.

"You've been going through something similar haven't you?" Sooz said.

"Not really."

"The loss part I mean; with your wife. I sense the divorce wasn't really your choice."

"No, it wasn't," I agreed, "I suppose it has been a kind of loss; a bereavement of sorts. I hadn't thought about it like that before. I did find myself getting upset when those first anniversaries came up after we split; the first Christmas, the first birthday. And I also found myself thinking things like, 'twelve months ago today we were doing such and such.'"

"Exactly," Sooz said, "And eventually you have to make the effort to start over again, otherwise what's the point of it all. That's what this trip is for me really; allowing myself to take pleasure in life again without feeling guilty about doing so. It's the first step to my future."

Four days ago I would never have said that Sooz and I had anything in common but here we were; both starting over again on our own. Mind you I couldn't really compare my recent problems to what she had had to endure over the years. I think she must have sensed what I was thinking.

"Please don't think my life hasn't been rich with happiness, because it has," she told me, "I have so many wonderful memories and it's those I wrap myself in at nights, when the world seems lonely."

"And you still have Josie."

"Yes," Sooz laughed, "I still have Josie. Speaking of which, I ought to be getting back. She'll wonder where I am."

"Hang on," I said, "I'll walk with you."

Chapter 10

Sooz took me on a different route back and the path we followed travelled around behind the hotel where there were more open fields and farmland. It was a stunning view and I wished my room was at the back of the house like Sooz and Josie's was. There was no way you could wake up to that wonderful vista every morning and feel grumpy. It really was a shame that The Grand didn't have more guests to admire the surroundings.

I let Sooz do most of the chatting as we walked. She told me more about the village she and Josie lived in. It turned out it wasn't a million miles from where I lived and yet I'd never even been there or driven through it before. There was so much of Britain that I'd never experienced. Holidays when I was married were always somewhere abroad with the other couples that formed our friendship circle, but even then most of the time was spent lying by a pool or propping up a bar so how much of the world had I actually seen, aside from some chlorinated water and the bottom of a beer glass? Thinking about it now I realised that I'd never actually got to pick a destination that we went to, I'd always gone along with the majority. This was the first time I'd ever selected a holiday for myself. Okay so I could have done a lot better in so many ways but Tenhamshire itself, with its gorgeous scenery, fascinating history and numerous places of interest hadn't been a bad choice of destination.

The path brought us out onto the main road on the other side of the hotel. As we walked back up and into the driveway so I saw Colin walking out the other entrance in the same direction I had taken earlier up to the church. Yesterday evening's speech came flooding back to me again. I kept telling myself it was only drunken ramblings but my brain just wouldn't accept that. His words last night had sounded sinister. He talked about not being noticed until his hands were on his mother and she had screamed. Now she was dead. Did Colin have a violent side to him? Maybe he was one of those quiet people that can only be pushed so far before they snap. My God, I'd shown the group those photos of him in the manure pile and we'd all laughed in front of him. He'd already been chased by the animals in the petting zoo and been covered in duck poo and we'd laughed at that as well. He'd had a go at me while on the stage last night. Was I the next victim on his list? Well, perhaps after Shauna.

Back inside the hotel Sooz bustled off to find Josie. There were still a couple of hours before dinner and I didn't really know what to do with the time. I remained in the hallway, staring at all the different touristy pamphlets on the stand by the lounge door. Mrs Goddard had re-tied the ribbon; I guess to stop any other nob with ridiculous ideas entering the room. But was I being ridiculous about Colin? He was drunk when he'd said what he had but that didn't mean he wasn't speaking the truth. I could hear him clearly in my head. 'Now you're dead mother, you and him. Hope you're happy!' My God, the guy sounded like some kind of psychopath.

"Freeze, Dirk. Don't move."

I was already on edge and jumped at the sound of Shauna's voice.

"Don't go in that lounge again," she said, walking across the hallway towards me, "The body's been moved."

"Very funny."

"Mrs Goddard told me about your investigation earlier. You really made her day, you dick."

"Yes, alright," I replied, "I know."

"She told me she was going to contact the chef later…by Ouija board."

"I'm glad you find it so amusing."

I let out a loud sigh.

"What's up, Dirk," Shauna asked, smacking me hard on the back, "Feeling the effects of the wine tasting; or thinking about the amount of money you shelled out for all those bottles you're never going to drink?"

"I was just thinking about Colin."

"Well that's bound to turn your stomach."

At the risk of more ridicule I confessed, "I keep thinking about what he said last night. You know, when he was drunk on the stage. It really sounded like he'd strangled his mother."

"This isn't a Cluedo-inspired murder mystery tour," Shauna said, "You do know that, don't you, Dirk? Colonel Mustard hasn't been bashing someone with the candlestick in the library while Miss Scarlet is upstairs in the bedroom, doing something unnatural with the lead piping. There are no murders and there aren't going to be any. I mean, no one's going to drop dead at dinner or anything like that."

"I know that, it's just…"

It was difficult to explain why I was letting this affect me so much, especially to Shauna who had been the one to tell me that all secrets are revealed on a coach trip. But the secrets I'd heard hadn't been told to her. I was the one hearing about the other passengers' lives and realising that my initial opinions of them had been wrong. Nagging Maeve was actually a caring wife; innocent, happy Sooz was a very modern lady who had seen a lot of heartache. Why couldn't hypochondriac, mummy's boy Colin turn out to be a murderer? I had to tell Shauna something but I didn't feel it was my place to mention what I'd found out about Maeve and Sooz.

"Well," I continued, "I'd be a bit worried if there was a murderer on our coach. After all, we don't know what he's capable of. His emotions have already been pushed; his outburst at us last night proves that."

That sounded plausible.

Shauna nodded. "I see your point, Dirk. The guy is a bit of a loner and obviously unhinged; but then who isn't in our merry little gang."

I waited for the, 'Present company excepted' line, but it didn't come.

"I guess we'll have to find out the truth about his mum," Shauna said, matter-of-factly, "And put your mind at rest, otherwise you're going to be a whinging tosser for the rest of the trip."

"Oh; and how do you propose we do that?" I asked.

She pursed her lips. "We could start by searching his room."

"You're not serious."

"Why not? Babs has a key behind the desk over there that opens any door."

"How do you know that?" I asked.

Shauna winked at me. "Come on," she said, "The sooner we're in, the sooner we're out."

"But Colin's gone for a walk. He could be back anytime."

"Then we'd better get started," Shauna replied, leaning over the reception desk and retrieving a small key.

"Come on," she said again, and began walking up the stairs.

I couldn't believe what she was suggesting; but I followed her anyway.

"Have you used that key before?" I asked, as I caught her up.

"Don't worry, Dirk; your night-time habits are safe with me."

I wasn't convinced she was joking.

At the top of the first flight of stairs Shauna turned left down a rather dark corridor. She placed a key in the lock of the second door along on the right.

"No, stop," I said, "We can't invade his privacy like this."

"He won't ever know," Shauna replied.

"It feels wrong."

"It's wrong to listen in at doors but that didn't stop you did it?"

"What? When?"

"Back on day one, Dirk," she said, "I told you the lezzas were at it. You can't tell me you didn't listen at their door."

"That was different," I told her, "That was to prove you wrong. Anyway, how did you know I listened in?"

"I didn't; until you confessed just now."

Shauna turned the key in the lock and opened the door.

"After you," she said.

A quick look round wouldn't hurt. We could be providing a great service to the public, unmasking a murderer. That's how I rationalised it to myself anyway as I stepped over the threshold.

Colin's room was lovely. It was a lot bigger than mine and had a large window overlooking the beautiful scenery at the back of the hotel. I knew for a fact he'd complained about it to Barbara Goddard, goodness knows why. The wallpaper was a heavy, floral pattern but in a large, bright room like this it looked elegant and tasteful. There was even space for a desk and chair under the window. Shauna made her way over to this now and began to look through the papers and books piled on top.

"Most of these are medical books," she called over her shoulder, "Blimey, 'The Immune System', 'Bowel Movements and How to Read them', 'Mucus and me.' One or two bestsellers here, I reckon. I won't start reading these; I might not be able to put them down again."

Shauna looked back over at me.

"Well?" she said, "Get checking, Dirk. We haven't got long."

"Where?"

"Start wherever you like. We've only got a short time to search the place."

I stared blankly around the room.

"You see that pile of clothes on top of the dresser?" she said, sitting down in the chair and flicking through an exercise book.

I walked over and picked them up.

"They're used, so don't touch them."

"Euugh," I said, dropping the lot onto the floor, "How did you know that?"

"He was wearing those dungarees that were on the top yesterday, Dirk. You're not very observant are you? If you're going to be my crime-fighting assistant you need to be a lump of clay that can be moulded. Right now you're acting more like a lump of shi…"

"Look, I'm new to this okay?"

"Just make sure you put them back up on the dresser the way they were," Shauna said.

I sighed and gingerly picked the pile up again.

"Oh God; I just touched his underpants!"

I heard laughter from across the room.

"From what he says about you in here, I think he'd rather you do that while he's wearing them."

I span round.

"What do you mean?"

"This is his diary," Shauna said, indicating the book in her hands.

She was sat right back in the seat, her feet up on the bed; looking for the entire world like she was there for the rest of the afternoon.

"You're reading his diary?"

"If there are any clues, they'll be in here," she said, flicking over the page, "Yep, Colin had a bit of a crush on you at the start of the week."

"I don't want to know," I said, opening the top drawer of the dresser to start rummaging.

"Thought you were kind and had nice eyes. Ah, rather sweet really. He's written he'd like to, oh; to rim you. That's less sweet."

"Sorry, what was that?" I asked, staring into a drawer full of potions, "I don't even know what that means."

"It's basically a tongue up the anus, Dirk," Shauna said, "You really are naïve aren't you."

"Oh Jesus," I turned round again to face her, "I don't want to know about that."

"You should feel flattered," she squinted at the page, "Sorry, my mistake. He said he wants to groom you, not rim you. Blimey, I think that sounds more sinister. His writing really is terrible."

She turned over another page.

"Hmm, the attraction seems to have waned by yesterday afternoon, after his manure incident. He now refers to you as an interfering, overweight cad. Such language; I'm blushing."

"Overweight?"

Shauna looked me up and down. "Well, maybe just a few pounds here and there, Dirk," she said, "Don't worry about it, porky; you can always start dieting when you get back home."

She returned to the book, flicking between pages and giving me a running commentary when she found something she thought was funny while I continued to search through the other drawers of the dresser, wondering how I hadn't noticed the weight gain and making a mental note to ask Karen about the latest dieting tips. Aside from a few clothes, the drawers were all mostly filled with jars of tablets, tubes of cream and bottles of different coloured liquids.

"**He** reckons Josie and Sooz are lezzas as well," Shauna called over.

"I'm sure he used politer terminology than that," I replied.

"Oh wait a minute. No, he suspects they're both thespians. The page is smudged. Ooh, I daren't tell you what he thinks of Angela."

"Then don't tell me."

"Stuck-up, vain and wears cheap perfume."

The little shit!

"I don't think he likes anyone," Shauna continued, "Karen's a fat moaner, Leroy's an over-confident charmer with a dirty mind, Dora's a windy, aggressive, old cow."

She shook her head, grinning as she continued to turn the pages back and forth, obviously enjoying herself.

"Listen to this; 'an over-bearing, foul-mouthed slag with the morals of an alley cat and about as much charm as an infected blister.' Blimey, who's that about?"

The smile faded a moment later as Shauna read the next line.

"The arrogant, little prick! I'm not a slag," she threw the book back onto the desk; "There's nothing in there, Dirk. We need the diary from when his mum died. That's not here. What have you found?"

"More medicines than a pharmacist stocks at any one time," I told her.

She sighed. "We're getting nowhere fast. Might as well take a quick look in the wardrobe and then go."

I opened the wardrobe door. There wasn't a lot hanging up in there but then Colin's suitcase must have been filled with all the books and medication. Surely he didn't use all of the tablets and potions at the same time? I moved a few hangers along the rail and then stopped.

"What have you found, Dirk?" Shauna asked.

I pulled out a hanger and showed her the tattered, purple, sequinned vest top and matching short skirt.

"One thing at a time, Dirk," she said, "We'll concentrate on the dead mother first."

I placed the outfit back inside and looked at what was on the floor of the wardrobe. Aside from shoes there were a couple of jumpers folded up in the right-hand corner. As I picked them up I realised they felt too heavy. I placed them on the bed and carefully unfolded them. Shauna leaned in as I uncovered something wrapped in tissue paper. We were silent as I undid the package, both feeling that we were about to reveal something important. As the paper came off so a large, silver photo frame was exposed.

"Oh my God," I said, looking at the picture, "That's Colin dressed in the purple outfit."

"No it's not, Dirk," Shauna said, "The photograph is far too old. Besides, look at the nose and the chin; they're both bigger. That's not him."

I looked again. She was right.

"Then this is…"

"His mother," Shauna finished.

We both stared silently at the image.

"God," I said, "That's ugly."

"Certainly is," Shauna replied, "Can't believe someone ever actually fucked that but I guess Colin's the proof."

I had to agree with her.

171

"But I also can't believe someone who carries around his mother's photo and clothes with him could have murdered her."

I couldn't argue with that logic. I wrapped the photograph up again.

"Mind you," I said, as a thought struck me while I put the jumpers back inside the wardrobe, "Maybe he carries them around with him because he feels guilty about what he did to her."

"You're like a dog with a bone, aren't you, Dirk."

"It's what he said last night," I told her, "I mean, if it wasn't true, why say it?"

Shauna looked around the room.

"Well, there's no more we can do here," she said, "Let's get the key down to reception."

We backed out of the room, making sure everything was in its right place. As we walked back down the staircase Colin came in through the front door. I stopped dead, guilt freezing me to the spot.

"Maybe there is still a way to find out what happened," Shauna whispered.

Before I could respond she shouted out, "Hey, Colin; good to see you. We were about to go and have a drink, weren't we, Dirk? Come and join us."

Colin's puzzled expression matched my own.

"I don't want a drink, thank you," he said.

"Well come with us anyway and have a chat," Shauna smiled, as she pulled me down the stairs behind her, "We haven't seen you all day, it will be nice to catch up."

I still couldn't speak. I didn't want to go and have a drink either, especially with Colin. I was having trouble looking him in the face after being in his room. I would hate it if someone entered mine without my knowledge. Mind you, he had called

172

me fat so he wasn't exactly Mr Nice Guy either.

"I suppose I could come with you if you really want," he said, "Oh, I just saw Gerald and Maeve sitting outside. Should I fetch them too?"

"No, forget them, they don't count," Shauna told him, before grabbing both my and Colin's arms and marching us through the dining room and into the bar.

Aside from Jim, who was sitting in the far corner on his own, the place was deserted. Glum barman was leaning on the bar looking totally bored and miserable as usual.

"Right," said Shauna, brightly, "Let's sit here in the middle shall we? Okay, what's everyone going to have, I'm buying."

As we sat down I whispered to her, "What's going on?"

"Go with the flow, Dirk," she whispered back.

Glum barman came over to the table.

"What are you going to have, Colin?" Shauna asked, "Anything you like."

"Oh ok then, I'll have a small tomato juice, please."

Colin smiled up at the barman who smirked back at him. It wasn't the most attractive look. Both lips disappeared completely, making his face appear like it had an ugly crack in it. Perhaps that's why he didn't do it too often.

"Come on you can do better than that," Shauna urged, "How about a brandy?"

"Ooh no," Colin winced, "I had enough of those yesterday. I don't usually drink."

Shauna looked a little deflated. "Okay, one tomato juice. What about you, Dirk?"

I stared blankly at her; not 'going with the flow' as she'd asked. She kicked me hard under the table.

"Ow. Sorry, I'll have a beer."

"Good choice. And I'll have a G and T."

Glum barman returned to the bar.

"Should we ask Jim over?" Colin asked, "He's all alone over there."

"No, don't worry about him," Shauna said, "He probably can't even see us at this distance. If we stay quiet he'll never know we're here."

Colin's face took on a knowing look.

"I realise what you're trying to do," he said.

I was glad one of us did.

"You're trying to butter me up so that I don't speak to your boss when I get home."

"Not at all," Shauna told him, "If I was doing that I definitely wouldn't have invited Dirk along. I'd have asked someone much more interesting."

"Well, just so long as you know, I'll still be phoning up and giving him a mouthful."

"That's your prerogative, Colin. Now tell us; what have you been up to today while we were out?"

"I had a quiet morning really."

Not surprising, I thought, after the skin-full he'd had last night.

"Mrs Goddard provided a lunch for those of us that didn't go to the wine tasting," Colin continued.

"That was nice," I said.

"It wasn't, it was garbage," he replied, "There was no butter on the sandwiches and the currant bun was something only a mother could love."

"Speaking of mothers," said Shauna.

Glum barman came over with the drinks at that point.

"Right, that's one beer, one gin and tonic and one tomato juice," he put the drinks down and then struck up a conversation with Colin, "So how are you this afternoon, feeling better?"

174

"Much, thank you," Colin told him, "I had a little snooze earlier while it was quiet and then…"

While they continued talking Shauna leaned over to me.

"We need to get him drinking," she whispered.

"Why?"

"To recreate last night of course. If we can get him talking about his mother again we might find out the truth."

"Oh right," I said, "I'm with you now. I wondered what we were doing in here."

"As a sidekick, Dirk, you're one player short of a full team. Now concentrate. We need him drinking and talking about his mother. We'd be halfway there now if silly bollocks hadn't butted in with the drinks."

Glum barman and Colin were still chatting away.

"Put this on my room tab," Shauna interrupted.

"Will do," Glum barman replied, before turning back to Colin, "So, as I was saying, they provide you with free drinks if you have the full massage…"

"Would hate for you to add it to the wrong bill," she continued.

Glum barman stopped his conversation again.

"Look around you honey," he said, "I don't think I'll get it mixed up with all the other tables I'm currently serving."

"How about you get my driver another drink?"

"He's been nursing that bitter for over an hour."

"Then he's probably ready for a fresh one."

Glum barman sighed and went over to Jim. Colin watched him go and then turned back to Shauna.

"Why were you trying to get rid of him?" he asked.

"He's staff, Colin," she said, "Now, what were we talking about before, oh yes; mothers…"

"He doesn't want one," Glum barman had returned.

"Well, now we know," Shauna nodded towards the bar, "Trot on then."

Realising he wasn't wanted, glum barman tutted and stormed off.

"I think you've offended him," Colin said.

"Yeah, well he should learn to hide it better," Shauna replied, "Honestly, finding good staff is murder. Speaking of which…"

"Ah, Mr Noble." Barbara Goddard walked into the room.

"Oh for fuck's sake!" Shauna shouted out. Colin baulked.

Mrs Goddard came over and sat in the chair next to me.

"There are four of us at the table now; shall we all link hands and try and contact the chef?"

She chuckled away but no one else joined in. The joke had worn rather thin for me so I didn't laugh along, Shauna was angry at Barbara's timing and Colin just didn't know what the hell was going on.

"Did you want something or did you just come in to annoy the fuck out of everyone?" Shauna asked.

"I'm just passing through," Barbara told her, brightly, getting up out of the seat, "Couldn't resist another little joke though, at Mr Noble's expense."

"Actually, while you're here," Colin said, "I'd like to talk to you about my water pressure."

As he went into complaint mode, Shauna turned to me and held up her index finger and thumb about an inch apart. "We were this close," she said, through gritted teeth.

It took a while for Colin to get through his latest list of complaints. By the time she left the room, Barbara's mood had soured.

"Right, how about another drink?" Shauna asked, "It's Dirk's round."

"Not for me, thank you," Colin said, getting up, "I'm afraid I still haven't finished this one but I really must go to my room to freshen up before dinner."

Damn; we weren't going to be able to find out anything. I tried to think of a way to make him stay and talk.

"Did you kill your mother?" Shauna asked.

Well, that was one way. Colin fell back into his chair.

"What did you just say?"

"What happened to subtlety?" I asked.

"We're past that now. It's almost dinner time."

Colin's bottom lip began to tremble.

"I can't believe you would say such a thing," he whispered, "Why?"

"Over to you, Dirk."

Great, thanks for that. Colin's reaction was already making me feel like I was about to make a complete idiot of myself again. I really hoped there had been a murder.

"It's what you said last night, when you were drunk," I began.

"I wasn't drunk, I was trying to cope with the events of the day," Colin said to me, accusingly.

"Okay, whatever. You talked about putting your hands on your mother and she screamed. Were you strangling her?"

Colin's hands flew to his cheeks as he gasped.

"Of course I wasn't strangling her," he replied, "Mummy didn't like being touched; that's all. That's why she screamed if I accidently brushed past her or wanted a hug."

He picked up his tomato juice and took a sip.

"You see Mummy's problem was…actually this is all a bit personal, you know. I'm not really comfortable discussing this with you," he turned to Shauna, "Especially you."

Shauna raised her eyebrows at me.

"Look Colin," I said, "The fact that you had this little outburst last night while you were drun…dealing with the day must show that this is playing on your mind. Wouldn't you feel better talking about it with someone? I spoke to Angela about my divorce."

"That's just because you want to get inside her pants, Dirk."

I ignored that comment. Colin appeared to be weighing up what I had just told him. I was speaking the truth. I had felt better after talking with Angela and not for the reason Shauna had said; although that would be an added bonus. I guessed that Colin was in a similar situation to me in that he didn't really have a social circle of friends he could talk to. He sighed.

"Well I might as well tell you the whole story now," he said, "But only because I don't want you thinking I'm some vicious, aggressive, homicidal nutter."

"We can't promise that."

"Ssh," I told Shauna.

"You see, mummy wasn't a very affectionate woman," Colin began, "She didn't like receiving affection and certainly didn't give it out. Don't get me wrong, she was wonderful in so many other ways, making me do all the housework so that I obtained new skills, leaving me on my own for a couple of days at a time so that I learned how to fend for myself; telling me I was useless so that I would try harder to become a better person."

"Bloody hell, I'd have strangled her years ago," Shauna whispered, to me.

"But affection wasn't very forthcoming," Colin said, "Unless I was ill and then she'd notice me."

That explained the hypochondria.

"The problem was that she never got over the death of daddy. I never knew him. Apparently they had one night together and the next day he was dead."

"Probably topped himself after he saw what he'd slept with in the cold light of morning," Shauna said, under her breath.

"What was that?" Colin asked.

"Nothing. Carry on."

"I think that's why mummy didn't show me much affection," he continued, "She'd given love to this one man and he died. She was afraid that if she loved me, she'd lose me too."

I think Colin was fooling himself but it wasn't my place to shatter his illusions.

"What happened to him?" I asked.

"He died in mummy's ring," he said.

"You can't get pregnant that way," Shauna told him.

Colin looked confused. "I meant that he was at work. Mummy's family owned a circus and they were both performers. Of course she gave it all up when she found out she was pregnant with me. A shame really as mummy had a rather unusual act for a woman. Daddy was a clown and he died in the ring, during his performance."

"How did he die?" Shauna asked, "Hit and run by a clockwork car?"

"No."

"Mauled to death by a balloon animal?"

"Of course not."

"He wasn't garrotted when his spinning bowtie went out of control, was he?"

Colin tutted and rolled his eyes.

"If you keep making jokes I'm not going to tell you anything. This is my father we're talking about here."

Shauna held up her hands in a gesture of surrender. Colin took a deep breath and continued on with his story.

"Daddy was murdered if you must know; halfway through a routine."

"Oh thank God for that," I said. There had been a murder after all.

Colin shot me a very disgruntled look.

"Oh, sorry," I told him, "I didn't mean a relief about your dad."

He carried on. "Apparently it was a packed house that night as it was during the school holidays and the clowns were performing a special children's show. It was the part of the act where the circus ring was plunged into darkness and the spotlight would then search out each clown individually and he would perform a quick routine. When the spotlight hit daddy he was meant to be sitting in a chair holding his balls."

"And this was a children's show," Shauna said, suspiciously.

"Of course. As soon as the light hit he would jump up and start juggling with all four of them. That's not an easy skill to master. Anyway, this particular night the light hit the chair and daddy was sprawled across it, his head stuck in a bucket."

"Had he been drowned?" I asked.

"No, it was a bucket of confetti. There was a knife in his back."

"Oh God."

Colin sighed. "What a terrible tragedy. The lights went up and the other clowns brought on a stretcher to take daddy away. When that broke and daddy fell into a bowl of custard halfway across the ring the audience laughed, they thought it was all still part of the act. Two of the other clowns bent down to pick him up and their trousers fell down," he shook his head, sadly; "It wasn't a very dignified exit, being dragged through the sawdust by two clowns in their pants, while five dancing toy poodles lapped at his custard-covered corpse. Still he got a standing ovation so perhaps that's the way he would have liked to go."

I very much doubted that.

"So who did it then," asked Shauna, "Who killed him?"

"Well there were lots of theories. He didn't get on very well with Tommy the Trapeze but he was in hospital at the time after an unfortunate accident with his partner during rehearsal. She was meant to somersault off of her swing and catch his hands in mid-air, but her timing was slightly out and she reached out and grabbed hold of whatever she could. Apparently they were never able to have children."

I crossed my legs under the table.

"And there was a long running feud over billing with Lionel but it couldn't have been him either."

"How do you know that?" I asked.

"Lionel was an elephant."

Ask a silly question.

Colin sighed again. "Nothing was ever proved," he said, "Eventually it became just another unsolved crime. I think that's why mummy never got over his death. Still, at least they're together now."

We all fell silent. I wasn't sure what I'd expected to hear from Colin but it certainly hadn't been that. Mind you, at least I could relax in the knowledge that he was no murderer and I wasn't on his hit list. I might still be in line for one of his mouthfuls of abuse but I wasn't about to die. Colin stood up.

"Well, I must go and get ready for dinner," he said. He was about to walk away from the table but stopped, "You may find this silly but I carry around with me an old photograph of my mother from her days in the circus, before I was born."

"I know," I said.

"Do you?"

Shit.

"Sorry, I meant to say I don't. I don't find it silly.

"I also bring along the outfit she's wearing in the picture."

"Why do you do that?" Shauna asked.

"Because she's smiling in the photograph," Colin told us, "I can't remember her ever doing that during my lifetime. She often used to stare at that picture herself; a reminder of past halcyon days I suppose. That's why I carry it around with me. It helps to know that she must have been happy once. Perhaps I'll bring it down later and show you."

"Yeah but not at dinner," Shauna told him, "I have enough trouble keeping down the food here as it is."

"Sorry?"

"That will be nice," I interjected, "I'm sure everyone will like to see the photograph."

Colin smiled at us and walked towards the door leading into the dining room. As I watched him go I realised, just as I had with Sooz earlier, that we weren't so different. He was on holiday on his own just like I was. It sounded like he'd had a rather lonely life so far with very little love and for the last few months I could relate to that. I wasn't sure how long ago his mother had died but I sensed it was recently. Perhaps he was also starting over again. I really hoped he would find some companionship and affection soon.

"Colin," Shauna called out.

Colin stopped in the doorway and turned round.

"You never did tell us what your mother's act was," she said, "You told us it was unusual for a woman to do. What was it? I'm guessing a bearded lady."

"Oh right," Colin replied, "No, she was a knife thrower."

*

We were all a bit quiet at dinner that evening on our table. Angela still had her headache, Jim was mostly staring down at the table, obviously embarrassed from entering her room earlier and I was thinking about the events of the afternoon. There had been a hell of a lot of talk about death what with Sooz's husband and stepson, the chef (although he wasn't actually dead) and then Colin's parents. I thought about the woman in the photograph. Surely it was too much of a coincidence that her husband died from a knife wound in the middle of his act and she knew how to throw them. Perhaps he'd been leaving his size fifteen shoes under other women's beds as well as hers. I tried to shake the thought from my head. There would have been an investigation at the time after all. I should be concentrating on my holiday. This was meant to be an enjoyable week away after all. I decided to engage Shauna in conversation.

"So, Ryan Harbour tomorrow."

"Yep," she replied, "All day."

"Why's it called that?"

"Geez, how the hell should I know?"

Well, I enjoyed that conversation. Chico appeared with the starters. He placed one of the bowls in front of Shauna.

"Here you go, sugar," he said, "I hope you find this fresh, tasty and hot!"

He gave one of his hip thrusts but was a little over zealous in his execution. As Shauna leaned forward to look inside the bowl so Chico's crotch smacked her up the side of the head. I thought she was going to deck him but instead she took hold of his hand.

"Ok, I give in," she said, "I admit it; I want you. I need you. I can't fight it any longer. Come to my room tonight at midnight; number four. Don't knock, I'll be waiting."

I thought Chico was going to pass out with excitement. He tried to form a sentence but couldn't. Instead he just stood there with a soppy grin on his face, drooling onto my starter. A nod from Shauna and he silently returned to the kitchen. We all sat watching her while she picked up her napkin and placed it in her lap. It seemed to take her an awfully long time. Finally she looked up at us.

"What?"

"Come on," I said, "What the hell was that all about?"

"I thought it might finally shut him up."

"But, you're not going to sleep with him are you?" Angela asked.

"Oh no," Shauna replied, "Number four is Colin's room."

I hadn't noticed the number on his door earlier. I guess this was payback for the 'slag' comment in his diary. This seemed to break the tension and we all tucked in to our meal.

"I must say, Louella's an improvement on the chef," Angela said, "This Calamari is delicious."

"Shame it isn't served without the groin thrust," Shauna replied, rubbing the side of her face.

"It could have been worse," I reasoned, "He could have hung them on his nob and served them that way."

"My aunt Mable choked to death on calamari," Jim had decided to join in the conversation, "She thought it was an onion ring. Not a nice way to go really."

Right, well that kept the atmosphere lively. We all fell silent again until the main course arrived.

"This steak pie is amazing," I said.

"Isn't it," Angela agreed, "The pastry's crisp and there's so much filling."

"Why the hell hasn't Louella been the chef all along?" I asked, "She's much better at cooking than waiting on tables."

Jim sighed. "I once found a toenail clipping in a meat pie."

I slammed my cutlery down. "Jesus Christ, can't we all just enjoy one fucking decent meal in this shit hole of a hotel?"

I realised I was standing up and it now wasn't just our table that was silent. I slowly sat back down. Fortunately Mrs Goddard appeared at that moment. She was looking rather cheerful and excited and I feared that was due to her getting the better of me earlier. I hoped she wasn't about to share with the group.

"Could I have everyone's attention," she said, in a loud whisper, "I found out that Louella's been working at the hotel seventy years today."

Bloody hell, how old did that make her?

"I've arranged a little surprise."

"I see she's not given her the night off," I said, to Angela.

Mrs Goddard held the door into the bar open and glum barman wheeled a trolley through with a cake on it. It was definitely a 'little' surprise; but the cake had been decorated nicely in white icing and had, 'Get Well Soon' written on the top in pink. I guess this had been a very last minute plan and Mrs Goddard had bought the only remaining cake in the shop. She tiptoed over to the kitchen door.

"Chico's going to bring her out in a second; I thought it would be nice for all of us to join her in this tribute."

She stood beaming beside the trolley and made a signal through the circular window in the swing door. Seventy years of service and not even a bottle of champagne or a balloon. It wasn't much of a celebration.

"Here she comes."

Mrs Goddard was practically jumping up and down with excitement. I felt this was the most thrilling thing that had happened to her since…well, probably since she got our booking. The swing doors opened and Louella hobbled in. We all yelled, "Surprise" and she dropped dead, right there on the spot.

Chapter 11

Louella's death put a bit of a dampener on the rest of the evening. Mrs Goddard was terribly upset, although she did seem more worried about who was going to cook breakfast; glum barman was upset as Louella was meant to have been helping him serve that night and Colin was upset because he didn't get any cake. The one plus was that Geoffrey Pilkington's 'Sheds of the World' slide show, scheduled as entertainment for that evening, was cancelled as a mark of respect. There were probably more fitting tributes after seventy years of service.

I wondered what sight would greet me in the dining room at breakfast time. It was surprisingly calm. The cereals were in their usual place and the eggs were congealing nicely under the heat lamp. The only excitement was when Mrs Goddard rushed in from the kitchen with fresh toast; well I say fresh. She obviously wasn't an early riser and was still in her night attire. She was wearing a mauve, quilted dressing gown, but when that accidentally flew open it revealed a pink Baby-doll nightdress underneath. Her hair was in rollers under a loosely tied head scarf and she had a cigarette tucked behind her right ear for later.

"I've managed to arrange some help for tonight," she said, while frantically looking for the end of the cord to re-tie the dressing gown, "Louella's elder sister, Valerie, has agreed to come back. She used to work here in the old days."

My God, how far back were we talking now; before man learned to make fire?

"Won't she be in mourning?" Sooz asked.

"Oh no, Valerie and Louella hated each other," Mrs Goddard said, "They fell out over some man who was dating both of them at the same time. Only found out when Valerie returned home early one day and found him bending Louella backwards over the vacuum cleaner. It was quite a rift that developed between them."

"I'm not surprised," Angela said, "How long has the rift been going on for?"

"Ooh, I'd say about three years now."

Only three years? Blimey, Louella was obviously a lot suppler than she looked…well, not now; obviously.

Josie sighed. "That's such a sad story," she said, "Now they've no chance of reconciling. Did the sisters not have any contact at all?"

"Well there was some; of sorts," Mrs Goddard admitted, "Louella always communicated on Valerie's birthday. She used to send her a nail with a note that read, 'Another one for your coffin you wrinkled, old trollop.'"

Wow, that was some rift. Barbara sighed, shook her head and returned to the kitchen.

"I'm glad I'm out tonight," I said to Angela, "I can't see dinner here being a success; not with some nymphomaniac pensioner in charge of the kitchen."

She smiled. "Yes, arranging to have that evening out with Pete and Leroy at Ryan Harbour has worked out rather well for you. And you'll never guess the extra treat me and the girls have here this evening?"

"What's that?" I asked, swallowing a spoonful of cornflakes.

"Postponed from last night; 'Sheds of the World.'"

"Oh damn," I said, smacking my hand on the table, "I can't believe I'm going to miss that. You will take some notes for me, won't you?"

"Keep that up and I'll make sure there's a repeat performance tomorrow night."

Mrs Goddard sidled back into the dining room again, looking a little shifty. She was carrying a long spoon and tiptoed her way over to the cereal table. If she was trying to be inconspicuous her elaborate creeping had quite the opposite effect. Once there she began frantically stirring the milk in the jug. We all watched, puzzled. What was she doing; seeing if the flash of her Baby-doll nightie had turned it? After about ten seconds of vigorous stirring, she visibly relaxed and sighed. All eyes were on her as she turned back round.

"My HRT patch came off," she confessed, "Thought it might have fallen in the milk jug."

I spat out a mouthful of cornflakes.

"Shit," I said, now vigorously stirring the milk in my bowl, "It had better not be in here."

"Don't panic, Derek," Angela said, "You'll be fine."

"Really? What happens if it is in here while I've been eating my cornflakes? Jesus Christ, what if I've swallowed it?"

"Please don't worry, Mr Noble," Mrs Goddard said, coming over, "You'd have known if you'd eaten it."

"Would I? You think a medically enhanced patch will taste different to the rest of the shit you're serving us? My God, what will happen to me? Will I grow breasts? Will I start to get irrationally moody once a month? Will I speak to a girlfriend on the phone for half an hour and then arrange to meet later for a proper chat?"

"Wow, Dirk, and you wonder why your wife left you."

Before I was able to throw the bowl at Shauna, Colin came into the dining room; last as always. He had a face like a gorilla who had misplaced his banana.

"Is this yours?" he asked Mrs Goddard, holding her patch at

one corner between his finger and thumb nails, "Looking around me here, I doubt anyone who should be on these, is. I just trod on it out in the hallway."

"Thank you Mr Cheeseman," Barbara said, taking it off of him, "I assume you're going to add this to your list of complaints?"

As he nodded, she turned and sheepishly returned to the kitchen.

"And I could use some more stationery in my room to write all this down on," Colin called after her.

"Is something else up?" I asked him, relieved that I wasn't changing sex at the breakfast table.

"Honestly," he said, "This place is getting worse. As if the old biddy dying and spoiling the party wasn't enough; last night I woke up, just after twelve, and felt someone creep into bed beside me. For a second I wondered if the house was haunted but then I felt an arm around me and…bare flesh pressed against my back. A voice whispered in my ear, 'I'll make all your dreams come true, sugar.' You'll never guess who it was."

"Mr Sandman?"

"Only that damned waiter."

"No," said Shauna, mockingly, "Well, looks like you got lucky, Colin."

"I wouldn't call a naked waiter invading my personal space lucky. He said it was a mistake."

"You mean it was just a cock-up?"

"I mean that after he screamed and muttered something unintelligible in Italian, he said he had the wrong room. Apparently he was looking for you," Colin looked down his nose at Shauna, "There's no accounting for taste."

"So what happened after that?" I asked.

"What do you think happened? He put on his leopard print

robe, pulled on a hairnet and left my room; taking the canister of whipped cream with him."

"Sounds like someone had a lucky escape," I said.

"Don't I know it?"

I was actually thinking about Shauna.

"Sexual harassment, that's what it amounts to," Colin continued, "I'm not sure what heading discarded HRT patches comes under but I'll be making a note of that too. The boss of Scrimshaw Travel is going to receive such a mouthful off of me next week with my long list of complaints." He walked off to get his breakfast.

I was glad Colin had found some new things to complain about; anything to take his mind off of my accusing him of being a murderer. I felt quite sorry for him now that I knew about his lonely childhood but let's face it; he was still a whiny hypochondriac who would soon be complaining of laryngitis after all the mouthfuls of abuse he was due to give people.

Jim was adjusting the driver's seat as I boarded the coach half an hour later. He had his back to me but I could hear whistling. That was a good sign, no superstitious crap today. When he stood upright and turned around I saw that one of the lenses in his glasses had cracked.

"I didn't realise this seat went forward," he said, brightly.

Oh my God.

"Thought I'd better try and move it because of this," he added, indicating the crack.

"How could you possibly break one of those lenses?" I asked him, "Surely even a laser couldn't get through it."

"I took my glasses off in the hallway after breakfast for a clean and put them down on the chair under that big mirror. While I was getting the cleaning cloth untangled from my lucky rabbit's foot, that big, old lady came out of the dining room and sat on them."

"Are you sure that rabbit foot works?" I asked.

"Definitely," came the reply, "I've not crashed the coach yet have I."

You couldn't really argue with that sort of logic.

"Now then," said Shauna, over the microphone once we'd set off, "Ryan Harbour isn't too far away; if you have a competent driver with a decent pair of specs. Anyway, when we eventually get there, whatever's left of the morning will be your own. We've got a set meal booked at one o'clock in the oldest pub in the area, The Smugglers Inn (that's original). The pub's on the harbour front next to where we're dropping you off so you can't miss it. Please make sure you're all on time for that because straight after lunch we'll be meeting up with a local guide who will be taking us on a tour of the old part of the town. The company is called 'Authentic Guides' so I assume he'll be some kind of prat in a costume. For those of you not staying on at Ryan Harbour tonight for a piss-up, we'll be leaving for the hotel around five thirty."

"It's sounding too well planned again," I said to Angela, "I wonder what's going to go wrong?"

"You should get professional help for that cynicism, Derek," she replied, grinning, "I'm sure it's going to be a lovely day. The morning's our own and I owe you a walk, remember?"

I smiled. "So you do," I said, "A walk, maybe some coffee; perhaps a croissant…"

"Don't push it. We'll watch where everyone else goes and then walk in the opposite direction so we can be on our own."

Oh yes, it was going to be a lovely day.

I think Jim's driving improved with a cracked lens although I guess that was essentially due to him moving his seat forward. Any journey will be smoother if the driver is actually sitting down whilst the vehicle is in motion. Had he been standing up all week? It would explain so much. We didn't get lost either but that was mainly due to him tailing a car that was towing a boat. Fortunately it was going to the same place we were. Maybe there was something to that rabbit's foot after all. The only blip came when Jim continued to follow the car down the slipway in the harbour and we almost ended up floating out to sea.

The harbour itself formed a crescent shape and we came straight through the middle of it via the town centre. To the right, where The Smugglers Inn was on the corner, lay the older part. Rustic fishing boats bobbed in the water; looked on by clapboard buildings from the sixteenth and seventeenth centuries. Some were guest houses; others speciality shops selling paintings and pottery. To the left modern day development had invaded. Coffee shops and trendy wine bars festooned that part of the crescent. Brand new apartments towered above with balconies surveying the large, expensive yachts moored below. Both halves were beautiful in their way but didn't really contrast well together. I remembered what Sooz had said to me yesterday in the church; 'Every generation adds something.'

Our group remained in the harbour, some going to investigate the old part and the others going off for a coffee in the modern.

"Back up into the town, then," Angela said, and we walked off the way we had driven in.

The town seemed busy but then we hadn't been in an area with a lot of people all week, only quiet, out-of-the-way places; so it may just have been our imagination. Then again it was Friday, the sun was shining and it was properly warm; which usually brought people outside. Angela and I walked up the high street and found yet another coffee shop that had an empty table outside so we decided to stop there. I couldn't help smiling while queuing for the coffee. We were finally alone together; at the busiest place we'd visited all week. We only had one more trip after today. It was definitely time for me to bring up the possibility of seeing each other once the tour was over. I had been planning on doing that last night but then Louella keeled over and it no longer felt appropriate. I guess there was no time like the present. When I walked back outside again I found a man sitting in my seat.

"This is Derek," Angela said, to him. She looked embarrassed and possibly even a little bit afraid.

The man immediately stood up so I could sit down. He was a hefty sort of guy with the look of someone who had probably played a lot of sports in his youth but whose body was now fighting against age and poor diet; and losing.

"Derek," he said, "I've just been hearing all about you from Angela here, haven't I sweetheart?"

I didn't like the way he used the word 'sweetheart.' He reminded me of Harry; a little too familiar.

"My name's Max," he said, holding out his hand, which I reluctantly shook, once I'd put the tray down, "Angela and I go way back, don't we, darling."

Angela nodded. "We knew each other a very long time ago," she said, quietly.

"She was just telling me all about this little trip the two of you are taking together," Max continued, his bushy moustache bristling as he grinned at me, "So glad she's finally settled down."

I was confused. As I went to open my mouth I saw Angela's eyes widen. It was a look that said, 'Go along with this.'

"Yes," I said, "Yes, it's wonderful isn't it."

"Such a lovely, generous woman," Max continued, staring intensely at Angela. His manner was unnerving.

"Yes, she is lovely," I replied.

Angela smiled warmly at me.

"Well, I mustn't take up anymore of your time. Amazing to see you again my dear."

Max took Angela's hand and kissed it, looking directly into her eyes as he did.

"Until we meet again," he said.

I saw Angela recoil. He stood back up and shook my hand again, almost crushing it, before patting me on the shoulder.

"Enjoy her, Derek," he said, and left.

That seemed an odd yet very disrespectful thing to say. I'd met his type many times before and even in this day and age, there were still plenty of them about. A woman was just a commodity to him. The wife was there to keep house and raise the children while the mistress was there for his pleasure as and when he felt like it. Why any woman fell for that kind of guy I didn't know and I certainly wouldn't have expected Angela to be one of them.

Neither of us said anything after Max's departure, both of us taking long sips of our coffee. I could tell she was embarrassed but I had to acknowledge his presence.

"Odd man," I said, eventually, "Bit over the top on the niceties."

"He's a dreadful man," Angela confessed, "A huge mistake from my past. I was so shocked when he came over. I thought he lived abroad now. A nasty, controlling man."

I liked him less and less.

"Would you like me to go after him?" I said.

A small grin appeared on Angela's face.

"Why?" she asked, "Are you going to beat him up for me?"

"Well I'd certainly go and find some big bloke and pay him to do it for you, if you want."

"My hero."

"We've all got our exes," I said, "But at least that's what they are now; exes that are no longer a part of our lives."

"That's true," she replied.

"So what did you tell him about 'our trip'?" I asked.

"Oh, well, I kind of made out it was just the two of us."

Angela's face reddened. My heart began to beat faster.

"I wish it was," I told her.

She looked at me shyly and smiled. I smiled back, holding her gaze until she turned and stared out onto the street, lost in thought. I returned to my coffee, giving it a stir.

"So, do you ever bump into your exes?" I heard her ask me. I looked up.

"That's a bit plural," I said, "It's only really my wife that I would class as an ex. We met in our last year at uni. I came out of a pub one night, really drunk. I fell into the gutter and there was Leanne, looking up at me."

"Derek!"

"Ok, it wasn't quite like that. I'd been really fortunate for the first two years of my studies as my parents had supported me, but in my final year I needed to get some work. I got a part-time job in one of the offices at the university and that's where I met her. We started dating but she wanted to go off on a belated gap year trip; alone. I was besotted and waited for her until she returned. We took up where we'd left off when she got back. I'd started work at an accounting firm by this time and helped support Leanne while she continued with her masters and doctorate. We eventually moved in together and got married after that, so there's never really been anyone else."

Angela seemed pensive.

"A bit pathetic really isn't it," I said, trying to sound like I didn't care about the past, "Only one ex at my age."

She shook her head. "No it isn't. I think it's rather wonderful."

I looked questioningly at her.

"I mean, it's wonderful to find someone you are so in love with and to be together for so long. I've never had that. I know you've had to endure a divorce, Derek, but still; all those years with the same person; that's lovely."

I wanted to grab her hands and tell her she was lovely. I wanted to tell her that she could have that long-lasting relationship; with me. I don't know what stopped me saying it. I even opened my mouth to speak. Perhaps it was the image of Max sitting in my chair only minutes before but I couldn't say those words and the moment passed. I picked up my cup.

It was pleasant where we sat, even though it was on the high street, so we had another coffee and chatted idly while we watched the world go by. There were a lot of pensioners and young women pushing babies in buggies going about their daily business and then a group of about fifteen lads dressed in football strips ran past us. They were each holding a can of beer and shouting about the beginning of their stag night. They were certainly starting early and, to me, looked so young I wouldn't have been surprised if they were bunking off school for it.

We still had a bit of time to kill before lunch so had a wander around the shops. I feigned interest while Angela looked at dresses and then we both stood in the card shop for twenty minutes, laughing at the funny ones before leaving without purchasing anything. As we walked back down the high street towards the harbour, Angela took my arm.

"It's actually rather lovely here," she said, "You have the

196

beautiful harbour and you still have civilisation around you. As much as I loved the settings of the farm and the vineyard, they were a bit stuck out in the middle of nowhere."

"Want to buy yourself a little place out this way?" I joked, "Here you go, an Estate Agents. Let's have a look and see if there's something in your price range."

Angela laughed, but we did stop and look anyway.

"There's a real mix in prices, isn't there," she said.

"And house styles," I replied, "Hey look, there's a penthouse apartment in one of those blocks overlooking the harbour. How much?"

"Derek."

"I wouldn't pay that for a two bed."

"Derek."

"Even though it does come with a mooring."

"Derek, look at this will you."

I looked at the property Angela was staring at.

"A barn conversion; is that what you fancy?" I asked.

"Don't you recognise it?"

"Should I?" I said, "Those ones all look the same to me; the ones covered with the blackened wood panelling. If anything it reminds me of the little church near our hotel."

"It's Harry's," Angela said.

"Harry's? Oh, you mean the one Margaret looked at."

"Exactly. The one Harry is meant to be having done up to live in."

I finally cottoned on.

"Oh. Are you sure it's his?"

Angela nodded. "Yes, don't you remember when Margaret showed us that picture on her phone last night? I commented on the fountain in the front garden. You can see it in this photo. Margaret's picture was taken from a similar angle."

"Maybe he's decided to sell," I said, "He's always going off to make phone calls abroad, perhaps his business needs an injection of capital."

"I wonder how much Margaret knows," Angela mused, more to herself than to me. I wasn't sure she'd heard what I'd just said.

"Why don't we ask him when we get back tonight?" I suggested, "Oh, I'm not going back, but you could ask."

Angela still wasn't listening. She walked across to the door of the Estate Agents.

"Or you could just check with Margaret," I called, following her inside.

*

We were the last to arrive at The Smugglers Inn. The pub was wide but not very deep. The bar ran almost the entire width of the room so that the majority of tables were along the windowed side, looking out onto the harbour. The interior was polished wood with all manner of boat related memorabilia on the walls; a ship's wheel, fishing nets, oars.

Two seats had been left at the bottom end of our group's table for Angela and me, but Margaret was sat right at the top with Dora. I stood at the bar to order drinks while Angela walked over and whispered into Margaret's ear. The two of them came over.

"This is all very cloak and dagger," Margaret said, grinning.

"We've got something we need to tell you," Angela confessed.

She didn't say anymore after that. Margaret was looking at us both so innocently it was difficult to burst her bubble.

"We went up into the town earlier," I said.

"Oh right," Margaret replied, "A bit of 'alone time' was it?"

"It was actually," I said, smiling, "We had coffee and then

hit the shops and then we…"

"Derek!"

"Oh right, sorry. We were making our way back here and looked in at an Estate Agents' window."

Margaret nodded, obviously still not on our wave length.

"We saw a barn for sale," I said.

"Harry's barn," Angela added.

Realisation dawned on Margaret's face.

"Oh right," she said, "Now I'm with you."

"I'm sorry but he doesn't own it," Angela continued, "We checked with the Estate Agent."

"I never thought he did."

Her response surprised both of us.

"You knew?" I said.

She nodded. "Oh yes. He must have borrowed the keys from the agency. I took the photograph as I was thinking of buying it myself. The man's an out and out conman. Didn't you realise? By the looks on your faces I guess not."

*

"I knew he was a wrong 'un the first day we got here," Margaret told us.

We'd moved a bit further along the bar, out of earshot of our group's table.

"But, but, but," Angela was having trouble composing a sentence.

"Please, didn't you notice the way he chatted to everyone in the dining room that first night; trying to get information out of them?"

"Erm, no," I said, finding my voice, "I was the last in that day."

"He was being so charming but was delving for knowledge," Margaret continued, "I spotted that straight off. Trained well by my father, I was. He didn't build up his business empire by being an idiot. No, as soon as mum mentioned selling dad's business, Harry was over like a shot."

"But, if you knew," Angela said, "Why didn't you say anything?"

"You've seen how much time I have to spend with my mother," Margaret told her, glancing over to where Dora was enjoying a large gin, "The old witch has me taking her here, there and everywhere. If it was up to me I'd have stuck her in a home years ago, but dad adored mum and made me promise to look after her. I was always daddy's girl and would do anything for him."

I couldn't speak now. I'd expected poor, lonely Margaret to be devastated that Harry had lied to her but instead she was quite chipper, and obviously a lot wiser than the rest of us.

"Harry's a great looking, charming man, so I thought I'd play him at his own game. String him along and enjoy having a bit of 'me' time for a while," Margaret said, "And I did. I liked looking around the barn, whoever owns it. Lunch at that picturesque, country pub was beautiful. And I especially enjoyed our efforts to break Mrs Goddard's bed back at the hotel afterwards."

That was a bit too much information. If she'd just finished her bedroom gymnastics when I bumped into her yesterday, where had her lips been before she kissed me on the cheek?

"Then of course he started giving me his spiel," Margaret continued, "Told me he had fallen in love with me and wanted us to be together. He said he knew I wouldn't just leave my mother and I would need some time to sort her comforts out first; but if we opened up a joint bank account straight away and both deposited some money in it; he could start getting things sorted for our future life together. Such an obvious con."

Margaret shook her head, remembering.

"So what did you say to him?" Angela asked.

"Oh I told him I knew exactly what he was and there was no way he was going to get money out of me. The charm soon disappeared after that. He called me a malicious, scheming bitch, so I told him I'd be on the phone to the police if he wasn't gone in half an hour. I must admit, I rather enjoyed doing that."

"So he's left the hotel?" I said.

Margaret nodded. "Yes. I don't think anyone realised last night after what happened to poor Louella, but they will."

"I feel sorry for Mrs Goddard," Angela said.

"She was never going to have him," Margaret spat.

"No, I meant I doubt Harry has paid his bill," Angela told her.

"That's not a problem; I'll pay her what Harry owes. It was worth it."

"But won't that seem a bit like you've just paid him for sex," I said, tentatively, "And without him even knowing it?"

Margaret let out a loud laugh and for the first time I could see a resemblance to Dora.

"Why not, Derek," she said, "Plenty of men do it."

That wasn't quite what I'd meant. I was thinking more how it seemed rather sad that this fake fantasy Margaret had created was the only way she could get some time away from her mother. Was Dora so controlling that Margaret really struggled to get, as she had put it, some 'me' time?

An image of my garden back at the marital home came into my mind. With a jolt I realised that had been my refuge; my 'me' time away from a controlling influence. Had my life with Leanne really been so different to Margaret's with Dora? Hadn't I always been kept busy running around after my wife while she led her life the way she wanted; picking her up from

Pilates every Tuesday and Zumba on Thursdays; collecting dry-cleaning; shopping for the dinner parties and then acting as coat attendant and wine waiter? Had I ever received a thank you or a show of affection in return? Of course I hadn't.

But at least I'd escaped that now and was starting over. Margaret's life was set to continue in the same vein. I'm sure Dora loved her daughter but, just like Colin's mum, she was a little sparse when it came to showing affection. For Margaret and for Colin it seemed they both lost the love they craved after their fathers died.

Angela and Margaret were still talking and I don't think they'd realised I'd drifted off, lost in thought.

"Harry's hotel bill won't exactly break the bank," Margaret said, "Dad's businesses were sold off for a couple of million."

"A couple of million?" I interrupted, more shocked at this news than at Harry's deceit, "Then what the hell are you doing on this shitty, little coach trip?"

Margaret laughed again. "It's mum's treat," she told us, "She thinks I needed to get away but obviously not without her. The tight, old cow won't pay out for anything expensive. She's never been abroad before; not even on the ferry."

Margaret looked at the two of us with some amusement.

"Dear me I've really shocked you with my behaviour, haven't I," she said, "Come on, down those drinks and I'll buy us another round."

Chapter 12

Angela and I remained pretty quiet over lunch; not really joining in the conversations of the rest of the group. Not that they seemed to notice, all chatting quite happily away to one another. Even Maeve, although not actually smiling, wasn't looking quite as grim as usual. The food at The Smugglers was cheap and cheerful; soup, chicken or fish with chips, followed by a cheesecake. After we'd finished eating we waited around for the tour guide; some staying inside the pub drinking coffee and the rest of us standing outside enjoying the sunshine.

"I'm still stunned," I told Angela, "I really thought Margaret was going to be devastated."

"Me too," she said, "Harry managed to fool everyone else. I thought he was a genuine, charming man."

He hadn't fooled me, I wanted to say. I'd never liked the guy. Okay, so that was down to plain, old-fashioned jealousy rather than to knowing he was a conman, but still. My instincts about people had taken a battering this week so it was good to know the initial feelings I'd had about Harry were right. I thought my opinion of Max was spot-on too. His manner had reminded me of Harry's. There was a little too much charm and sliminess. Was he a conman as well? Had he cheated Angela? She'd looked frightened when he'd shown up earlier on. I didn't like to think of him being in the same place as we were. Hopefully he was only visiting. I didn't want to bump into him again today.

"Oh dear," Angela said, looking over my shoulder, "I think our tour guide has arrived."

I turned round and saw a man dressed up in a pirate outfit

talking to Shauna. The costume looked homemade, all silk scarves and wellington boots. A pencilled on beard and soft toy parrot completed the look.

"Dear God, have we really got to walk about with that?"

The answer to my question was, yes. Shauna indicated that we should all gather round and she banged on the window to alert the rest of the group still inside the pub.

"Arrrgh, my hearties," said the tour guide, once we were all together, "Hello shipmates, I'm…"

"Look, Long Gone Sylvia," Shauna said, "I think I speak for the whole group when I say we can do without the performance."

The tour guide smiled. "Oh thank goodness for that," he said, now in a very plummy-sounding voice. He took a swig of water from a large, plastic bottle he was carrying, "I'm more used to doing the Stately Homes tour dressed as the first Duke of Tenham. I've only just been moved onto the Booty tour. It's been stressful enough learning all the facts, without also trying to perfect my 'arrrgh.'"

"The Booty tour?" I whispered, to Angela.

"Don't get your hopes up, Derek," she whispered back, "I think it refers to loot rather than to arses."

I guess the only arse on this tour was going to be the one wearing the pirate costume then.

"Right," said the guide, taking another drink from his bottle, "My name is Andrew. We're standing here at The Smugglers Inn. Of course back in the day it was known as The Three Crowns…"

"Why was that?" Lauren interrupted.

"Well, the smuggling was done in secret," Andrew told her, "If the place was already called The Smugglers Inn the local law enforcement would have known that this was where the contraband was stashed wouldn't they."

"Contraband? Pete, isn't that what you wore with your tux at the wedding; around the waist?"

"Let's move on, shall we?" Shauna said.

Andrew took another gulp from his bottle. Did he have a sore throat or something? I hoped his voice was going to last out for the entire tour.

"Okay," he said, "Well, long before the smugglers came on the scene the area was known as a place for pirates to bring their loot. I say pirates, they were sailors who had a, shall we say, agreement in place from the reigning monarchs of the day to share the booty in return for backing."

I must admit my mind wandered while Andrew spoke. I think I'd have paid more attention if he'd ditched the pirate costume altogether; but standing there with a fake parrot and plastic sword; carrying a bottle of water and calling himself Andrew, I couldn't really get too interested in what he was saying. I thought about Margaret and how wrong I'd been in thinking her a mere drudge rather than as a particularly astute woman. This led me to mull over what I'd also learned about Colin, Sooz and Maeve, which brought Shauna's words from day one back to me again. 'Your lives, your secrets; they'll all be revealed eventually. It always happens on a coach trip.' I really hoped there weren't going to be any more surprises this week.

The others began to walk past me and I realised the tour was moving off. Was it me or was Andrew swaying a little?

"And because he wasn't any good at growing facial hair, he was known as Captain Crapbeard."

"I think our guide might be improvising," Angela said.

"I think our guide might be swigging more than water from that bottle," I replied.

We made our way around the crescent of the harbour and came up to some stone steps that led down towards the water below. They looked rather slippery and uneven. On the outside there was an iron railing that worked as a bannister rail. The inside had hooks drilled into the rock and a thick rope had been threaded through them to hold onto.

"And so now we're going to descend down into one of the secret passages the smugglers used to use," Andrew called.

"Looks like the tour is over for me," Dora said, "Margaret; take me to that bar opposite The Smugglers; the one on the good side of the harbour."

"I'm not going, Gerald," I heard Maeve say; "You can if you like, but if you slip over and break your leg; don't come running to me."

"I don't think I should risk it either," said Lauren.

Margaret turned the chair around and wheeled Dora back the way we had just come, followed by Maeve, Lauren and Colin; who informed us that he couldn't go down the harbour steps and into a secret passage either because of his vertigo and claustrophobia. I was tempted to chase after them but Shauna grabbed my arm.

"Come on Dirk," she said, "We can't lose anyone else."

The irregular steps were really steep and, being at the back of the group, I took extra care as I began to descend. If I slipped and fell I'd take the rest of the party with me.

"I wish now I'd given my camel toe a good massage this morning," I heard Josie call out, as she gingerly stepped from one stair to the next.

"It's a hammertoe, isn't it dear," Sooz told her.

While each member of the group held onto the rail for dear life, Andrew's tight grip was just around his water bottle. How he managed to walk down those steps unaided I'll never know.

The lower we went the louder the sound of the water lapping against the stone wall got. Ahead of me, all I could see were the steps disappearing below the surface. Just as he reached this point, Andrew turned to the right and disappeared. I waited to hear a yell and a splash but it didn't come. As I watched, each person in the group in front of me did the same thing. When I finally reached the bottom I saw there was a big hole in the side of the rock, leading into the tunnel. At some point electric lighting had been added but it still retained its gloom and murkiness. We walked up the narrow passage until we entered a wider, circular space. Andrew stopped and we all crowded round him. He took another drink of his 'water.'

"Now," he said, smacking his lips, "This is the last surviving, secret tunnel of the smugglers. We believe there used to be another four thousand of these…no that's not right; another four of these, but they've all since caved in. They're gone. Completely vanished. Don't go looking for them because you won't find them."

"I think they've gone," Angela whispered, behind me. I laughed and the sound reverberated up the tunnel. It felt dank and close where we were.

"So," said Andrew, taking another hefty mouthful from the bottle, "Oh my God, that's good stuff. Anyway, this tunnel is rumoured to be haunted by one particular, infamous smuggler who was head of a local gang. He was a foul man by all accounts and was known to everyone as Friendly Fergus…no, that can't be right either."

Andrew scratched his head, trying to remember.

"Foul Fergus," he shouted, and we all jumped as his voice echoed around the space. If this guy did haunt the tunnel, I think Andrew had just invited him over.

"Foul Fergus," Andrew said, again, "Yes, that's right;

anyway, he really was an evil son of a bitch. He shot his own father for losing two barrels of rum, he sold his sister to a rich merchant and he cheated the other members of his gang left, right and centre. Finally, they'd had enough and plotted revenge. One night they tempted him down here onto this very spot."

"I'm starting to feel uneasy," Angela whispered.

I was starting to feel terrified. There was definitely an ominous sensation in the atmosphere but I smiled back at her and said, "Don't worry, I'll protect you."

"There were five that turned on Foul Fergus, that night," Andrew continued, hiccupping every so often, "But he didn't go down without a fight and took two of them with him to the grave. Legend says he still walks the tunnel to this day, looking for the other three members of his gang to carry off into hell."

Angela grabbed my hand at this point and I screamed. I didn't shout, I actually screamed. Josie and Sooz were right in front of me and they screamed too and then everyone else joined in. Andrew was the loudest and still going after everyone else had stopped.

"What the fuck," said Leroy, giving Andrew a shove which finally made him shut up, "Derek, why the hell did you do that?"

"I, er; Angela grabbed me," I said, pathetically.

"And you made that noise?" Shauna said, "Where did she grab you?"

Andrew downed the rest of his bottle.

"Right," he slurred, "Shall we move on?"

We carried on walking up through the tunnel and eventually came to a wrought iron gate that separated us from the outside. We waited while Andrew searched for the key and then waited some more while he tried several times to get it into the lock.

Once through we found ourselves standing at the back of The Smugglers Inn by the pub car park.

"So this is where the contraband was brought," Andrew said, "Oh wait, she meant cummerbund not contraband. Worn around the waist; tuxedo. That's very funny. Where'd she go?"

I didn't think this tour was going to improve. Andrew stopped turning around looking for Lauren and stared at his empty bottle in dismay. He sighed before throwing it over his shoulder.

"Talking of ghosts," he continued, swaying so much on the spot he made me feel seasick, "Foul Fergus had a girlfriend who worked here in the pub as a wench. She was killed when he threw her out of that window up there. He found out she was cheating on him with a local man from the village. They reckon she haunts this area; searching for her true love. What did the bitch expect? She was cheating on a nasty piece of scum. Got what she deserved if you ask me; filthy slag."

"Ok," said Shauna, "I think we've had enough of the tour for one day."

"Really?" Andrew questioned, "Because I've got tons more. I haven't told you about the local witch, Winifred. She used to burn faeces in her cauldron so was known as Winnie the Poo."

Shauna began pushing Andrew out through the side gate of the pub and back onto the pavement, shaking her head as he continued talking.

"Then there's Billy No Bollocks. Played poker and the stakes got a little too high. What about Kinky Ken, the cross-dressing accountant? No wait; he's not part of the tour, that's my flatmate."

"Honestly," Shauna said, patting him hard on the back, "It's been great. I'll be telephoning your boss later. Now you get yourself home."

Andrew staggered off.

"And get yourself to the job centre first thing in the morning," she called after him.

We now had some time to kill due to the premature end of the tour. I guess we could have sat down on the harbour steps, discussing art, culture and life in general but instead we headed straight for the bar where Margaret had taken Dora. Shauna tried contacting Jim to get him to bring the coach back a bit earlier but he wasn't answering his mobile. As we reached the entrance I pulled at Angela's sleeve.

"I don't really want to go for a drink," I told her, "Especially as I'll be drinking all evening with Pete and Leroy."

Angela nodded. "I agree," she whispered, "I'll be having a few with the girls back at the hotel later. Let's escape for an hour, shall we."

Great, some more alone time; just the two of us.

As we turned round we bumped straight into Josie who had been lagging behind the rest of the group.

"Are you not going in?" she asked, "Very wise. A little early for a drink I feel. Where are you off to?"

Shit.

"Oh; we're just going to take a walk along this side of the harbour," I told her, "I know the rest of you have already spent time down here."

"That sounds like a good idea," she said, "Perhaps I'll tag along too, if that's okay."

Bugger.

"Haven't you already explored this bit?" I asked.

"Not really, we only stopped for a quick coffee this morning and then moved on to the older side of the harbour."

Oh God; why hadn't I said we were going to the old part?

Josie leant over my shoulder and called out loudly, "Sooz;

Derek and Angela are going to take a walk along the modern side of the harbour. Are you coming?"

"Ooh yes," Sooz called back.

Karen was standing beside her. "Why don't we all go?" she said, "The road continues on at the corner and there's a little amusement arcade up there. That will pass some time."

So much for a quiet, intimate stroll. In the end Gerald and Maeve stayed behind in the bar with Dora (they were on coffee; she wasn't) while Pete and Leroy headed off to check out a few pubs and clubs for me and them to visit later on. The rest of us began the walk up to the corner. It was a good job the road did continue around on this side of the harbour as the fifteen seconds it took to walk to the end wasn't really killing time until the coach arrived. It was only as we reached the far corner that we could see the stretch of road that Karen had mentioned. It wasn't very wide and ran diagonally back towards the shoreline.

The old-fashioned-looking parade of amusement arcades wasn't really in keeping with the modern bars and shops we'd just walked past. There weren't that many people in them either; the pedestrianized road in front seemingly used just as a cut through from the town to the harbour front by the locals. A lot of the signs over the top of the different arcades were faded and the paint on the wooden facades was beginning to peel. I didn't like to say it but I suspect it would have been better to have knocked these down and incorporated the space into the new development that backed onto it.

We wandered into the first arcade and had a look round. This was mostly made up of old-fashioned fruit machines, like the one-armed bandits where you put the money into the slot and pulled the lever. Fortunately I knew how to play these. I didn't know how to use the modern electronic ones of today.

Whenever I had a go on them I just put my money in and kept pressing the button until I'd lost it. I guess that was the point; the quicker you put your money in, the more of it you lose. The next arcade along was a bit more up to date inside and had a lot of, what I still call, video games.

"Oh look Josie," Sooz said, "This looks like some kind of horse riding machine."

"It is," I said to her, "You sit on this saddle here and the horse race happens on the screen in front of you. The saddle moves up and down so you can pretend to be the jockey."

"Have a go Sooz," Josie said.

"Dare I?" Sooz giggled, "I don't know if I should."

"You're playing a game, not getting a tattoo," I told her, "There won't be any permanent scarring."

With a lot more giggling Sooz climbed on and Josie put the money in. As the saddle rose so she let out a little scream and then started laughing again.

"Go on Sooz," Angela called, "The game has begun, you need to start riding."

Sooz began rocking backwards and forwards on the saddle; chuckling all the time. It was funny to watch and we all ended up laughing. Suddenly her voice seemed to change. It deepened slightly.

"Oh yeah baby," she said, "Come on you big beast, ride it hard."

Only Josie continued to laugh, the rest of us felt we were watching something that perhaps should have been a bit more private.

"That's it, faster boy, faster. Come on, ride this one for momma."

We all kept looking around, not making eye contact with each other but checking that there were no strangers overhearing what was going on.

"Yes, yes; that's it, we're almost there. Where's a whip when you want one. Yes, yes, Oh yes!"

The race was over. Sooz sat where she was for a couple of seconds, leaning forwards over the saddle and breathing heavily. When she sat back up she looked at us all quite innocently.

"That was marvellous," she said, "I might have another go."

We left her and Josie to it and wandered over to the opposite side of the arcade, out of earshot. I suspected Sooz might need a few minutes to herself after another go; maybe to pop outside for a cigarette.

We enjoyed a few more of the games in the arcade. Lauren had a go at the basketball one where a ball is thrown down a small alley into a basketball net at the end. She threw it a bit too hard and it ricocheted out, smacking Colin up the side of the head. Yes, I particularly enjoyed that one. Margaret had a go at a driving game and revealed a propensity to road rage, surprising for someone who drove her mother everywhere. I'm not even sure what some of the words she shouted out meant, but they still made me blush.

Sooz and Josie joined us just in time to watch Shauna and Colin go head to head on a dance mat. Shauna shook all the talents her parents' genes had given her while Colin stood stock still, only moving his feet onto the relevant pad as required...he won.

Josie wanted to have a go on something before we left and fortunately she didn't want to return to the horse racing game. We wandered around for about ten minutes while she stopped at each machine, asked how it worked and then decided against it. Finally she settled on a duck hunting game. She pointed the plastic gun at me.

213

"Hands up Mother Tucker!" she said, "Is that the correct term, Derek?"

"Actually," began Shauna, "It's Mother Fu…"

"You're close enough to it," I interrupted.

Josie beamed and turned back to play the game. I don't know whether she'd ever used a real gun before but she was bloody good, although the way she kept shouting, "Die, Die" at the ducks belied her nature-loving persona. I was quite happy to return to the bar now but there was only one more arcade to go in.

"Oh, look at the soft toys in that crane machine," Karen said, as we reached the entrance, "They look really good. Lauren, what change have you got left? I always manage to get the claw to grab something. Let's have a go."

We all stopped and watched Karen's first few failed attempts before leaving her to it. Lauren and Shauna stayed with her while the rest of us went inside. The majority of the inside space was given over to bingo. There was a raised stand in the centre of the room where a man was stood beside an old fashioned bingo machine full of ping pong balls with the numbers on them. A long tube inside was where the balls were sucked up one at a time so that the man could retrieve them and read out the numbers. It was very reminiscent of the club where my grandmother used to go and play every Saturday evening when I was a child.

Surrounding this raised area were a large number of square bingo boards where the numbers were marked off by moving a little black door across the front of them. In front of each board was a stool and we all decided to sit down and have a game; all except Colin who said the stools were too low and would probably start off his sciatica. There were a few elderly ladies already playing and so we remained silent until the game finished and we were all able to put our money into the slot, ready for the next one.

"I've never played this before," Angela said, "Is it easy enough to follow?"

"Yes," I told her, "The numbers on the board are all shown in numerical order and that machine he's using is pretty slow so there'll be plenty of time to find the numbers and mark them off."

Margaret was sat the other side of Angela.

"Mum loves her bingo," she said, "But she really moans if one of her friends wins and she doesn't. I'm surprised they've not come to blows."

"Is it that competitive?" Angela asked.

"No, it's great," I said, as the woman opposite who'd won the last game received her prize. Her friend gave her such a look of loathing she could have been turned to stone, "My grandma used to play and it was loads of fun going to watch."

"Ok Ladies and Gents, we're ready for our next game," the man in the centre said, through his microphone, "Eyes down and looking for a full house."

"Here we go," I said.

"Sssh!" hissed the old lady sitting on my other side. Blimey, he hadn't even called a number yet.

"Three and one, thirty-one. Two and eight, twenty-eight. Kelly's Eye, number one."

"It's just the same as when I was a child," I whispered to Angela.

"Shush," the woman beside me said again.

I turned and stared at her but she was gazing intently at her board.

"You've just missed thirty-four, Derek," Colin said, behind me.

"Oh shit." I quickly pulled the door across.

"Six and five, sixty-five. Two fat ladies, eighty-eight."

"He must be talking about those two over there," Colin said, a little too loudly. The two women he pointed at shot us both a nasty look.

The game continued on. I loved that the man was using all the old terminology.

"Doctor's Orders, Number nine. Was she worth it, seven and six? Meal for two, sixty-nine."

I don't remember that last one.

"Two little ducks, twenty-two."

"Quack, quack," I shouted.

That's what was done when I was a child. The silence of the room told me it wasn't what was done here.

"Are you deliberately trying to put me off?" said the lady, beside me.

"I'm sorry," I replied, "It's just that when I was a kid I…"

I stopped talking as I noticed her board.

"Twenty-two," I said, "You've got a full house. Hey, she has a full house."

"Will you keep quiet," she said.

"But you've won."

"Do we have a call over here?" the man with the mike said.

"No, we don't," the woman said, blushing, "I'm not actually playing."

"What!" I shouted.

"I'm not playing. I didn't put any money into the machine."

"Are you calling then sir or not?" the man said to me, but I wasn't listening.

"Why the hell have you been telling me to be quiet when you're not even playing?" I was riled. I'd been cheerfully reminiscing about a happy, childhood experience and this old witch had spoilt it.

"I don't like your attitude," she said, to me.

"And I don't like yours, you stuck-up cow."

"Excuse me sir, you're disrupting the game." The bingo caller had come over.

"Me? She's the one," I shouted, pointing my finger right in the old woman's face.

"Calm down, Derek," Angela whispered, "Remember the happy times watching your grandmother."

"Oh, she just enjoyed gambling and getting pissed every week!" I snapped.

"If you can't control yourself sir, I'll have to ask you to leave," the bingo caller told me.

"What about her?" I said, incredulously, "She's sitting here, telling us to be quiet and she's not even playing. You're not making any money out of her."

"Yes sir" he replied, "But she's the owner of the arcades and so it doesn't really matter."

There wasn't any way I could win this argument so I stood up and left with as much dignity as I could; which wasn't much as Colin was in my way and we had one of those moving in the same direction moments; so it took me a while to get out of the arcade.

I walked back to where the crane machine was while the bingo game finished inside. I found Karen alone, with her arm up the prize chute.

"What are you doing?" I said.

"Fifteen pounds I've put in here," she told me, "I'm not leaving with nothing."

"But you can't just take a prize," I said, putting my hand in the chute to try and pull hers out, "It's stealing."

"Stealing? I'll tell you what stealing is," Karen said, miffed,

"Fifteen pounds and not so much as a proper grab at a toy; that's stealing."

At that moment the rest of the group emerged from the bingo, along with the bitch of an owner. I guess it looked shifty from their point of view, both my and Karen's hands up inside the crane machine but I still think it was a bit much for her to threaten us with the police. She finally settled on a life time ban of her arcade, which was fine with me. It was definitely time to go and get a drink now.

Back at the bar we all sat round two circular tables pushed together, apart from Pete and Leroy who were playing on a quiz machine over in the corner. Maeve was talking to Dora and Margaret at the far end. I say talking; with the music and Dora's deafness she had to shout and I could see the effort of this was exhausting her. Karen and Lauren were sat next to Angela and me, and Josie and Sooz were opposite. Shauna was stuck in the middle with Gerald and Colin, who was talking nineteen to the dozen at them; probably reliving the story about his big win on the dance mat.

"How long is it until the coach leaves?" Sooz asked me, from across the table.

I checked my watch. "In about twenty minutes."

"Good," she said, "It's a bit noisy for me in here."

The place was filling up with people who had finished work for the week. The stag party group that I'd seen in town earlier were standing along the bar, just beyond where we were sitting. It was obvious they'd been here the entire afternoon. They weren't causing offence; they were just loud in their chatter and laughter. Josie kept glancing round at them. Eventually she leaned over towards me and asked,

"Do you think there's something wrong with that woman in their group? She hasn't said a word and it looks like one of the boys is holding her up. Is she drunk?"

"No," I replied, "She's inflatable."

Josie's mouth dropped open. Actually her expression looked very similar to the one on the woman's face.

I finished off my lemonade. I was steering clear of alcohol until I headed off for the evening with Pete and Leroy. About ten minutes later Jim walked in through the main door that was beside our table. His glasses were steamed up and when he looked down at me his face showed no recognition. Before I could say anything he turned and walked off. He tripped over the leg of Sooz's chair as he tried to pass round her and fell into the stag party group. They all cheered and helped him stand upright again. Jim thanked the inflatable woman, who was right in front of him. He did a double take and smiled.

"Ah, there you are, Shauna," he said to her, "Are you ready to go?"

Chapter 13

By the second pub of the evening I'd started to relax. When the coach had left earlier I'd almost run after it (although with Jim's level of driving I could probably have overtaken it). My being so much older than Pete and Leroy had niggled away at me ever since Angela had suggested this night out. I didn't want people to think the guys had brought their dad out for the evening. But now; after a few drinks, I was getting into the swing of things. Pete and Leroy weren't bothered about the age gap so why should I be? I hadn't eaten anything since lunchtime but I'd probably be okay if I just stuck to drinking beer.

"Here you go, Derek," Leroy said, "Have a shot."

Well, one won't hurt.

Leroy smiled as I downed mine and held his glass up to me in a cheers gesture.

"The first of many," he said, and gulped it down, "Let's have another."

After a few more, Leroy informed me that pub number three was going to be a special treat. He then winked which set alarm bells off in my head. Had he and Pete found some illegal den on their tour of the town earlier? Were they about to take me to some all-night rave where drinks and drugs flowed easily and I'd end up coming to in a strange bed sometime tomorrow afternoon, with a pierced nipple and a whore called Roxie? Okay maybe my imagination was running away with me slightly. I was relieved but also quite surprised when we turned up back at The Smugglers.

The atmosphere inside was completely different to lunchtime. The place was lively and full of men, including the stag party guys who were crowded together at the far end of the bar. They all started cheering at the same time. I wasn't sure why until a gap appeared in the crowd and I caught a glimpse of a small, square, slightly raised area of floor, covered in carpet and with a long pole on one side on which a naked woman was currently hanging upside down. She slowly manoeuvred herself to the ground and did the splits. Somehow she was able to gyrate while in that position and I worried about carpet burns. I turned to Leroy and Pete and they both grinned back at me.

"Surprise," Leroy said.

It seemed so odd for this historical pub, which had lots of boating memorabilia on the walls to have women stripping in it of an evening. Perhaps they kept the nautical theme going. The woman currently on stage was certainly giving the whole room a good look at her poop-deck.

I bought drinks and left Pete and Leroy enjoying the entertainment. Strippers weren't really my thing. I preferred to get to know a woman first before she took her clothes off; and then I'd rather she did it just for me and not for a group of horny, pissed-up men.

I noticed a middle-aged woman sitting just across from where I was standing. She looked uncomfortable and I didn't know why she remained in here. The lady caught my eye and smiled. I smiled back and she indicated the chair opposite her.

"I'm not stopping here long if you want to sit down," she said.

"Thanks," I replied, pulling out the chair, "I was here at lunchtime today. It's a bit different now."

She smiled. "Yes it does change over pretty quickly. I'm just having a quick drink before I go to work."

"I'm on a bit of a pub crawl with some friends," I explained, "I didn't know this place was a strip club in the evenings. It's not my sort of thing really."

"It's not for everyone," the lady said, "Although that guy seems to be enjoying it."

She pointed behind me and I turned to see Leroy on Pete's shoulders, whooping loudly and waving his jacket above his head.

"Yes it does seem to be his thing," I replied, "Whoever he is. It must be intimidating for the girls though."

"Absolutely," the woman told me, "It's not a dignified way to earn a living is it, getting paid to swing your bits in a man's face; make a few groaning noises before sticking a finger up your own ass."

"Oh, well, erm, I guess not; no." I hadn't expected such a detailed explanation.

"Massaging your minge, licking your own tits and then bending over backwards to show off every little bit of yourself."

Was it me or was it getting hot in here?

"Gripping a pole with your thighs and rubbing your oiled body up and down it whilst spanking your arse. It's pretty disgusting if you ask me."

I was so turned on right now. Another cheer went up behind me.

"Thanks to Saucy Sarah there," the compere shouted out, "Up next, Juicy Janine."

"Well," said the woman, downing her drink and standing up, "That's me. I'd best go get ready."

It took some effort to move Pete and Leroy on to pub number four. After talking with her I didn't really want to see what Juicy Janine did, although the quick glimpse I got as I closed the pub door behind me showed a woman in very good shape for her age and I was surprised at how quickly she made the banana disappear.

The drinks flowed well at the next pub but I felt I could still hold my own.

"Yeah, when I was your age it was anything that moved."

I could certainly still lie.

"Go Derek, my man," Leroy said, "I used to be the same. I did it in a field once while a horse watched. I think he felt pretty inadequate, if you know what I mean?"

"Did he have a long face?" I asked, and threw my head back, laughing at my up-to-date sense of humour.

"I meant my cock," Leroy said.

"Yes, I know what you meant."

It was mostly Leroy and I making conversation. Pete threw a comment in every so often but for the most part he remained rather quiet. He was a lot more cheerful though.

"How about we hit a club now?" Leroy said, "You can show us your chat-up techniques, stud."

I turned round to see who he was talking to and realised he meant me. I wasn't that drunk.

"No, I can't do that," I told him, "It would be wrong. They'll all be young girls in there."

"Not always," Pete piped up, "You often get old women in their fifties and sixties turn up at these clubs, desperate for it. They'll go with anyone. You'll be fine, Derek."

I preferred it when he was quiet.

"Come on," Leroy said, "Let's go anyway."

I couldn't remember the last time I'd been clubbing. It had to be before I was married and even then I must have been pressurised into going. They were always places where I felt uncomfortable, self-conscious and really untrendy. It would be even worse now. A part of me wanted the bouncer to not let me in so that I had an excuse to move the evening elsewhere; but the bigger part of me feared the humiliation of being refused entry on the grounds of being too old and having to do the walk of shame past the other people in the queue.

"This'll be great," Leroy said, as we waited outside, "A few drinks, a dance with a beautiful woman or two."

"What about Karen?" I asked. Not that it was really any of my business.

"Only a dance, Derek. I like to know I can still pull. Karen's the only one for me."

"I won't be chatting up anyone," Pete told me.

"No; really?"

"Honestly," he replied, missing the sarcasm in my voice completely, "I'm a married man now; with responsibilities."

I was feeling more and more apprehensive as we moved nearer to the front of the queue, tucked behind a group of giggling, young girls who had gone way over the top with their make-up to try and look older than they actually were. They were shivering away in thin, wispy outfits with not a coat or jacket in sight. A part of me wished Maeve was here. She'd have got them wrapped up in cardigans and vests quick enough.

I was pretty sure the bouncer did a double take as I walked past him into the club but I guess it could just have been my paranoia. The reason why the shivering girls weren't wearing coats became apparent when I went to check in ours.

"Two pounds fifty per item?" I said, incredulously, looking at the three jackets I was holding plus Pete's umbrella, "That's ten pound. I've already paid fifteen quid a head just to come in here."

"That's the rules," was the response from the spotty youth behind the counter.

"Rules? You're a teenager, aren't you? You're meant to be breaking them."

I refused to pay out for that and we headed off to the main

area. I still seemed to be holding all of the jackets. I couldn't believe the noise when we walked in. Had the music always been played this loudly? Even Dora wouldn't have any trouble hearing it. She'd love it in here.

The room was vast, but rather dark. There was a large, circular opening in the centre which looked down to the floor below where the dancefloor was. Two spiral staircases led the way down. Leather sofas and comfy chairs were set out in the corners of the room where we were but around the safety rail, that surrounded the circular opening, the seating was mainly stools and tall tables. We made our way across to one of these now, close to the bar and beside one of the spiral staircases. Leroy went to the bar and bought the first round of beers and shots. Before I could say thank you he'd headed off to chat to a group of girls.

"He doesn't waste any time, does he," I shouted at Pete, hoping he could hear me over the din.

Pete moved a stool closer to me and sat down. "I know," he said, "I wish I had that confidence. He used to drag me along with him but I always hated it. I felt so uncomfortable trying to think of something clever to say, and it was horrible when the girls just laughed at me."

Leroy walked by with one of the girls from the group. He winked at us as he walked down the stairs to the dance floor. As the evening progressed I noticed that each girl Leroy chatted up got one dance and then they were escorted back to where they had originally been standing. He came back to the table every so often to catch up on his drinking. Pete was turning into quite the talker.

"I really love her," he told me, "Meeting Lauren was the best day of my life."

"I know, man." I seemed to be gaining an American accent.

I'd almost used the word 'dude.'

"I mean, Lauren is the dippiest girl I've ever met," Pete continued, "I'm talking really thick. She thought a smuggler was someone who could keep three balls in the air. But I don't care. I love her."

"I hear you, bro," I said, swigging from my beer bottle.

"I knew I wanted to marry her as soon as I saw her. The baby's brought that forward but we would always have got married."

"Respect dude."

Yeah, I'd just tipped over the edge. I tried to perform a high five but only succeeded in smacking Pete on the forehead. Fortunately he didn't appear to notice.

Leroy came over to our table with two girls. Both were slim and wearing short mini-skirts and tight, low-cut tops. One was blonde, the other brunette. I guessed the evening was progressing too rapidly for him so he was now taking two at a time.

"Derek, this is Melanie," Leroy said, indicating the blonde.

"Hey there, Lemony," I slurred.

"She likes the older guy."

"That's handy, there's an old folks home next door."

Melanie laughed and grabbed my arm, almost pulling me off the stool.

"Come on Derek, let's see your shapes," she said, and dragged me away from the table.

I found myself down on the dance floor, moving. I call it moving as I don't think it comes under the heading of dancing. As I looked around me I realised no one was staring so it couldn't have been that bad. I relaxed a little and let myself go. It was probably a mistake to throw in the spin. I lost my balance and nearly went head first into a couple joined at the lips but Melanie managed to grab my arm.

"You're funny, Derek," she said, squeezing my hand; just like Angela had been doing.

"You should see my act," I replied, "How about a drink?"

"Sure."

I was so glad to leave the dance floor. We walked past Pete who was sitting on his own, staring at a photograph of Lauren. I bought drinks and to make conversation, I started talking about the trip. It sounded a lot funnier chatting about it than actually living through it. Melanie seemed to be enjoying herself.

"Come on," she said, eventually and grabbed my arm again. I really didn't want to dance.

She led me back past Pete, who grinned knowingly, and out through a door at the end of the bar. It was dark but cool and the monotonous thud of the music lessened. I realised we were outside. I think it was some kind of garden area. I could hear the rustling of leaves but also a lot of moaning and groaning, similar to the noises Sooz had made on the horse racing machine earlier.

Melanie led me to the far end by the wall. She turned round and before I could ask where we were she was kissing me; her tongue inside my mouth and her arms and legs clamped around me like a limpet. I found myself responding. How had this happened? A young, attractive woman with her pick of young men had chosen me. It was a massive ego boost and I felt like the cock of the hen house. Yep, that was the phrase alright. Our mouths broke apart and while I gulped in some air, Melanie moved around to kiss my cheek and bite my ear.

"I don't have a condom," I whispered. Well, apart from the emergency one in my wallet but that had been there since my university days.

"It doesn't matter," she breathed back.

I froze. So did Melanie.

"What's wrong?" she asked.

I looked into that young, innocent face staring up at me.

"It does matter," I said, "It matters a lot. There's no reason you should never use a condom. It's morally the right thing to do and you should always insist on safe sex. You're a lovely girl, Melanie and you should respect your body, and yourself."

"I meant it doesn't matter because I have one in my purse."

"Oh, ok; that's alright then."

I moved in for another kiss. Melanie pushed me away.

"Fuck you, grandpa," she said.

"Yes please."

She shoved past me and disappeared. I gave it a few minutes and then made my way inside again. Leroy was back at the table.

"That was quick," Pete said, "Did you, you know, have a problem...getting it up?"

"No I didn't," I snapped, "We...I don't want to talk about it, okay? Now, who wants another drink?"

By the time we left the club I was having trouble focussing.

"Where the fuck has the cab rank gone?" I asked.

"I don't think there was one," Pete said, swaying a little on the spot.

"Are you sure?"

"No, not really."

"There was one," slurred Leroy, "And I'll take on anyone who says different."

"Different," I said, and howled inanely at my razor sharp wit.

We staggered up the road together, Leroy and I leaning on each other to keep ourselves upright.

"How much is a cab going to cost?" I asked, "I've only got a ten pound note left in my wallet. It's my emergency one. I keep it next to my condom. Where's the cash point?"

"I don't think there was one," said Pete.

"Are you sure?"

"No, not really."

"There was one," Leroy slurred, "And I'll take on anyone who says different."

"Shit! How are we going to get home?" I wasn't finding this funny anymore.

"We'll walk," Leroy said, determinedly, before falling over, "Or maybe we should call Jim the Limb to pick us up in the coach," he added, from the floor.

"Give me that tenner, Derek," Pete said.

I passed over the condom first but then managed to get hold of the ten pound note and switch them over. Pete took it and walked off down to the high street. I picked Leroy up off the floor and followed. By the time we caught up he was in the Chinese Takeaway, ordering food.

"What are you doing?" I said, "That's all the money I've got."

He ignored me.

"That's ten pound fifty," the man behind the counter said.

Pete routed around in his pocket for some coins and paid the man. Great, we were well and truly stuck now.

"Can we have that delivered?" he asked, "It is free for orders over ten pounds isn't it? That's what it says in the window."

The man behind the counter nodded. Well this was marvellous. The takeaway was going to get back home safely even if we weren't. We all sat down in silence, waiting for the food. I didn't know what we were going to do. I took another look in my wallet in case I'd overlooked some money. All I found was a two-for-one voucher for Epsom salts I must have been given at some point. Perhaps if we found a cab driver with chronic constipation we'd still have a chance of getting home tonight.

After fifteen minutes the order was brought out and given to one of the drivers.

"Where to?" he asked us.

"We'll show you," said Pete, getting up, "Come on you two."

We followed him outside and watched as Pete settled himself into the passenger seat of the car. The bewildered driver looked over at me. I shrugged my shoulders and helped Leroy into the back. It worked out as a pretty good deal really; ten pound fifty for a ride to the hotel with a meal thrown in. I grew rather fond of Pete after that.

It was eerily silent when we walked in through the front door. I'd spent most of the car journey dozing. Leroy had found a hipflask in his jacket pocket that he didn't remember owning and he and Pete continued on with the party. We gave it to the driver as a tip when we got out. He was still looking confused by the situation and took a nip before driving off.

"Where the hell is everybody?" Leroy said. He didn't shout but he wasn't quiet either and his voice reverberated around the hallway.

"Ssh. Everyone's in bed," I whispered.

"What, the same bed?" asked Pete.

"Wahey, orgy night," said Leroy, rubbing his hands together, "Bags I get Dora."

"You're welcome to her," I said, "But no, everyone's in their own rooms. It's time for bed."

"That's a good idea, Dennis," Leroy said, "Where is my room?"

I don't know how I managed it but I dragged the two of them

up to the first floor. I wasn't totally sure which rooms were theirs but sod it; they could work that part out for themselves.

"Thanks Derek," Pete said, throwing his arms around me, "I wish you were my dad."

He fell instantly asleep on my shoulder and it took a while to wake him enough to lean him on Leroy and point them in the direction of the right hand corridor. I just hoped their rooms were that way. I didn't hear any screaming as I continued on up to the second floor so I guess they made it ok.

I realised I was still holding the Chinese takeaway. It was in a plastic bag, slung over my wrist and the handles were digging right in. I couldn't have sobered up that much as I thought it would be a great idea if Angela shared it with me. I didn't even consider that it was probably cold by now. I walked up the staircase leading to her room and knocked gently on the door. Nothing. I knocked again, a bit louder. I heard a giggle from the other side and then the door flew open.

"Hey, it's Dirk!"

"Ssh."

I think Angela's evening with the girls had gone well.

"Are you hungry?" I whispered.

"Ravenous," she said, still talking loudly, "Have you seen the slops they serve here?"

"I've got Chinese," I said.

"I **love** Chinese. Get in here."

Angela grabbed the front of my jacket and yanked me inside her room. It was the mirror image of mine except she had a double bed. We sat on the floor and ate some of the lukewarm food. It was congealing but still a lot tastier than most of the stuff we'd eaten so far this week. Angela produced an almost full bottle of wine and we drank that as well, swigging from the bottle as there were no glasses. I can't remember half of what

231

we chatted about, but it was all hilariously funny.

"The Sheds of the World slideshow didn't go too well," Angela said, "As soon as the projector was switched on, the shadow puppets started. The horse with his 'fifth leg' was brilliant; I still don't know who did it."

"Probably Sooz," I said, "Reliving the ride at the arcade. Did she start moaning again?"

"No but Colin did. He really is a right old misery. He reckons he's got concussion from the basketball smacking him up the side of the head."

"So he's going to give Lauren a mouthful now as well."

"Bless her, I don't think she can spell concussion, let alone know what it means," Angela said.

She took another swig from the wine bottle and then remembered something else.

"Dora sat with us after the slide show. I bow down to her level of alcohol consumption. The woman's amazing but God, she knows some filthy songs."

"I know," I said, taking a sip from the wine bottle before handing it back to Angela again, "I still recall Mary from the Diner."

"Oh blimey, she finished that one off," Angela told me, "I don't want to give too much of the story away but Mary and Rod were soon joined by her friend, Debbie; from The Ritz. Guess what she had a massive pair of."

I laughed.

"Karen and I were still downstairs drinking together at one o'clock," Angela continued, "That camp, old queen behind the bar wasn't happy, but fuck him."

I laughed again.

"Someone should," she mused, "Might cheer him up a bit. A cock, right up his arse, that's what he needs."

"It's a shame the chef left with his chopper."

Angela grinned. "Yeah; that would sort him out," she agreed, "A big piece of that. Touch your toes and up it goes."

"I'm not so sure it would be a smile that was brought to the barman's face though, if that happened," I told her, "The chef certainly wasn't average...at least I hope he wasn't."

"I bet you only have to drop your trousers to see a nice, big cock, Derek."

"Maybe wearing Jim's glasses."

"Come on," Angela said, crawling forwards, "Let's have a look."

"No," I shrieked, sounding like a frightened virgin on her wedding night.

"Come on, Derek, give us a look."

Angela kept trying to knock my hands away from my groin. We were both laughing.

"Go on," she said, "You show me yours and I'll show you mine."

"I really hope you don't have a cock," I told her.

Angela stood up and unzipped her dress, letting it fall to the floor in front of me. I stopped laughing. She was beautiful; her body lithe and supple; not an ounce of fat anywhere. From where I was on the floor, her breasts loomed over me. I felt sure that if she took off her bra, they wouldn't sag an inch. I stood up and pulled off my top. She wasn't laughing now either, thank goodness.

We stood looking at each other for what felt like an eternity before finally succumbing. The first kiss I felt nervous, just like when I'm in the dentist's chair; my mouth is open and I don't know where to put my tongue, but I quickly got over that. Our lips locked again and our hands began frantically pawing away at each other's bodies. The taste of her was beautiful, even the

233

faint hint of sweet and sour prawns.

"I don't have a condom," I told her, as we parted for air.

"It doesn't matter," Angela said.

Suddenly I was back in the garden at the nightclub. I quickly blinked the image away. That was then and this was now; and now felt so right.

"I have one," she whispered.

The best three words in the world. Better than, 'I love you' or, 'Chelsea win league.'

Our love making continued. Soon we were both naked, my socks being more of a pain to get off than Angela's bra. I was worried my hopping around the floor as I tugged at them would ruin the moment but fortunately it didn't. Angela moved her lips expertly over my body and I gasped at her touch. She obviously knew exactly what she was doing and I hoped I would be able to perform well after all that booze.

We stepped over to the bed and I began to explore her body, enjoying every inch. There was a momentary lapse in concentration when I spied an intimate tattoo that said, 'Slippery When Wet' but I quickly moved away from it. This was no time for reading in bed.

The kissing and caressing continued until Angela climbed on top and began to ride me hard. God, I could see why she was so good on the horse the other day. She pulled my hands onto her breasts. We were both groaning; I didn't care how loudly. The bed creaked, a spring latched onto my arse, but we didn't stop. This was the best sex I'd ever had and I didn't want it to end; but when it did it felt like we both exploded with pleasure.

We fell back, panting afterwards; not in each other's arms like in the movies, we were too sweaty and slippery for that. I thought again about that tattoo and then an image of Max appeared. Had he enjoyed such great sex with Angela too? I shook the thought away. We all had pasts; hell you could be seventeen and have a past these days. I'm sure Melanie had one.

We lay there in silence while our breathing returned to normal. I started wondering if Angela wanted me to leave or stay. Would she be offended if I brought the subject up? Could I put an arm around her now? I realised I'd got married to avoid these sorts of questions and situations, no wonder it hadn't worked out. I turned my head to ask if I could stay and saw Angela was already sleeping. I gently pulled the duvet up over both of us and promptly fell asleep myself.

Chapter 14

I awoke to the sound of moaning beside me. I hoped Angela was enjoying a private moment on her own, reliving the night before; sadly no. She was lying there with her hands over both eyes. Not a good sign. Any minute now I expected to hear that immortal phrase, 'What have I done?'

"I think my head has split in two," she wailed.

I was feeling pretty terrific.

She groaned again. "I tried to look around the room just now but it was spinning too much. And I think I'm seeing double."

"Let's check," I said, "How many fingers have I got up?"

"Up where?"

"No, I mean how many am I holding up, in front of you?"

"It had better not be two."

"Oops; sorry."

Angela moved her hands away from her face. Lipstick was smeared across her cheek, her hair was sticking out in every direction and she squinted up at me through what can only be described as two piss holes in the snow. She still looked beautiful.

"That is you, isn't it Derek?" she asked.

"No," I said, in my best Italian accent, "It's Chico. I've come to give you an early morning sausage."

I thrust my hips at her. Angela laughed and then grabbed her head again.

"My God, I've not had a hangover like this since the great Ouzo challenge of ninety-seven. I'm still banned from Corfu."

"That's a story I want to hear more about later," I said, getting out of bed, "But right now I ought to be getting showered and dressed and let you do the same. You are still coming on the trip today aren't you?"

"It's why I booked the holiday in the first place," Angela said, "I'm coming, Derek."

"Ooh, and that's just with me standing here, naked."

It took a second for her to realise what I meant but then she smiled, threw a pillow at me and told me to get out. I quickly dressed and left. I was glad I didn't see anyone as I snuck back across the landing to my room. Last night I hadn't cared what noise I made but this morning I really hoped we hadn't been too loud. I wanted this to be about us, not anyone else.

Once I'd showered I felt even better. Maybe great sex was a hangover cure. In that case why did Angela feel like crap? God, I hope that theory was wrong. I found myself whistling as I skipped down the stairs to breakfast. Dora was leaning over the chair in the hallway, picking an earring up off the floor. Her vast bottom was facing me as it had done in her room the morning of the wine tasting. What a funny memory that seemed now.

"Give us a smile, Dora," I called, as I passed.

"Ooh Derek; wait 'til I've got my teeth in," she replied.

It was strangely silent in the dining room as I entered. Or was that because I had entered? Had the group been discussing Angela and me just before I walked in through the door? Surely we hadn't been so loud that they'd all heard us? I sat down in my usual seat. Shauna gave me a very innocent looking smile. Jim didn't acknowledge me at all but as I hadn't made a noise as I sat I don't think he was aware I was actually there. Angela wasn't down yet and I decided to display a nonchalant attitude. I smiled warmly back at Shauna and casually poured myself a cup of instant.

I scanned the room. Nobody at the other tables was trying to surreptitiously glance my way so I don't think there had been any talk about my actions last night. Taking a closer look at everyone I assumed the quietness was due mostly to the number of hangovers the drinkers of last night were suffering. I felt sure Leroy's vest over his shirt was a mistake rather than trendy new look. Karen had moved her untouched bowl of cereal to the side of the table and was resting her head on a placemat. Pete had somehow managed to doze off in the middle of his breakfast, a spoonful of cornflakes halfway to his lips. When Lauren noticed she gave him a nudge. He jumped in fright, sending the contents of the spoon up into the air. A splodge of cold, milky mush on the back of the neck certainly woke Karen up.

Mrs Goddard's newest member of staff entered the dining room with a plate of toast. Valerie moved a lot quicker than her late sister but then she did have the advantage of a motorised scooter. I'm not sure how long she'd been using it for as her driving wasn't the most accurate, although I still think she could have given Jim a run for his money. Valerie drove across the floor towards the cereal table in little bursts while she fiddled with the buttons on the handlebars. I really hoped pizza was on the menu this evening, it would feel like we were getting it delivered.

As she neared the cereal table Valerie's hand slipped and she flew forwards, bashing into the leg and sending the milk jug crashing to the floor. In reverse mode she maintained the same speed and went flying backwards right into the back of Josie's chair, sending Josie face first into her porridge. Yep, Valerie was going to fit in very nicely around here.

I noted Harry's absence and had a quiet word with Margaret by the buffet table while the travesty behind us was being cleared up. Everyone was aware he'd disappeared now. Mrs

Goddard had been beside herself yesterday and was found by Chico with her head inside the oven. Fortunately for her the village wasn't on mains gas and she'd been lying on the floor for four hours with her head inside an electric oven. She had stamina, I'll give her that. Margaret, as good as her word, had taken her aside, explained the situation; and paid Harry's bill.

"So at least she's not out of pocket," Margaret continued, "Do you know, Derek; I think she was really counting on that money. I don't think this hotel has turned a profit in years. I told her she should think about selling up but from the little Barbara said to me; I reckon this place is carrying a rather large mortgage."

"I suppose she's too proud to throw in the towel," I replied, "Besides, what would this sell for with so much needing to be spent on it."

Margaret nodded. "I know. I think her only way out now is an insurance fire," and she laughed.

Angela entered the dining room at that point and I returned to my seat. She was still looking pale, but more alive than earlier.

"You're looking better," I said.

Angela's eyes opened wide and I realised the mistake I'd just made.

"Er, than when I saw you earlier on this morning…when I knocked you up. I mean, when I knocked at your door…to see if you were ready for it…for breakfast."

Smooth Derek, I thought, drinking another mouthful of what passed for coffee around here. As usual, Colin was last down.

"No visitors last night, sunshine?" Shauna asked him, as he passed by our table.

"I might just as well have had," he said, "Didn't get a wink of sleep due to all that awful noise."

239

I spluttered into my coffee and Angela took a great interest in her napkin.

"The yelping, the scratching, the high-pitched howling; it sounded like a bloodbath."

Geez, the guy should calm down, it was just a bit of sex. I can't help it if I howl.

"A bucket of cold water, that's what the two of them needed."

A smack in the mouth is what Colin needed.

"And as for the stench; I had to close my window in the end."

I wasn't taking any more of this.

"Right, that's it," I said, standing up, "Ok, so Angela and I had sex last night. Actually, we made love. We weren't that noisy and the stench you refer to was a Chinese takeaway I'd brought in with me. We're both consenting adults and have done nothing to feel ashamed about. Quite frankly if you indulged in a bit of rumpo once in a while you might find it cured your headaches and stopped you being such a whinging tosser!"

Colin stood there, open mouthed; staring. The whole room was silent again, only this time all eyes were definitely on me.

"Erm Dirk," said Shauna, "There were a couple of foxes fighting in the garden last night about half past two. I think that's what he's referring to."

Ground, please open up and swallow me now. I looked back at Colin, smiled and then said; as casually as I could,

"Oh ok, we're obviously talking at cross purposes, forget I said anything."

I sat back down. Angela's hands were once again covering her eyes. Breakfast remained a quiet, somewhat muted affair after that; the only sound being the beep of Valerie's scooter which was now stuck in reverse.

I'd hoped to be first on the coach after breakfast so that I could disappear down into my seat and avoid having to see anyone, but I'd left my camera up in my room. I couldn't go to the gardens without it so I had to go back upstairs. Only once I was back down in the hallway did I realise that my notebook wasn't in my jacket pocket and so up I went again. As I ran out the front of the hotel I could see that the rest of the group were already on board. Jim even had the engine running. Shauna was waiting by the coach door.

"Sorry," I said to her, panting heavily from all the rushing about, "I had to run upstairs to lay my hands on a couple of things."

"I'll bet," Shauna said, "Couldn't you both have left recreating last night until later; I do have a schedule to keep to?"

It was going to be a day full of comments like that, I could tell.

"So is Angie coming along or have you tied her to the bed as a little treat to look forward to later on?"

I opened my mouth to answer but couldn't think of any retort. Instead I turned and boarded the coach. Jim looked like he gave me a wink as I got on; so did Leroy while the rest of the youngsters all smiled knowingly. Dora pinched my bum as I went past and Maeve, Gerald, Josie and Sooz couldn't make eye contact, although I was having trouble with that part myself.

As I sat down I saw Angela rush out the front door. It was just long enough after me to make everyone think we'd planned it that way. As she reached the bottom step her handbag twisted and a make-up bag fell out, sending lipstick and brushes and other items across the driveway. After swearing loudly she picked up what she could in her hands and ran over to the coach.

"Sorry, sorry," she puffed, as she and Shauna boarded, "I was just, well…" she looked at the stuff in her hands, "I was just doing a bit of touching up."

"No need to explain," Shauna said, "Dirk's already told us."

Looking puzzled, Angela made her way up the coach. As she reached me she remained standing.

"I'm going to lie down on the back seat, Derek," she said.

I didn't think the next sentence was going to be, 'Would you like to join me.'

"I still feel dreadful."

"Oh, ok," I told her, "See you later on."

Shit; had I blown it? Had Angela already started regretting last night before I'd inadvertently told everyone about it? Would we be able to move on from this? We pulled out of the driveway and Shauna switched on the microphone.

"Right, well here we are on our final excursion. I was going to say let's go out with a bang but a couple of you have beaten me to that already."

I sank lower into my seat.

"On behalf of Scrimshaw Travel I'd like to say I hope you've all enjoyed your week away with us. Personally I've found it more painful than the time I had my bikini line waxed by a young lad on work experience at my local beauty salon; but that's just me for you."

She really did have a lovely way of putting things.

"Anyway, today we're going to the ancestral home of the Dukes of Tenham. I've got a bit of information for you so, in the words of Dirk to Angie; 'Let me fill you in.'"

My God; tomorrow couldn't come soon enough.

"The house and grounds are now run by a charitable trust as the family line no longer exists. The last surviving member

242

died back in the nineteen fifties and was well-known as being; what was termed back in the day, 'a bit of a whoopsie;' so he never managed to marry or have any children to inherit the title and lands."

I turned in my seat to whisper a comment to Angela, before remembering she wasn't sitting with me.

"The current Tenham House was built in the mid eighteenth century after the previous building was destroyed by fire. The place is most famous for its landscaping and gardens; the main one of which was designed by Calamity Jane. Hang on, that's not right. Bugger. I knew I shouldn't bother trying to learn this shit. Where's that poxy leaflet gone? Ah, here it is. The main garden was designed by Capability Brown. I wasn't that far off. Anyway, there are a lot of different areas to see, if you like that sort of thing. The house is also of historic interest…look, this leaflet is free when you get there; just read that, will you. I really can't be arsed today. We'll be there in twenty minutes."

She switched off the microphone and sat back down. It did only take twenty minutes but felt much longer sitting on my own. I'd got used to having Angela beside me. I wanted her beside me all of the time.

After passing through the front gate, where Shauna was given our tickets and the all-important leaflets, we drove up to the house on a path that meandered through the park-like grounds designed by Capability Brown. The vast, smooth expanse of grass, planted sporadically with native trees stretched right up to the front of the property. I loved the simplicity of the clever design and couldn't wait to see what other delights the rest of the gardens had to offer.

Tenham house itself was smaller than I'd imagined but still an impressive and beautiful Georgian building with two large wings jutting out either side of a central entrance to give that classic symmetrical appearance. The numerous windows on the first two floors were the same height as the front doors leading into the hallway while the third floor, within the roof space, contained a large number of impressive dormer windows, all perfectly aligned with those on the two floors below. Right in the centre of the roof stood a dome-shaped clock tower, its faces surveying the land and countryside that surrounded the property.

Shauna handed out the leaflets and tickets as we alighted from the coach. Once off, I waited for Angela while the rest of the group headed in different directions; some to explore the house first, and others the gardens. She smiled at me as she walked down the steps. That was a good sign.

"I've been thinking, Derek, it's probably best if we split up today," she said.

My stomach lurched. I didn't know we were 'together' and already she wanted to split up.

"You really want to see the gardens and I really want to see the house, so we may as well do those on our own."

"Oh, right," I said, relieved in one sense but still disappointed in another.

"I'd hate to think that I was holding you back looking at the gardens and I'm sure you'd feel the same with me in the house. I know I'll be in there for hours."

I guess I knew what she meant.

"Maybe I'll see you in the café at lunchtime," Angela said. She smiled again and disappeared off into the house.

I still wasn't sure where I stood. There was no definite time made to meet for lunch. I hadn't yet had a chance to apologise about my outburst at breakfast. Was she still embarrassed about that or, what seemed more likely to me; was she regretting the whole damn thing?

I opened up the leaflet which contained a map of the grounds. They were vast and I doubted I would get to see all of it before lunch. I remained standing where I was, trying to plan out which gardens I really wanted to see. There were paths everywhere. I think the idea behind it was that you could pop in and out of different gardens at your leisure without having to walk through a load of other areas you didn't want to visit. However, to me it just seemed to over complicate things. I must have spent ten minutes marking paths on the map before giving up and heading off to the Garden Walk which was situated around the back of the house.

I was feeling rather melancholy but I had to get a grip. The main reason for booking this tour was to see the gardens here at Tenham House. I'd been looking forward to it all week and had always expected to be walking around them alone. I'd certainly not planned to meet someone on this holiday. Angela and our relationship, whatever that was or wasn't going to be, would have to wait. I got out my notebook, pencil and camera and began the tour.

There were actually quite a lot of people walking around. It was Saturday and the day was warm and sunny although cloud and rain, and a potential storm, were forecast for this evening. Once I concentrated on the gardens I did begin to enjoy myself. The first area behind the house was set out more formally than at the front. Two large, square areas of ground had been framed by metre high Box hedging and the insides of both had flower beds dug into them in a symmetrical pattern. Each was filled with an abundance of bedding plants. Colourful geraniums wrestled for space beside vibrant petunias and striking begonias, their fight for supremacy overseen by majestic purple alliums.

Beyond this area a path zigzagged up a gently rolling slope passing all manner of shrubs and trees and giving teasing views of the pastoral scenery beyond the grounds. Golf carts and drivers were provided for those less able-bodied and I spotted Maeve and Gerald in the back of one as it passed by. Gerald waved when he saw me; Maeve was looking out at the view and enjoying the journey. She wasn't actually smiling but there was something about her today; an air of contentment and radiance.

As I reached the top of the slope so the land flattened out again. There were now three different paths I could take, one back around to the front of the house and Capability Brown's design, another to the dry garden, which I did want to inspect and the central one that led up to the koi pond. I wasn't sure where to go until I heard a sudden yelp and a splash ahead of me.

The koi pond formed a large, rectangular shape with a rock garden at one end which had a cascading waterfall snaking through it. The pond itself was full of water lilies not yet in flower but there was now a clear space over in one corner besides which a small crowd had gathered and two men were pulling a third out of the water. As I moved closer I realised it was Colin who was now dripping onto the concrete slabs that surrounded the pond. I heard him saying, "I don't know what happened. I must have lost my footing." Just beyond the group I spied Shauna. She caught my eye and smiled; the same innocent smile she had given me at breakfast. Perhaps Colin hadn't lost his footing after all.

I walked around on the opposite side of the pond from the commotion and made my way through a gate and into an area that was surrounded with mature trees. I followed the path alongside a modern day stone wall where rocks of differing size were packed tightly into wire cages. Personally I wasn't keen on this effect but if I wanted to design gardens I would have to be aware of other people's tastes.

I kept stopping along the way, taking notes and photographs of plants or designs that caught my eye and time passed quickly. I walked through a pretty water garden and then, as I rounded a corner, so I came to a bridge crossing a small stream. Karen and Lauren were on the other side. Karen smiled as I walked over to them; Lauren was sitting on a bench and too busy studying a shrub with greenish-yellow flowers on it to notice me. I sat down beside her.

"Euphorbia," I said.

She looked at me with a puzzled expression on her face, before saying, "No Derek; it's me, Lauren; from the coach."

"Yes I'm aware it's you."

"So why did you call me…oh, is this another baby name suggestion; like Vagina?"

"It was Fanny," I said, correcting her, "But I was referring to the shrub you're looking at."

"Oh right," Lauren turned back to the plant, "So this is called Fanny?"

"Euphorbia."

"Fanny Euphorbia? Actually that is a pretty name for a girl."

"Where have you left the boys?" I asked Karen, desperate to move the conversation on.

"They found a Frisbee and have stayed out at the front of the house where the park is," she replied, "It was a bit too warm out in the sunshine for Lauren so we came around here to the shade."

"Don't know why I feel odd today," Lauren said, "I suppose I didn't get to bed until late last night; that could be it."

"You went up before me and Angela," Karen told her.

"Yes I know," she replied, "But when I got upstairs I tidied the room and re-made the bed."

"Why?"

She shrugged her shoulders. "Just felt like it."

Karen shook her head. "But that bed in your room is vast," she said, "It must have been awkward."

Lauren giggled. "It was. I did find myself bouncing around on it grunting and moaning."

All three of us remembered my outburst at breakfast at the same time. Karen and Lauren both took a sudden interest in the mulch on the floor. I made my excuses and slipped away.

The path continued on and then veered off to the left which brought me back towards the koi pond. Before reaching that it turned again and I came out through the trees and into a rose garden. There were all manner of roses here of different colours and styles. A pergola walkway led through the middle and climbing roses had been trained either side of it to look like garlands hung up for a special occasion.

This was obviously a popular area of the grounds and a small refreshments kiosk had been set up with a number of tables and chairs dotted about in front of it. Margaret and Dora were sat at one and waved me over. I bought a coffee in a small paper cup and sat with them in the sunshine; chatting about what we'd seen so far.

"We did start off at the house," Margaret said, "But it's not really designed for wheelchair access."

"I hate this bloody thing," Dora said, hitting the arm of the chair.

I'd always imagined Dora liking the attention she got from being in the chair but realised that was a ridiculous notion to have. Why would she choose to spend her time in one, having to rely on someone else to help her get about?

"You won't need it for much longer," Margaret told her, "Once you've had the hip operation and a bit of physio."

"Huh, we're still talking months," Dora moaned.

"A bit more exercise and proper eating would help you not need it so much right now," Margaret said, "That's what the doctor told you."

"Doctors, what do they know," Dora replied, "Have you ever seen one warm his hands first before a breast examination?"

"He's right about the diet, though," Margaret said, "The way you eat; I don't know how you've made it to eighty-five."

"I eat the odd rice cake, that's healthy."

"Not when you make a chip sandwich out of two of them it's not."

I laughed and took another swig of the coffee. I don't know where Mrs Goddard bought hers from but I was just glad that no-one else in the county purchased from the same supplier. Margaret got up to fetch some extra napkins. As soon as she had gone Dora brought up Harry.

"I suppose you heard about him running off?" she said.

I nodded.

"Bloody con man. I knew he was a crook, you know," Dora continued.

"Did you? I thought you got on rather well with him."

"Well, you have to be sociable, don't you," she shook her head, "No, he was a definite wrong 'un. To be honest with you I'm quite glad he's left. You may not have noticed it Derek but I think my Margaret was rather keen on him."

"No," I said, in mock surprise.

"Oh yes. I'm razor sharp on things like that. She's led a sheltered life has Margaret. I'm sure if he'd stayed, Harry would have had money out of her."

"Do you really think so?"

"Oh yes. I mean, why else would someone like him look twice at my Margaret?"

That was a bit harsh.

"No, I'm glad he's gone, before things got out of hand."

I was going to respond but Margaret returned to the table. Instead I drained my coffee cup and made to leave but Dora tugged my sleeve.

"By the way Derek; don't let any embarrassment of this morning cause friction between you and Angela. You two go very well together, we both think that, don't we?"

Margaret nodded. I suddenly felt very choked seeing these two women smiling up at me. I smiled back and nodded, afraid that if I opened my mouth to say something I'd actually start crying.

I left the rose garden behind and crossed over an access road, just where a child was sobbing to his mother about a lost Frisbee and entered the allotments area. This was a small, fenced off space with a shed and various individual beds where different vegetables were being grown. On the far side by the exterior fence was a row of scarecrows and beyond that I could see open fields. In the central plot a member of staff was giving a talk and I wandered over and mingled with the rest of the listening group.

"And so this year we're experimenting with growing potatoes in different ways, which is why you can see plants being grown in bags around the site."

A hand shot up on the opposite side from where I was standing. I realised it was Josie. From the way the man rolled his eyes I didn't think it was her first question.

"So what advice have you got on growing tomatoes?" she asked.

"I can speak to you about that afterwards, madam; but we're talking potatoes just now."

"But tomatoes grow in bags," Josie reasoned.

"Yes," said the man, "Yes they do."

He turned back to the rest of the group to continue his talk.

"Are these Jerusalem Artichokes growing over here?" Josie hadn't finished with him yet.

"What? Oh, yes they are, but back to potatoes…"

"Give me terrible wind."

I wasn't sure Josie realised she'd said that out loud. A woman standing beside her took an interest.

"Do they really?" she said, "With me it's onions."

A man beside me joined the conversation.

"Is that just fried onions?" he asked, "Because that's my problem."

"It used to be," the woman said, "But it's getting now that it's any kind of cooked onion. I guess that's just one of the symptoms of getting older."

"I was like that with cauliflower," another lady chipped in, "Used to be just raw cauli but now cooked affects me exactly the same way. I don't care for myself but it's not pleasant for the residents of the retirement home where I work. Still, at least I can always blame the smell on one of them."

"With me it's Hummus," piped up someone else.

"That's very interesting…"

And so the potato talk was forgotten as everyone preferred to discuss their farting habits instead. The member of staff gave up and disappeared into the shed. Fortunately Josie only spotted me after the conversation had died down so I wasn't asked to contribute; although after the beer and takeaway last night I had been doing; silently.

"I left Sooz asking one of the curators a question back at the house," Josie explained.

I hoped it wasn't how vegetables affected his digestive system.

"Have you been in the house yet, Derek? It's very

interesting although some of the rooms are out of bounds so the tour didn't take too long."

"I haven't," I said, "I've been making my way around the grounds."

"Lovely aren't they? I definitely prefer them to the house. Angela looked to be enjoying the inside immensely but then she's into her history isn't she?"

She stopped talking and, probably remembering my morning speech, looked down at the floor. Was everyone from the group going to inspect the ground when they saw me today? Just at that point, Sooz joined us.

"Isn't this lovely," she said, "Did you come via the rose garden? Isn't it stunning?"

"Yes," Josie replied, "I was just telling Derek, I prefer it to the house."

"Me too," Sooz said, "I must say, the inside was a little disappointing. I don't like seeing cabinets full of stuffed animals; I think those regency chairs on show were replicas and as for the Victorian stool collection..." She shook her head.

Josie wrinkled her nose. "Ooh yes," she leaned in towards me, "If I were you, Derek, I'd give that a miss. I'd expected furniture but it was a collection of human stools."

"Right," I told her, "Thanks for the tip."

"It's not the sort of thing one expects in a stately home is it," she continued, "It was rather unpleasant and I'd just eaten an éclair at the cafeteria."

I couldn't think of a response to that.

"Oh look at those funny scarecrows over there," Sooz said, "Aren't they sweet?"

"They were part of a children's competition," Josie told her. Sooz walked over to them.

"They're adorable. Oh look at this one's grumpy face. That

one's got a carrot nose, just like a snowman."

She made her way along the row, making comments at each one. Finally she reached the end.

"Oh look at this. What a state, all wizened and grey-haired. And look at the scruffy clothes. Isn't it ugly?"

The scarecrow moved.

"Do you mind, madam," it said, "I'm the head gardener."

I rushed forward, just in time to catch Sooz as she fainted.

Chapter 15

I thought Josie's smacking of Sooz's face was a little rough but put it down to fright and panic at seeing her friend faint like that. Plus, it did have the desired effect of bringing her round pretty quickly.

"It was such a shock," Sooz said, gently touching her reddening cheek, "You don't expect scarecrows to start talking like that."

"You do realise it was a real person, don't you?" I had to ask.

"I know that now," she replied, "I feel so embarrassed; calling him ugly."

"To be honest you weren't wrong," I told her, "I've not seen nostrils that big since we went horse riding."

We helped Sooz up and the three of us walked back across to the rose garden where the kiosk and seating area were. I left the two of them there with a pot of tea and headed off to the café for lunch. I hoped Angela would be waiting for me. If she wasn't then I'd just have to wait around for her. I didn't care how long for.

The café was at the back of the house in a conservatory. To reach the seating area I first had to pass through the self-service section so I bought a sandwich and drink on the way. The conservatory was large and the columns that supported the ceiling had been painted white and were draped with green foliage. There were lots of plants in colourful pots spread around the space to make it feel like you were eating outdoors.

As I scanned the rather busy room, holding my tray, I couldn't see Angela anywhere. I saw Maeve and Gerald sharing a piece of fruitcake and Colin (now dry) wolfing down fish and chips but no sign of her. I sighed and walked over to where there was an empty table. As I did I noticed that the room had a large bay window to the side that was hidden from view until you were practically standing in it. Angela was sat there at a table drinking a glass of orange juice; looking ever more beautiful bathed in the sunlight that was gently radiating in through the open blinds. I approached and she looked up. She smiled warmly at me and I felt such a rush of relief.

"Is this seat taken?" I asked.

"It is actually," she replied, "I'm waiting for the Duke."

"Not that whoopsie?"

Angela laughed and I sat down.

"I'll just park myself while you wait for him then. Hangover gone?"

"I feel so much better," she said, "It must have been the snooze I just had."

"What, in the house?"

Angela winked at me. "Well there was this very comfortable-looking, old, four-poster bed up on the first floor that no one was using."

"How convenient."

"It was, except a lot of other people kept walking past and staring."

"Maybe you should have got under the covers once you'd taken your clothes off," I told her.

She smiled. "That might have been it. It also didn't help keep hearing the guide saying, 'This old thing has been here for over two hundred years.'"

"And had many Dukes in it."

Angela's smile wavered for a split second before reappearing.

255

"So, how has your morning been?" she asked.

"Before that can I please apologise for my outburst at breakfast," I said, "I've wanted to do that all day."

Angela waved her hand, dismissively. "You don't need to apologise," she told me, "To be honest I thought Colin was talking about us as well. I was ready to give him a fat lip when you stood up. It's quite funny really."

She started to laugh. I did too and then neither of us could stop. What the other diners thought I didn't care. When we did eventually compose ourselves I realised all my worries about us had evaporated.

"That felt good," I said, and began to eat my sandwich; talking between mouthfuls.

"I thought you were regretting everything this morning," I told her, "Especially when you sat up the back of the coach on your own."

"No that really was just for my hangover. I felt dreadful."

"And then suggesting we split up our tours as well."

"To be honest with you I didn't really enjoy the house as much as I thought I would," Angela confessed.

"Yeah I've heard all about the stool exhibit."

"Oh God, that was disgusting," she said, wincing at the memory of it, "No I meant I didn't enjoy it because I was on my own. The rooms we were able to go in were beautiful and the artwork and antiques absolutely stunning; but I realised I wanted to share the experience…with you."

I smiled, well actually it was more of a grin; the widest grin I could do. Angela smiled shyly back at me.

"And?" she asked, "How about you?"

"I had a great morning," I said, "Best day ever."

She waited for the 'but' line. I just sat there, still grinning and finishing off my sandwich.

"You're a bastard, Derek," she said, eventually.

I laughed. "Of course I wanted to share the morning with you," I told her, "I've wanted to share every waking moment with you since we met. I want us to share so much more."

"Oh Derek," Angela said, "This seems so crazy, I mean; we hardly know anything about each other and there's so much to say. I really should tell you about…"

"There's plenty of time for that," I interrupted, "This is the last day of the trip. Let's just go and enjoy the afternoon; together."

I held out my hand. Angela looked at it for a split second and then took it. We stood up and walked out of the café.

There were still a lot of the grounds to see. We took the path through the dry garden where there were lots of colourful, drought-loving plants set decoratively amongst rocks and gravel. This led us into another section, surrounded by a large Yew hedge which had also been trained to encroach into the area at certain intervals; thereby creating pockets around the entire space for planting. We spent some time here as I attempted to impress Angela with my plant knowledge. I decided we should move on when I caught her yawning.

We crossed over a bridge that spanned a dry ditch, which had been filled with lots of evergreen shrubs, and found ourselves in a wooded area. As we turned a corner we bumped into Josie and Sooz. Upon seeing them Angela and I instinctively gripped each other's hand tighter, both of us wanting to show that we were together now. When they saw us they smiled and Josie beckoned us over. Sooz placed a finger on her lips to ensure we remained quiet. I don't think they'd even noticed our hand holding and had obviously forgotten about my outburst at breakfast. They were standing next to what looked like a pile of old pallets and some other tat.

"We're just watching the birds," Sooz whispered, and pointed ahead of her.

Looking in that direction I saw a bird feeding station had been set up in an old oak tree. The branches were full of different sized feeders containing various nuts and seeds. There were more people standing the other side watching too.

"What's that next to you?" Angela asked Josie, indicating the pallet pile.

"It's a wildlife hotel," Josie whispered back, "It's mainly to entice insects to hibernate here over the winter. Isn't that a good idea? Look, there's even an area at the bottom for Hedgehogs. I think I'm going to set one up in my garden."

"What birds have you seen?" I asked Sooz. I wasn't that interested but I was in such a good mood I felt like indulging them.

"Oh there's been so many," she replied, "Chaffinches, Blackbirds, Sparrows."

"Look now," Josie said.

We all looked. I couldn't see anything from where I was standing as a branch was in my line of sight.

"What's there?" I asked.

"Can you see it, Derek?" Josie said, "Just look to the right of the peanut feeder. You should be able to spot a Great Tit?"

"Do you mean that man wearing socks with sandals?"

Angela sniggered.

"No, the bird on the...oh it's gone."

"As are we," Angela said, "Come on Derek."

We left the bird watchers behind and continued on up the path. After only a few yards it stopped at a small opening in the trees. We walked through and found ourselves out in open countryside. After the shade of the wood the fields seemed bathed in golden sunlight.

"Oh, isn't this marvellous." We hadn't heard Josie and Sooz follow us but they too had just emerged from the trees. As much as I liked them I really hoped they weren't about to tag along with Angela and myself. I wanted us to be alone.

We must have been up on a slope as we could see for miles across rolling hills stretching out to the horizon where the green of the land met the white of the cloud that was building up in the sky. The field we were in was only grass but it was about a foot high and rough paths had been cut through it. Beyond we could see distant tree lines and the roofs of farmhouses and barns spattered here and there; nestling into the landscape.

"Oh, bee hives," said Josie, looking to the right of where we were standing.

There were three hives inside a large, wire cage that had a gate in the side for the beekeeper to enter and exit. They were very pretty and painted a delicate duck egg blue. I stepped forward to get a better look but Angela didn't move.

"What's wrong?" I asked.

"I'm not too keen on bees and wasps. I was stung as a child and it bloody hurt."

"Bees are ok," I said, taking her hand again and gently walking her forward, "They don't want to hurt you. The trick is not to move or make a fuss when they buzz around you."

At that moment Sooz came running past waving her arms around and yelling, "Bee, bee."

"A visual example of what not to do," I said.

Josie joined us as we watched Sooz double-back on herself, trying to confuse her pursuer. As she did, there was a rustling in the grass beside where she was dancing about and a quick flash of brown darted away across one of the paths.

"Oh, a hare," Josie exclaimed, beaming, "I've not seen one of those in years."

We watched as it ran off to find a safer area to rest in. Even Sooz stopped jumping to look.

"I wonder what the term is for a group of hares," Josie said.

"What do you mean?" I asked.

"Well most animals have a collective noun to describe a group of them. There's a pride of lions, a parliament of owls and I believe it's a knot of toads. I wonder if there's a term for a group of hares."

"I think it might be a merkin," I told her.

Angela had to walk away.

"Really?" Josie asked, a look of contemplation on her face, "Do you know I think you're probably right. A merkin of hares. I've definitely heard the term somewhere before."

I placed my arms around Josie and kissed her on the cheek.

"Don't ever change," I said.

She obviously didn't know why I'd done that but she still smiled and said thank you before I walked away.

"Poor Josie," Angela smiled, as I came up to her.

"Yep," I replied, "For someone so innocent I'm amazed she ever got married and had children. She'll probably get back home and tell everyone she saw a merkin in a field. I wonder what they'll say to that."

"With all her talk of phalluses at the church picnic I suspect a pubic wig holds no surprises for the local congregation."

Angela and I walked through one of the paths cut into the grass and eventually came up to a small copse. There was a gap in the trees and a sign that said Woodland Walk. We decided to continue on as it looked like somewhere we could be on our own. It wasn't a trail that saw many visitors and the lower branches on some of the trees hadn't been clipped this year.

"How far do you think this goes?" Angela asked, pulling another branch aside to get past, "It's becoming a bit wild."

"It must come back out onto the field somewhere," I said, "I don't think it would be wise to turn back now. Let's press on and see where the journey takes us."

"It's a woodland walk, Derek; not a trek across the Antarctic."

I grinned at Angela. "You know, if you want to stop for a while, there's no one else around; we could always…"

I left the sentence hanging in mid-air. Angela stopped walking; a hint of a smile on her face.

"Derek; are you suggesting what I think you're suggesting?"

"Why not? We could try it sober and without the stench."

She laughed. "Knowing our luck, we'd be discovered."

"I don't care anymore," I said, "Let them see. Let them watch. Let them all come and watch."

"I'm pretty sure that's called Dogging."

"I thought you needed a car for that. Anyway, how about it? Might be fun to do it, al dente."

"Al Fresco."

"That's what I meant."

I could see Angela thinking it over in her mind.

"Oh go on then," she said.

"Really?"

"Yes, but let's be quick."

"I'm sure I can manage that."

We ran off the path and through the trees, giggling like naughty school children.

"This should be far enough in," I said.

We began kissing. Our passion was soon aroused and it wasn't long before we were tugging down our jeans and underwear. I really didn't care now if someone did come along the path. I was with Angela and I wanted everyone to know about it. When our lips broke apart for a brief second, she said,

"It's a bit rough."

"I'm sorry," I replied, "I'll try and control myself."

"Not you, the bark of this tree against my back."

"Oh, right. Hang on; let's see if we can find a smoother one."

It was difficult to move with a woman wrapped around my middle and my pants wrapped around my ankles but I managed to jump over to another tree.

"Better?"

"Worse."

I jumped across to another; a young tree with a much thinner, smoother trunk.

"That's better," Angela said.

We got going again. As I began to thrust harder so we pushed right up against the trunk. It was too much for the sapling which bent over and snapped. Angela and I both yelped as we fell into the undergrowth.

"Just keep going, Derek."

I had a mouthful of mulch but I did my best, spitting it out onto the ground rather than into Angela's face whilst also trying to maintain a steady rhythm. Angela squealed. She hadn't made that noise last night.

"Stinging nettle," she said.

I moved us a bit to the left.

"Ah, now don't move your head," I warned her, "There's some squirrel poo just beside your right ear."

"Oh God!"

"This outdoors sex isn't all it's cracked up to be, is it," I said, trying to manoeuvre us both away from the animal excrement.

"Flatterer," Angela smiled, "Can you keep it up, Derek?"

"Pardon?"

"The rhythm."

"I'll try," I told her.

We kept going. Really, it was just great to be together. I smiled at Angela, she grinned back and then her eyes widened.

"Oh God, Derek."

"Yeah baby."

"No, there's a squirrel in the branch right above us. He's sitting there, watching."

"Let him," I breathed.

We continued on although I could see Angela's eyes kept flicking over my shoulder every so often.

"Horny little beast," she said.

"Thanks babe."

"No, the squirrel. He's just jumped down to a lower branch. He's still looking."

"He's a squirrel. He's probably never seen it done face to face before."

"Well let's not run before we can walk, Derek."

I could feel the end approaching. I didn't bother trying to prolong it as we needed to get out of the shrubbery. Just at that moment the inquisitive squirrel decided to say hello and he jumped off the branch and onto my arse. I yelled and so did Angela although not due to the final throes of passion.

"Jesus Christ, don't let it go for my nuts," I called out.

I felt him run up my back. He climbed onto my head and sat there.

"Oh God," Angela shouted, "I'm being fucked by Davy Crockett."

We gave up after that. I couldn't concentrate on what I was doing with a squirrel clinging on to me that no amount of shaking would dislodge. Angela tried to help by waving the broken tree trunk at it but only managed to whack me up the side of the head instead. I crashed to the ground in pain but at least that finally did the trick and the squirrel ran off through the undergrowth and back up another tree.

I think we both felt a little dejected as we pulled up our jeans and dusted ourselves down. We made our way to the end of the woodland walk. Every time I looked behind me or up into the trees I saw that same sodding squirrel following us. Naturalists tell us that animals can't smile. Well I'm bloody sure that little grey bastard was grinning from ear to ear.

Angela was keen to see the rose garden so we headed back that way. We didn't see any other members of our group as we walked along, only other visitors to Tenham House and I liked the idea of them thinking of us as just another couple on a day out. Ok they were probably more interested in the plants but I still enjoyed the thought.

After walking around the rose garden there was time for a coffee before we were due back at the coach and so Angela headed off to the kiosk and I looked for a seat. The area was much busier than it had been that morning and there were at least two people at each of the tables. As I tried to find us a seat I heard my name being called. I turned round and saw Gerald had half stood up over at a table on the far edge and he was beckoning me over to him and Maeve. It was very nice of them but as I walked over I couldn't help thinking that I would rather have sat somewhere else. I'd not really spent much time with the two of them over the course of the week and I wondered what we would find to talk about.

"How's the 'no smoking' going?" Maeve asked me, as soon as I sat down.

"The what?"

I saw Gerald's face change to panic and remembered the conversation back at the Farmers' Market in Baddlesbury.

"Oh right," I said, "It's going really well, thanks. I can

honestly say; I've not smoked a single cigarette since I spoke to you in the market."

Maeve nodded approvingly. "Good," she said, "Good. It's just a case of willpower. There are a lot of people who could take a lesson out of your book, Derek. I've been smelling smoke all week."

Either Maeve's sense of smell was becoming more acute or Gerald needed to buy a new container of fabric freshener.

Angela had just been served and I saw her looking for me. I stood up and waved. Someone else waved back from a table just in front of the kiosk. It was Colin, who thought I'd been motioning to him. He got up from his table, almost knocking the coffees out of Angela's hands as she tried to pass him, and headed over to us. He sat down with his tea; totally oblivious to the fact I was waving at Angela, even when she arrived at the table with two coffees.

"I'll just go get another chair, shall I," she said, through gritted teeth as she put the drinks down.

"So glad you spotted me, Derek," Colin said, "That old couple over there were boring me rigid with stories about all their aches and pains and illnesses. I could feel one of my migraines coming on."

Angela brought another chair over and placed it between me and Maeve. As she sat down, Maeve squinted at her for a second and then reached up and pulled a twig out of her hair.

"Oh, how did that get there?" Angela said, her face reddening, "I said that woodland walk was a bit overgrown, didn't I Derek."

"Yes," I replied, "It was wild in places wasn't it."

We both exchanged a secret smile.

"I think today has been the nicest of all the trips," Gerald said, picking up a packet of sugar.

265

"You've got enough of that in your tea already," Maeve told him, "Put it back."

"I agree with you, Gerald," I said, "I think the grounds here are spectacular."

"You've enjoyed it too, haven't you dear?" Gerald asked his wife, placing the packet back in the little container, "I know you're a little tired now."

She did look really pale again but obviously I couldn't say anything about that. Maeve nodded.

"Yes," she said, "It is lovely here but I'll be glad to get back home again tomorrow; not that I'm looking forward to the coach journey."

"How about you, Colin," I asked, "What's been your favourite part. I heard you made a bit of a splash earlier."

He groaned. "Oh don't talk to me about that."

The others were all looking puzzled so I felt it was my duty to enlighten them. All three held their cups up to their mouths to hide the smiles, even Maeve.

"I hate to think of all the germs that live in that pond," Colin said, "I still don't know what happened."

I had a shrewd idea.

"I must have slipped or something. I've taken some pictures of the area and if I spot a raised paving stone then there'll be hell to pay. Someone at the charity that runs this place will be receiving a mouthful from me."

He shivered. "Ooh, it was awful. Fish carry so many different bacteria. And as for all of that green stuff…"

"Duckweed?"

"Oh, don't mention ducks to me either," Colin winced.

I'd forgotten about that one, the duck crapping all over him on the boat trip. What with that and the fall into the horse manure at the farm I guess it was difficult for Colin to pick out a highlight of the week.

It was soon time to return to the coach. Surprisingly, I did feel a pang that this was the end of the last excursion; but I guess that had more to do with my feelings for Angela than the actual holiday being over. After all, once home and with Angela at work and me at college, we wouldn't be able to spend all day every day with each other. We all walked back to the car park together; Angela and I holding hands again. We were at the back of the group, purposely walking slowly to make the moment last longer. Shauna was waiting by the coach steps as usual. She watched us walk over but didn't say anything. I really thought she'd have a comment ready. As we passed her she called out, "You've got grass stains on your arse." Both Angela and I automatically reached out to check. We were both clean. I turned back and saw Shauna's satisfied smile.

The first two seats on the coach were empty.

"Where are Lauren and Pete?" I asked.

"The hospital," Karen said, "Lauren went into labour."

"But it's not her time."

"I know. I hope everything is ok, we haven't heard yet." Karen looked worried.

"I'm sure everything will be fine," I told her, soothingly, and continued walking down to my seat.

"That's a bit worrying," I whispered to Angela, once we'd sat down, "I hope the baby's going to be ok."

"And Lauren," Angela said.

"They can do a lot for premature babies now though, can't they? She may already have had it."

"Little Fanny?" Angela winked.

I smiled. "I hope not if it's a natural birth."

We pulled away and Shauna switched on the microphone.

"Just a heads up; for those of you who may not have heard,

Lauren and Pete are at the hospital. Once we have any news about the baby, we'll let you know. The human gremlin up here did kindly offer to drive them to the hospital but I felt the baby would probably be at university before he found it so we called an ambulance instead. Also, as it's our last night at the hotel Mrs Goddard has arranged a special evening. We scarily don't have any details but what I do know is that dinner will be a buffet style meal, so at least you can select which slops you want to eat rather than having them thrust into your face by an undersexed, Italian wanker."

"Do you think she meant to say waiter?" I asked.

"Probably not," Angela replied.

"What do you think this special evening is going to be?"

"Something you shouldn't get your hopes up about."

The rest of the drive proved uneventful. I think Jim had finally got the hang of the coach driving but, like Maeve; I certainly wasn't looking forward to the long journey home tomorrow. I also wasn't looking forward to saying goodbye to Angela. I knew it wasn't going to be forever, but how often were we going to be able to get together? I didn't even know how far away she lived from me. We'd not even swapped phone numbers yet. She said she travelled a lot with work. How much time did she spend out of the country? Those were questions for tomorrow. Tonight, regardless of whatever crap Mrs Goddard had planned; I was going to enjoy myself.

When we got back to the hotel we found it altered. Dusty old banners and balloons had been put up in preparation for a celebration. Mrs Goddard stood in the hallway beaming at us all. She'd had her hair done again and the two-piece, charcoal-grey suit looked new and expensive. Obviously she had been spending Margaret's money but it certainly wasn't on the decorations. Still, she looked so pleased no one had the heart to tell her the whole place looked tired and shabby so we all murmured our approval.

"Oh, it's nothing really," she said, "We do it all the time. Now, if I could have your attention for a few minutes. There will be a party for you in the dining room this evening."

A party sounded good, even if there weren't many of us.

"It's a fancy dress party."

Oh shit. There was a collective groan.

"I knew you'd all be excited," Mrs Goddard continued, "Now then, you each have a choice of two costumes. They've been laid out in your rooms for you. We like to do something different for our guests at this hotel to make sure you never forget us."

There was no danger of that happening.

"The party starts at seven o'clock, sharp. I look forward to seeing you all there."

She disappeared before anyone could say anything. We all trudged dejectedly upstairs.

"I don't suppose you want to go out tonight?" I said, to Angela, "We could get a cab to...well anywhere."

She laughed. "One more night, Derek. You won't be able to escape. Mrs Goddard has probably locked the door behind us now anyway. Besides, I want to be around to hear any news on Lauren."

She squeezed my hand. "I'm sure it will be a funny evening," she said.

I had no doubt about that.

269

Chapter 16

My fancy dress choices were laid out side by side on the bed. After the week I'd spent in this hotel I was expecting musty, old outfits styled very much on the Victorian era. I put the rabbit costume to one side and stared at the other one. With all of the reflective rhinestones it appeared to be staring back at me. I guess Elvis was in the building this evening. The suit was pretty snug. I put on the wig and oversized, gold-rimmed sunglasses and looked at myself in the mirror. The look was definitely, 'Elvis – The junk food years.' I tried a pose and swore never to do it again when I saw the result. I had a crack at curling my lip and couldn't do that either; but was it Elvis who curled his lip; I couldn't remember.

I sighed. I looked ridiculous; a middle-aged man, carrying a few extra pounds; trying to squeeze into a sparkly, fitted costume and failing. Why hadn't Mrs Goddard provided a girdle or something to go with it? Still, it was definitely preferable to dressing up like an extra from Watership Down. If I wore the rabbit suit Jim would probably try and cut my foot off to keep as a lucky charm and Josie would spend all evening telling everyone I was part of a merkin.

I very reluctantly made my way downstairs. Mrs Goddard was standing by the doorway into the dining room, greeting her guests. As I approached the door she clicked the heels of her red shoes together and it was only then I realised she was meant to be Dorothy from the Wizard of Oz; a Dorothy who really hadn't aged well under the Kansas skies. Unfortunately she couldn't manage the full three clicks so her greeting more resembled an enemy soldier in a nineteen forties war movie. I didn't know whether to shake hands, salute or take her hostage.

I walked into the dining room. Angela was already there, wearing a white dress and blonde wig. She tried to stifle a laugh when she saw me but only succeeded in letting out a loud raspberry sound instead.

"Elvis the rheumatic pelvis," she said.

"Thanks."

"Are you going to strike a pose?"

"No."

"So," she asked, indicating her outfit, "What do you think?"

"Uncanny," I told her, "Chico's serving the drinks, where's Groucho?"

"You cheeky bastard," she said, "I'm Marilyn Monroe, not Harpo Marx!"

I grinned. Chico **was** actually serving the drinks but following the Wizard of Oz theme he was dressed as the Tin Man. Glum Barman made a very miserable-looking Scarecrow and I did worry that Sooz might have another fainting fit when she saw him. I don't think Valerie was working this evening, which was a shame really as she'd have been great dressed as the wicked witch, flying around the room on her motorised scooter; although maybe not if it was still stuck in reverse.

"Is that the dress that gets blown up over the air vent?" I asked Angela.

"I reckon so," she replied, "There was a mini fan and some masking tape with the costume, but I didn't put that on."

"Too shy?"

"No, I just didn't want to walk around with a whirring appliance under my dress all evening."

"I see your point," I said, "Or rather I can't see it."

"Drink!" Glum barman had come over to us with a couple of glasses on a tray. They were half-filled with an orange liquid which I assumed was The Grand's attempt at a cocktail.

"Thanks scarecrow," I said, taking one, "When I go home, I think I'm going to miss you most of all."

"God, I hate this fucking costume," he confided, "I wanted to dress up as one of the Go Go Dancers but Mrs Goddard wouldn't let me."

"There aren't any Go Go Dancers in the Wizard of Oz," Angela told him.

"You watch your version, dear," he said, "And I'll watch mine."

He headed off to the bar to refill his tray.

The only other members of the group in the dining room so far were Colin, Margaret and Dora. Colin was wearing the costume of an annoying hypochondriac; in other words, he hadn't bothered; while Margaret was dressed as a very embarrassed-looking cowgirl and Dora as Queen Victoria. She was sat, regally by the buffet table; Chico at her side holding a tray of rapidly disappearing glasses of orange cocktail. I felt a tap on my shoulder and turned to see Josie and Sooz. They were wearing matching outfits of body warmers, green wellingtons and floral headscarves.

"The Queen at Sandringham," they chorused, and walked off to talk to Margaret.

"I'm not the only one thinking they're wearing their own clothes am I?" Angela asked.

I shook my head.

"Actually there are quite a lot of old queens in here now aren't there?" I said, just as glum barman passed by us with a tray full of drinks, "Oh sorry; I didn't mean you."

He shot me a very disgruntled look and carried on walking.

"Nice outfit, Dirk," I heard a voice say behind me, "Are you going to curl the lip?"

"No," I sighed, turning round again, "Wow, Shauna. You look amazing."

"Yeah; I know," she agreed, running her hands admiringly down the sides of the tight fitting Wonder Woman outfit.

"That's a great-looking costume," Angela said, "Where did Mrs Goddard find that?"

"It's my own," Shauna replied, adjusting the gold tiara, "I wouldn't wear the shit they've supplied here. Who knows the last time they were cleaned."

I suddenly felt very dirty.

"You carry around your own Wonder Woman costume," I questioned, surreptitiously scratching myself.

"Of course," Shauna replied, like I'd just uttered the stupidest sentence in the whole world, "It doesn't take up much room in the luggage and, well; it's come in handy hasn't it? Oh shit."

Shauna had just spied Chico and he her. His silver-painted face lit up as he strode across the room towards us. Glum barman was in his path and got roughly elbowed out of the way. We watched as the poor guy lost his balance and did a spectacular twist on the spot. He stumbled sideways and fell onto a seat beside Dora. None of the drinks on his tray were spilled and the whole room broke into spontaneous applause. Dora, already under the influence of a vast number of cocktails was laughing away at him. As he stood up she gave him a hearty smack on the back that sent him flying through the swing doors into the kitchen. A split second later we heard the sound of glasses smashing. Colin rushed in to check he was ok.

Chico had sidled up to Shauna. He was panting and trying to study every inch of her.

"I have some lovely drinks for you on this tray," he puffed, "How about a large, stiff one?"

Shauna sighed. "Look here tin nob; the only thing large and stiff I want now is a baseball bat; which I'd use to knock your bollocks up into your throat."

"I love a gutsy woman," Chico breathed, "You're a naughty girl and I want to spank you."

"You even try and your teeth will be back in Italy before you are."

She grabbed a drink from the tray and stomped off. Chico remained rooted to the spot, watching her go.

"Could you move?" I asked him, "You're drooling on my foot."

I don't think he heard me but he moved off anyway. I turned back to Angela. I was hoping we could discuss our future. Tomorrow on the journey home would probably be a better time than at a party but I just couldn't wait that long. Before I could speak there was another tap on my shoulder. I really needed to move away from the dining room entrance. A hand appeared in my line of vision. It was black and furry. I jumped and span round. A large, shaggy, black and white dog waved at me.

"Who the hell's that?" I spat.

"It's me," said a muffled voice, which really didn't help answer my question.

Karen appeared beside the dog, spilling out of a Bo Peep costume. She had a crook in one hand and was holding a cuddly toy sheep under her other arm.

"Leroy," I said, "Was this really the best outfit?"

"There were two black suits with bowler hats," Karen told us, "But city gents' costumes seemed a little boring."

"They were probably meant to be Laurel and Hardy."

"Who are they?"

Seriously?

"They were a comedy duo," I explained, "Made films in the

nineteen twenties and thirties."

Karen looked at me, blankly.

"They wore suits and bowler hats. One was thin and the other fa...funny. Doesn't matter; any news from the hospital?"

"Nothing yet," Karen said, "We've tried calling Pete's mobile but there's no answer."

"No news is good news," Angela told her, "I'm sure everything will be fine. Try and enjoy the evening."

"We will," the shaggy dog said. He nudged me in the ribs with his elbow, "I'm planning a lot of panting on all fours later; if you know what I mean."

I shouted into the mouthpiece of the costume, "Yes, I know what you mean."

"Doggy style," he called out, while giving us a Chico hip thrust. Karen grabbed his paw and the two of them walked off to get a drink, although how Leroy was going to manage refreshments in that outfit I didn't know. Finally I could talk to Angela.

"So," I said, "After tomorrow, when can I next see you again?"

"Oh Jesus."

That wasn't the response I'd been expecting but I noticed Angela was focussing on something behind me. I turned round once more. Maeve and Gerald had entered the room dressed as Robin Hood and Maid Marian. Maeve still looked pale and really unhappy, but maybe that was because she'd wanted to come as Marian.

"Hello Derek, Angela," Gerald was beaming, "What do you think, isn't it a scream?"

"That's certainly what I want to do right now," I said.

He still had his glasses on which didn't help improve the overall appearance.

"Well, my legs were too long for the green tights," Gerald explained, "And the other choice was caveman and cavewoman but Maeve is allergic to fur."

I think I'd have still gone with that myself.

"I thought this would cheer everyone up."

"You go girl," I told him.

Gerald took Maeve off to find her a seat. I'd completely lost my train of thought now and so instead of talking; Angela and I joined in with the party.

Mrs Goddard had outdone herself on the buffet. It seemed like all the leftover food from the past week (and let's face it, there was a lot of that) had been used to make up the spread on the table. Those meatballs surely couldn't still be fresh. I even spotted some of the sweet and sour prawns from the takeaway that I'd left in Angela's room last night. Not a lot was eaten but the cocktails went down a storm as most of us were drinking them like shots.

Half an hour later and the evening started to feel like a proper party. As I stood with my back to the swing doors into the kitchen I surveyed the lively scene in front of me. Bo Peep and the shaggy dog were dancing together and laughing at the moves made by Dracula Jim. Three queens were sitting in the corner, chatting away happily to Robin and Marian. Wonder Woman, cowgirl and Marilyn Monroe were stood together by the dessert table, knocking back orange cocktails. I smiled. It hadn't turned out to be such a bad week really, had it?

Of course it had. We'd been driven to a crummy hotel in the middle of nowhere by a partially-sighted driver and a courier who really couldn't give a shit. This had been nothing like the holiday advertised in the brochure. Still, I guess the trip had proved to be the distraction from my own problems that I'd wanted it to be, just not in the way I'd expected. Instead of losing myself in pampered luxury at the spa hotel I'd spent the week getting in and out of scrapes and hearing about the lives of my fellow travellers. So many of the group had gone through or were dealing with their own issues and I'd come to realise that I'd underestimated them at the beginning of the holiday. I really wasn't so different from them.

I wondered how everyone else was feeling about the week. Looking around the room now it seemed like a good time had been enjoyed by all; well, maybe not Colin…Colin, where was he? He'd disappeared into the kitchen an hour ago and I hadn't seen him since. I opened the swing door a crack and heard groaning. Perhaps glum barman had really hurt himself on the smashed glass. The rest of us hadn't even thought to check. He could be bleeding to death for all we knew.

I opened the swing door fully and entered the kitchen. It was pretty dirty in there and my stomach did a somersault as I thought about everything that I'd eaten this past week having been prepared in this shit hole. I could see the smashed glass had been neatly swept up into a dustpan that was laying on the countertop, beside the drinks tray. There was no sign of any blood but also no sign of Colin or glum barman. Where on earth had they disappeared to? Was the barman in pain? I could still hear moaning.

As I stepped forward so I heard Colin's voice call out, "Take it all." Perhaps he'd made some hot sweet tea for shock. He sounded pretty insistent that the drink should be finished. I walked towards the sound of his voice. Maybe I could be of some assistance. As I reached the end of the counter I stopped dead. Colin was standing the other side of the aisle, leaning back against a fridge-freezer. His trousers were around his ankles and a scarecrow was kneeling down in front of him, seemingly doing an impression of a woodpecker. There was

277

straw everywhere but I don't think Colin was too concerned about hay fever at that moment. I guess he'd decided it was time to give the barman a mouthful. This was certainly a situation where I couldn't be of any help and I quietly backed out of the room.

The drinks continued to flow, the buffet continued to decay and the night continued to progress. Angela and I joined Karen and Leroy on the dance floor but I could tell Jim's jumping around her was getting on Angela's nerves. I found him rather funny. Eventually we stepped aside to grab another drink.

"You were right about tonight," I said, talking loudly to be heard over the music.

Angela looked questioningly at me.

"You said it would be a funny evening."

"What can I say, my predictions are never wrong," she told me.

"What do you predict for us for the future?" I asked.

Angela just smiled and winked.

I turned back to look at the dance floor. Jim appeared to be attempting a Paso doble; swirling the Dracula cape around his head. It got stuck and took him a while to untangle. When he eventually got himself free he had such a funny grin on his face that I couldn't help laughing.

"I think he's high on brake fluid again," I said, but Angela didn't laugh.

Ok, so it wasn't my best line but I thought it would at least raise a smile. Maybe she'd just had enough to drink, or had enough of the loud music. Just so long as she hadn't had enough of me. Jim was still dancing but he kept looking over in our direction and grinning. Eventually he bounced over to us.

"Can I bite your neck?" he asked Angela.

I laughed, but she said, "Get lost, Jim."

"Oh go on," he urged, "How much do you normally charge for that?"

It took a moment for that sentence to sink in. The smile left my face.

"What was that?" I asked, "What do you mean?"

"Nothing," Angela interrupted, "He's clearly drunk."

"Come on, Derek," Jim said, draping an arm around my shoulder, "We're both men of the world. There's nothing wrong with paying for a little action now and then, is there."

I was confused but several images from the past week flashed through my brain; Jim's flirting with Angela at breakfast on the second morning, his winking across the table before the wine tasting excursion, Max at the harbour town and his final comment of, 'Enjoy her Derek,' and then Jim again, emerging from Angela's room and apologising. Hadn't she said she'd been in the shower? Why had her hair been dry? I couldn't form any words. I stared at Angela. She was gazing back at me, looking scared and biting her lower lip.

"Angela?"

She turned and bolted. I ran after her, calling her name. I chased her through the hallway and out the front door onto the gravelled drive. I called her again and she stopped beside the coach. As I walked over to her so a streak of lightning lit up the sky, followed closely by a loud clap of thunder.

"What did he mean?" I said; when I reached her.

Angela was still facing away from me. I saw her take a deep breath before she turned round. Tears had already smudged her mascara. It wasn't a cold evening but she shivered in her thin Marilyn dress. I wanted to hold her; to warm her, but I couldn't move.

"What did he mean?" I repeated. I was beginning to suspect the answer, "What are you?"

That bit came out wrong. Angela shot me a look but then her face fell.

"Oh Derek, I've wanted to tell you so often this week; I've tried so many times but…no, not this way; not now."

She walked past me back towards the house. Shauna's words flew into my brain again. 'Your lives, your secrets; they'll all be revealed eventually.' This wasn't meant to include Angela. I felt a rush of anger.

"Oh I think now is the perfect time to tell me," I called out. Angela stopped walking.

"I'll help start. Did Jim pay you money for sex? It's a simple yes or no answer."

She turned and faced me. It began to rain. Angela nodded slightly and then looked at the floor.

"Yes," she whispered, and sniffed, "He knew…what I did, through a friend of his. He recognised my name."

"You're a prostitute."

"In a manner of speaking."

"What, in the manner of having cheap sex for money?"

Angela looked up again. There was hardness in her eyes that I hadn't seen before.

"I don't hang around on street corners," she said, "I travel the world where wealthy clients pay good money for my services."

"You're a prostitute."

The rain was coming down harder. It seemed really dark too; until I realised I still had the Elvis sunglasses on. At least they hid my tears.

"And Max?" I asked, "Is he one of your clients?"

"He used to be. He was from my early years before I set up my exclusive list."

"And there was I worrying that you'd been in an abusive

relationship and wanting to hold you and take care of you."

"Max had some special interests, he liked it when I…"

"For fuck's sake Angela, I don't want details!"

"I'm sorry."

I was having trouble controlling my temper. Why the hell was this happening now; just when everything seemed to be going right? I'd started feeling happy again and was looking forward to the future; a future that I thought was going to include Angela.

"A wealthy client list," I said, "So where does Jim fit into this? He's not wealthy."

"No of course he isn't," Angela snapped, "But he was going to tell you what I did unless I gave him a discount and let him...he wouldn't leave me alone; always winking and smiling knowingly at me. I didn't know what to do and I panicked."

"Oh boo hoo. The man's a blind, old fart. Who would have believed him?"

"You did just now, didn't you?" Angela said, "I couldn't risk him doing that when we were becoming so close. I needed to tell you when the time was right; and now certainly isn't that time."

"It's too late," I told her, "I want…need to know it all; now. I mean, do you even realise how that makes me feel; us having sex after you'd slept with Jim?"

"I didn't sleep with him," Angela said, "The stupid, little tosser couldn't get it up."

"I'm sure you have ways of helping with that," I spat.

Angela opened her mouth to retort but her whole face crumpled. She put her head in her hands and cried. I still couldn't go to her. I just stood there, watching the woman I'd fallen in love with sob her heart out.

Another clap of thunder made us both jump. Angela reached

inside the top of her dress and pulled out a tissue. It was already sodden from the rain but she still used it to wipe her eyes.

"I thought you were a museum curator or antiques expert," I said, quietly.

"I never told you that, Derek. I haven't lied to you."

The anger rose again.

"Well, you've been a bit bloody economical with the truth," I erupted, "You've talked about travelling the world and loving antiques and doing a history degree, what was I supposed to think."

"It's all true, Derek. You came up with my job spec, not me. I needed to earn money to help finance my studies. I worked bloody hard to get my degree. We don't all have wealthy parents who help us through the first two years, you know. Life hasn't exactly been kind to me."

"Well join the club, sweetheart," I spat, "Life's a pain in the arse for everyone. I've learnt that this week. I've just lost my wife, home and job and am slowly trying to pick up the pieces but I'll tell you; after some of the things the rest of the group have told me this week, my life is still a walk in the park compared to theirs."

I should have walked away then but the anger kept me rooted to the spot.

"And by the way," I added, "In reference to your 'wealthy parents' comment, you should know my father died in my second year at university, leaving behind a heartbroken wife and debts."

"Well how was I meant to know that?"

"You weren't," I continued, "All I'm saying is, I also worked hard for my degree; but never on my back."

Angela gasped, but I hadn't finished yet.

"So you paid for your degree by prostitution. I can almost accept that, but why continue with it after you'd graduated? What a fucking waste of the education you supposedly fought so hard for. Was the money too easy, or was that just you?"

"How dare you," Angela exploded.

"You'd got your degree, why not use it? But no, you went after the fast, easy money instead."

Her eyes narrowed. "You think it was an easy decision to make do you, Derek; to sell my body to seedy men? Do you not think I regularly questioned what I was doing? I've worked damned hard to get where I am today; to be able to keep just a few select clients; gentlemen who appreciate the company of an intelligent woman and not just some random guy who wants a whore to fuck! I've struggled and fought all my life. You know nothing about me."

"That's becoming more obvious by the second."

Angela let out a loud sigh.

"This is exactly why I didn't tell you earlier. I should have known you'd react this way, just like all other men. I thought you were different, Derek. I thought your surname really suited you. I felt such a connection between us right from the start."

"So you gave me a freebie last night did you?"

Angela gasped again.

"Hang on," I said, reaching for my wallet, which I obviously didn't have in a rhinestone jumpsuit, "Let me pay you the going rate."

"Don't Derek."

"No, no; I insist. Let's make it all fair and square. How much do I owe you?"

"Alright, eight hundred pounds!"

"What?"

"An all-nighter with sex included and no extras, not

including travel costs and other expenses; that's eight hundred pounds. I told you, Derek; I'm not cheap. You know, I'm not ashamed of what I've done to get where I am today. Yes, my life isn't conventional, yes it's not what I'd planned when I was growing up, but it's left me with no debts, a home that I own and plenty of time to spend on my hobbies. The only thing it's ever stopped me doing is settling down with the right man and having a family."

Angela's tears were flowing again.

"I told you once Derek that I wasn't too bothered about the husband and kids thing but that was a lie. I never had the normal, proper family life growing up. I knew that the lifestyle of my profession would mean I couldn't have children and I dealt with that, but now I've turned forty I'm scared about the future. I'm leaving my…job, because I've had enough and besides, who wants to pay top money for me at my age when they can have a young, pretty twenty year old instead. I've spent the last fifteen years travelling the world, seeing some wonderful places, but I've always been alone or felt alone even when I've travelled with a client. I want to start over again now and I've realised my future needs to be shared with someone; and then I go and meet this amazing man on a coach trip who I thought was really special."

"And how has deceiving him helped?" I said, "You may not have lied, Angela, but you've certainly been economical with the truth. I've told you about my wife, my divorce, my redundancy. I've spoken about my fresh start but you've told me nothing about yourself. You've just left me guessing."

"But how could I drop my past into the conversation?" Angela asked, "I saw the look on your face at Ryan Harbour when you spoke to Margaret about paying for sex with Harry."

"This isn't about your past," I said, "Well it is to a degree, but the real problem is the deceit of now; sleeping with me **before** I knew about the past. I don't know; maybe if we hadn't moved things on so fast…"

I left the sentence hanging.

"But Derek I…"

Angela stopped speaking as a taxi came into the driveway. It pulled up and Pete flew out of it and into the hotel. We looked at each other, our fight forgotten. The baby.

We both ran back to the house. Just as Angela reached the steps in front of me a freak gust of wind blew her dress up and I cursed myself for getting turned on. We ran into the dining room, just in time to see Pete punch the shaggy dog. Leroy went down and the head fell off. Bo Peep screamed and all eyes turned in that direction. Even the music seemed to stop.

"You bastard," Pete shouted, as he jumped on top of Leroy and started punching him again, "You fucking bastard."

Karen was screaming, "Get him off; get him off."

We all came to our senses. Chico and I rushed forward and pulled a struggling Pete off of Leroy. He was still shouting and kicking out.

"Pete, Pete!" I said, wrenching his head around to make him look at me, "Calm down."

He stopped struggling.

"Now, tell me what's happened."

"The baby," he said, bursting into tears, "The baby. Not premature at all. Eight pounds two and fucking black."

I let go of him, shocked. Were these secrets and revelations ever going to end? There was another loud shriek and Leroy shouted out again in pain, only this time Bo Peep was on top of him, slapping any part she could get to.

"You lying, cheating bastard," she yelled, each word coming with a smack.

"Karen, stop it doll," Leroy pleaded.

"I knew it," she said, the fight going out of her, "I just knew something like this would happen."

She began to cry.

"Babe."

Leroy put his hand up and stroked her hair. Karen reeled back and began slapping him again.

"Bastard!" she yelled, "Don't ever touch me again."

"That's enough!" screeched Mrs Goddard, above the din.

Startled, we all turned around to where she was standing in the doorway out to the hall. She pulled her wig off and ruffled her own hair, giving her the look of a crazy, wild woman.

"That's enough," she repeated, "I've had it with you people; I can't take anymore. What have you done to me? I used to run a lovely, little hotel, but you lot," she gestured round to all of us, "You fight over board games, you get pissed every night; my staff are dying around me."

To be fair, I didn't think we could be blamed for Louella's death but Mrs Goddard wasn't in a reasoning mood right now.

"I've tried my hardest to remain upbeat and positive. My floor fell through, my window broke and a con man cheated me. I can't take it anymore."

"Mrs Goddard," Shauna said, walking over to her, "You're becoming hysterical, try and calm down."

"I don't want to calm down," she replied, "I want you to leave. I want you all to go; right now. I can't take anymore."

"Leave this to me," said Jim, pushing up his sleeves and striding over to her as well, "I know what to do. I've seen it in the movies."

"You all need to go and pack your bags," Mrs Goddard continued, "You people, you damned, awful people."

Jim pulled his hand back to smack Mrs Goddard across the

face. He seemed to pull it back an awfully long way. I didn't think this was going to stop her being hysterical, more knock her out cold. Shauna stepped forward to prevent him but the timing was out and she got the full force of Jim's smack. Her head snapped back, sending the wonder woman tiara spinning across the room. To be honest, it did silence Mrs Goddard but Shauna wasn't best pleased. She looked at Jim while she gently felt her cheek. I heard him whimper.

"Oh boy," she said, her eyes narrowing, "Have you had this coming."

It was one of those moments you see in slow motion. As Shauna punched Jim full in the face we all watched him leave the floor and fly backwards. His glasses split in two while he was in mid-air and he crashed down right on top of the dessert table. A shame really as the trifle had looked the only decent thing worth trying.

As the table collapsed the world came back into regular focus again and I realised Karen was still hitting Leroy. I pulled her back off of him, just as a cry of, "No" went up behind us.

"Jesus Christ, what now," I called out, realising I'd pulled Karen up by the tits and was still holding both of them in my hands.

I quickly let her go before turning round. Gerald was on the ground, cradling Maeve in his arms. She was wincing in obvious pain.

"Is it her heart; it must be her heart," Gerald said, hiccupping with emotion, "Not now my love. It's not meant to be now."

"Someone phone for an ambulance," Shauna called.

Mrs Goddard sprang into action but I feared it was already too late. We all crowded round Maeve and Gerald. She looked so pale and weak; the strength she'd used to get through each painful day having finally deserted her.

"I'm not ready to let you leave me," Gerald whispered, gently stroking her cheek.

It wasn't really a dignified way to go, lying on the floor dressed in green tights; being cradled in the arms of a Maid Marion drag queen whilst Elvis Presley, Marilyn Monroe and Wonder Woman looked on and yet I think Maeve sensed the situation through her discomfort. She looked round at each of us in turn and then rested her eyes on Gerald. She smiled; the most beautiful smile I've ever seen. She giggled, closed her eyes and died.

Chapter 17

It was a ghastly way for the holiday to end. Not that the evening was over for us, especially Shauna. She showed herself to be a true professional at her job. She took complete control of the situation, calming everyone down, arranging separate rooms for Leroy and Karen and sorting a doctor and all the necessary paperwork for Maeve. She found out all the relevant information required for getting the body taken back to Gerald's home town and then also arranged further accommodation for those members of the group who needed to stay on after tomorrow to sort out their problems.

Angela and I didn't speak again that night. We both tried to help Shauna as best we could but made sure our assistance meant we didn't have to come into contact with one another. The following morning most of us gravitated to the dining room as we had done each day that week. Nobody wanted to eat, which was just as well as nothing was prepared. Some tables had been pulled back to their usual position but mostly the room was still as it had been the night before. The detritus lay all around; empty glasses, ripped banners and the mess where Jim had fallen into the desserts. He had two beautiful, black eyes this morning and after the way he had treated Angela, I wasn't sorry about that. As I walked into the room Josie and Sooz were just leaving.

"Got a bit of last minute packing to do," Sooz told me, although I felt they were really just trying to escape the oppressive atmosphere that lingered throughout the ground floor.

Jim was sitting on his own in one corner with his broken

glasses and a packet of plasters. Margaret and Dora were sat on the opposite side of the room from him; Dora looking much the worse for wear after the number of orange cocktails she'd downed last night. We never did find out what was in them. Josie & Sooz's table was one of those that had been placed back in its usual position. I was surprised to see Gerald sitting there.

"He was there when we came in," Josie said, seeing where I was looking, "The poor man's a wreck."

"Hardly said a word," added Sooz.

My mind returned to the conversation with Gerald at the top of the church tower in Baddlesbury. He'd told us Maeve had been preparing him for when she was no longer here. I hoped all her hard work hadn't been in vain.

"He just looks, well; lost," said Josie, "He did manage to tell us that he's staying on until Maeve's body is driven back to their home. He says he wants them to make that final journey together."

"I think he just needs time on his own for now," Sooz added.

If anyone knew what he was going through at this moment it was Sooz, but I couldn't just ignore him. After the two ladies left I walked over. As I reached his side I realised I didn't know what to say. All I had was a head full of clichés. Gerald didn't look up but I sensed he knew I was there. I placed my hand on his shoulder and gently squeezed it. Without looking at me, Gerald raised his hand up and patted mine. We'd both said all we needed to.

I pulled a table over to where I usually sat and waited for Angela. I felt sick with nerves thinking about what had been said and what was still left to say. The whole room was silent, until Colin came bouncing in, whistling.

"Good morning," he called. No one answered.

"You're very chipper," I said to him, as he walked past the

table, "Looking forward to getting back home and giving the travel company a piece of your mind, I suppose."

"Why would I want to do that, Derek," he asked, "I love this place. In fact, I'm going to stay on here for a while."

At that moment glum…actually not so glum, barman came out of the kitchen, dressed in his every day clothes.

"There you are, Rupert," called Colin, "Ready to go?"

"Ready dear," he replied.

"Is that what you're wearing?"

"Don't start with me. What's wrong with it?"

"A little too bright, perhaps," Colin said.

"Better to be colourful than boring, dear," glum barman replied.

Colin sighed. "I suppose you'll be able to blend in," he said, and turning to me added, "We're off to the flower show."

"Aren't you worried about your sinuses?" I asked.

"Oh Derek, you are funny," he told me, "Have a good trip home."

He and Rupert left the dining room as Angela walked in. She stopped when she saw me but gave a hint of a smile. I smiled back.

"Is this seat taken?" she asked, after walking over.

"It is actually," I said, "I'm waiting for the Duke."

"Not that whoopsie?"

We both laughed and Angela sat down.

"Oh Derek, what a complete mess."

"I know. Everything is a shambles. Poor Gerald, poor youngsters; poor us."

"We're not going to have a happy ending are we," Angela said.

I shook my head. "I don't see how we can. I don't think I can ever truly forget what you do as a job."

"But I'll be giving it up completely soon, I said so last..."

"I know, I know; but no matter what, it will always be there," I told her, "Even if we did get together and were happy, I'd still know. Every time we had a row it would come up. I've been through a divorce recently and I know how bad things get at the end. Even if we got together; I still think there would be an end. It's painful enough now to let you go, I don't think I could cope with that further down the line."

"I understand," Angela said, "I truly do. It's not like I haven't heard that before."

She reached for a tissue in her handbag. I tried desperately to swallow the lump that had risen into my throat.

"You're looking for someone special who can cope with this," I told her, "That's someone a lot more special than me. But I do hope you find him one day."

Angela managed a smile through her tears. "Thank you," she said, and squeezed my hand.

We didn't hang around long in the dining room. When we walked back out to the hallway together to go and get our cases Angela stopped me before going up the stairs.

"Derek, I can't bear the thought of saying goodbye in front of everyone else on the coach. Can we do it now?"

I hadn't prepared myself for this. For the second time that morning I couldn't think of anything to say, but I nodded. We both stood there in silence, neither wanting to be the first to speak; but then we realised how silly we looked just standing there. We smiled and hugged, clumsily.

"Goodbye Derek," Angela said, sniffing and wiping her eyes again.

"Goodbye Angela." The words wanted to stick in my throat.

I watched her walk up the stairs. At the top she turned round.

"Can I ask one favour, Derek?" she said.

"Of course."

"You'll be getting off the coach first. When you do, please don't look back."

I nodded. Angela gave one last smile and then she was gone.

*

It was going to be a very quiet journey home, I realised, as I walked back down the stairs with my case. The coach had been empty enough coming but would be virtually desolate on the return trip.

Mrs Goddard was in the hallway making sure that everyone gave her their room keys back. She was still in costume from last night and hadn't bothered trying to tame her wild hair. I did feel sorry for her though. I remembered how happy she had been upon our arrival. She'd expected so much from our booking but this week had been as much a disaster for her as it had been for the rest of us. I tried to make her feel better.

"Honestly," I lied, handing in my key, "Things aren't as bad as you think."

"Mr Noble, two people have died in the hotel this week."

"Well, yes; yes they have; but you can't blame yourself for that. These things happen. Look at how well you coped with getting the lounge window sorted out after the floor caved in. The glaziers were here the same day."

Mrs Goddard thought about that.

"I suppose that's true," she said, "I did get onto that straight away, didn't I."

"Yes you did," I replied, "And I'm sure the room is going to look a treat once it's cleared and decorated. The glass in the bay window looks spectacular."

Mrs Goddard smiled at me.

"Thank you Mr Noble," she said, "You've helped remind me

of why I entered this industry. Every day is a challenge and it's all about meeting those challenges head on. So long as the guests are happy, it's all worth it."

After what had happened I doubted any of us were happy. If there were any smiles this morning it was just because we were finally leaving this place, but I didn't voice that opinion out loud.

"You're definitely right," she continued, "The new look lounge is going to be stunning. I've picked out some wonderful paint colours. I think I'll get on to the plasterers again later today."

I smiled and turned to go but Mrs Goddard called me back.

"Mr Noble, this is for you."

She handed me an envelope. What was it, a little leaving gift?

"It's your bar bill," she said, "Cash or card. We don't accept cheques."

"Oh, right; yes." Damn; I'd forgotten about that.

After parting with what I felt was a suspiciously large amount of money, I was more than ready to leave this place. I carried my suitcase outside into the drizzling rain. As I got to the bottom of the porch steps I heard a commotion. Shauna had someone by the scruff of the neck and was throwing him off of the coach. It was Chico.

"You're not coming with me," Shauna shouted, tossing a pink rucksack that was shaped like a pair of boobs after him.

Chico picked it up off the floor. "But sugar," he said, "We are made for each other. Don't make me stay here. We go together like mozzarella and tomato; like pasta and bolognaise; like…"

"Listen pal, if you want to talk analogies; you're like a fly to my shit!"

294

"That works for me, baby."

"Piss off!"

As Chico joined me by the front steps so a convertible pulled into the driveway and three young women climbed out. They were all tall, slim, and blonde. Even though it was raining they wore sunglasses and were dressed for a long day on a hot beach.

"Excuse me," one of them called, "We're looking for a couple of rooms. Do either of you work here?"

I looked down at my case. Surely that suggested I was holidaymaker rather than staff. When I looked back up Chico was already helping them with their matching luggage. He whispered something and the three girls all giggled. I guess he was over Shauna.

I walked over to where she was waiting beside the coach. She looked tired after the organisation of the night before and I doubted there'd been much chance for any sleep. I had a new found respect for her. Everyone else seemed to have changed in front of my eyes this week why should Shauna be excluded?

"Hope you haven't got the Elvis costume in here," she said, throwing my case into the hold.

"No, I went for the rabbit one instead," I told her.

She laughed. "Hop on Dirk, not long now until we're all home."

Seeing Jim with his glasses perched precariously on his swollen nose, taped together with a couple of plasters; I felt sure the journey home was going to be very long indeed. Margaret waved at me as I got on.

"Derek, are you and Angela ok? I mean I don't want to pry but you both look like your worlds have fallen apart."

I forced a smile onto my face.

"Don't worry," I said, "It's nothing; just a little disagreement." I wasn't about to tell her everything that had happened.

Margaret sat back in her seat, relieved.

"Good," she said, "You two are made for each other."

Dora gave my bottom a friendly pinch as I passed and then I overheard her say to Margaret, "I think Shauna said she'd found out Angela was a bore. I always thought she was rather interesting to talk to."

I was surprised to see Karen sitting in her usual window seat. Her eyes were still puffy and red from crying.

"I thought you were staying behind," I said to her.

"Nothing to stay for," she replied, pulling a tissue out of her bag and wiping her nose, "It's for the three of them to sort out."

"All four of you surely," I said, sitting down in Leroy's seat.

Karen looked at me as if I'd just said something really stupid.

"Why?" she asked, "What has this got to do with me? Pete and Lauren are married and Leroy is the father of Lauren's baby. I'm nothing; always have been."

"Don't say that," I said, "You're not nothing. What about you and Leroy?"

"What about us? That's over."

"But he loves you."

Karen snorted, tears welling up in her eyes. "Yeah, of course he does. Nice way of showing it too; shagging one of my friends."

"I'm sorry," I said.

"He gave me the old, 'It was only once, we were drunk; it will never happen again' speech."

"Maybe he was telling the truth."

"What if he was?" Karen's voice rose, "I don't care. The guy's always been a flirt. I knew he'd go too far with someone one day. I didn't expect things to turn out like this though."

She snorted again, shaking her head. "That stupid bitch got her dates confused; can you believe that? She thought the doctors were out with their timing; genuinely thought the baby was Pete's. That poor guy is devastated. And I introduced him to the silly cow."

"It's not your fault," I said.

"Oh don't worry Derek, I'm not blaming myself. I just feel so sorry for him. He's so in love with her."

"And you love Leroy. And he loves you."

Karen gave me a pitying look.

"Oh Derek, I thought out of everyone you would understand how I'm feeling right now. You're wife's having a baby with someone else isn't she?"

"Well, yes; circumstances are different but…yes; I can understand exactly how you're feeling. But even so, don't give up on it all. You're angry now, obviously and have every right to be, but later; once the baby has been brought home; at least hear Leroy out when he calls you; because he will. All I ask is that you make no rash decisions now."

Karen remained silent which I took to mean that she'd heard what I'd said and might take my advice.

"I can't promise anything," she said, finally, "I mean I know when you truly love someone you should be able to forgive them but come on Derek, this is pretty unforgivable isn't it?"

I couldn't deny that and I also couldn't deny how, what Karen had just said, resonated with me. 'If you truly love someone you should be able to forgive them.' Maybe that was advice I should heed.

"I'll leave you alone," I told her, and got up.

"You know the worst thing, Derek?" Karen said, "Leroy has always told me that he loves me whatever my size and that I don't have to lose weight for him."

297

"I know; I've heard him say it myself."

"But when he cheated on me with Lauren, I was three stone heavier. Lying bastard."

I had a feeling it was this point, rather than the baby, that Karen would find the hardest to forgive.

"But surely you're happier in yourself now that you've lost the weight," I said.

"Happier? No Derek, I'm not happier. I'm just as miserable only in a smaller jeans size. I'm on this coach, alone. All I've got to show for the last year is a few weight loss stickers from my diet group. When I get home I'm going to have a bloody big meat pie with chips."

I walked down the coach. I could see the top of Angela's head, in a seat towards the back so I sat down in the middle, a couple of rows behind Josie and Sooz.

We were ready to leave. Mrs Goddard appeared at the top of the porch steps. She'd changed into one of her business suits and had tidied up her hair. She was talking to the three girls who had just arrived and was pointing at the newly fitted window; obviously trying to impress them with the improvements she'd made. When the engine of the coach spluttered into life Barbara turned and began waving; glad and relieved to finally see us off. Jim pressed down on the accelerator pedal…and back we flew.

Everyone yelled as we felt the bang and heard glass smashing. When we dared to look we found we had a rather good view down the coach into Mrs Goddard's lounge. I could see the original pile of debris still heaped up against the back wall, which now had a nice coating of freshly broken glass across it. Jim eased the coach forward. It didn't have a scratch on it. He got out his lucky rabbit's foot and kissed it.

It took Shauna quite a while to calm Mrs Goddard down

again; especially while the car with the three girls in it was disappearing out of the driveway; Chico running after them with his rucksack. We had to wait while Shauna contacted the glaziers and left insurance details for Scrimshaw Travel, but once that was done and she'd smacked Jim around the back of the head, we were ready to leave again. I did hear, some months later, that the hotel burned down in a mysterious fire. No one was hurt and Mrs Goddard moved to Tenerife.

We were finally on our way. I had a lot of time to think on the journey home. At the beginning of the week I'd been feeling sorry for myself and thought I was in such a unique position having to start my life over again but really, most of us on this trip were in the same boat. I guess everyone has their problems to deal with and it's not always easy to tell when someone is going through a distressing time.

I thought about the four youngsters, so happy and so in love at the start of the holiday. Pete and Lauren were on their honeymoon for God's sake. One stupid mistake nine months ago had led to this fall out; but it was one hell of a mistake. How were they going to move on from this? Would they each have to start over again down separate paths?

I thought about Gerald; fifty years of marriage and now alone. He had his children and grandchildren but I didn't know how often he saw them. Besides, no one could take the place of Maeve. I couldn't help thinking that he may be one of those people who die not long after their partners because they just can't go on without them. Had Maeve wondered that herself and was that why she'd tried her hardest to get him ready for her demise? She wanted him to go on; to start over again without her.

I thought of Josie and Sooz. They'd probably got the most enjoyment out of this trip. I think they were two people who always found what pleasure they could out of life no matter what was thrown at them; and Sooz had had some tough things thrown her way. It was the holiday the two had planned and exactly what Sooz needed. She and her husband had had to rebuild their lives after the death of his son and now she was doing the same thing again on her own, just like Gerald. Maybe he had a friend like Josie.

Speaking of getting enjoyment out of this trip brought Colin and last night's kitchen antics to mind. It looked like he too was about to embark on a new chapter in his life with glum barman. I was pleased for him after all his years of loneliness. I hoped he and Rupert had many years of happiness to come, bickering and arguing with one another.

I couldn't leave out Margaret and Dora. Margaret's life, like Colin's had been lonely since the death of her father. As much as she was a Daddy's girl though, I think she'd still be mortified when Dora was no longer here and miss her dreadfully. I don't think she hated running Dora about quite as much as she made out. They were more alike than either of them would ever have admitted. Margaret had mentioned buying the barn Harry had pretended to own. Perhaps she was planning a new life for herself. I hoped her plans included staying in touch with Angela. The two of them could be good friends.

And then there was Angela herself. My God that woman had driven me to distraction. I'd spent most of the week thinking about her, unable to concentrate on anything else. I'd fallen in love and yet now I was full of anger and confusion after what I'd discovered last night. I still yearned to be with her. I wanted to run to the back of the coach right now, take her in my arms and tell her I'd always love her; but then I thought about what she did for a living and I couldn't. I wasn't judging her morally, not now. If that's what she did, so be it. If it's worked out well for her then great but at the end of the day would anyone want their partner or spouse sleeping with other people? My ex-wife was already sleeping with someone else and that fact still riled me. Even if Angela was giving up this career, well...there's having a past and there's having a past. We'd said our goodbyes. It was probably best to leave it at that.

We stopped a couple of times on the journey back, once just for toilets and the other for lunch. Fortunately we made it to the proper motorway services this time which were large enough for Angela and I to eat at different restaurants and avoid each other. The hour and a half spent there dragged by. Even though I'd eaten nothing at breakfast time I still wasn't particularly hungry and it took a lot of effort to swallow half a sandwich.

Afterwards I wandered around aimlessly, checking my watch every few minutes to see when it was time to return to the coach. I thought of reading the funny cards in the card shop, but that only reminded me of being with Angela at Ryan Harbour. In the supermarket the high prices in the wine section reminded me of the two of us at the vineyard. I walked out the back of the service station but the small copse I found reminded me of our attempt at lovemaking at Tenham House. Everything reminded me of her.

Finally the hour and a half was up and I boarded the coach again. I thought I could pass the final leg of the journey by going through all of my e mails from the past week on my phone but I only had three. That wouldn't see me out of the Service Station car park let alone get me back home. The first one was from my bank asking if I'd like to extend my overdraft, the next was from the local gym asking if I'd like to extend my membership and the final one was from a spam address asking if I'd like to extend my penis. I hit delete on all three.

The last leg of the journey felt the longest of the entire trip but eventually we pulled up into the bus bay at my drop-off point. I took a deep breath and stood up, a lump in my throat. As per Angela's wishes I didn't look back as I walked up the coach. Josie and Sooz both waved. Josie placed a piece of paper in my hand.

"Our addresses," she said, "If you're ever in our neck of the woods, do knock us up."

Karen managed a smile as I passed and Margaret got up and hugged me. I bent down and gave Dora a kiss. She grabbed my arse with both hands and had a final squeeze. I ignored Jim, who was staring out of the windscreen. I reached the top of the steps and stopped. This was the moment, the last chance to turn round and face Angela. She'd asked me not to. What would happen if I did? Would she be looking my way? Would we run down the aisle toward each other? Would she ignore me completely? I took a deep breath; and walked down the steps.

It was still drearily overcast; a miserable day to reflect how I felt. Shauna had already got my case and my wine purchases out of the hold and placed them onto the pavement.

"It's all over, Dirk," she said.

"Yes," I replied, staring at my case, "Yes it really is."

"I'm sorry, Derek, about you and Angela."

I looked up, sharply.

"You called me Derek."

Shauna smiled. "Well, you look so down; I didn't have the heart not to."

"Did you know about her?" I asked.

"Angela?" Shauna shook her head, "Not until last night, after you both ran outside. Jim told me everything."

"Everything?"

"I almost feel sorry for him, the horny, little toad," she said, looking up at the coach door and smiling, "I don't think he's seen a woman in ten years."

"Or a road sign."

She laughed, but then added, "I am sorry though."

"I do believe you are."

"I'm not a nasty bitch, Derek, whatever you might think. I can do this job standing on my head. All my little comments, they just relieve the boredom. I like to see how far I can push things. Most of the time people don't even notice."

"Maybe you should change your career," I told her.

"What and miss out on all this glamour?" She grinned and then whacked me hard on the back, "Oh well, must get these other old codgers dropped off pretty sharpish. My period's about to start and I tend to lose my sweet-natured side when that happens."

I was glad I was the first drop-off.

Shauna climbed back onto the coach.

"See you around, Dirk," she said, giving me a wave.

I smiled. Perhaps my fresh start should include a name change. The name's Noble; Dirk Noble. Shauna poked her head back out of the door again.

"Hey Dirk," she called, "I meant to say."

"What's that?"

"If you ever want to go on another coach trip…don't call us."

She winked and disappeared inside the coach. The doors closed and I watched it gently kangaroo hop away. It was only as it disappeared from view that I realised the colossal mistake I'd just made. Angela was gone. The woman I loved and who had made me happy all week had just been driven out of my life; and I'd let it happen.

Did it really matter that she had been a prostitute in her past, I reasoned, while I stood there on the pavement. She wasn't going to be one in the future; Angela had told me that herself. Why was I being so high and mighty about it? There'd been plenty of times that my ex-wife had dressed in short skirts for certain male business clients to ensure they signed up with her company again. She'd told me once how she had got out of a speeding ticket because of her low-cut top. She'd used her body to her own advantage and I had applauded her cleverness and ingenuity. Hadn't Angela done exactly the same thing? Well, maybe she'd taken things a little further than Leanne had but still; she'd been clever, resourceful and brave in her choice of job. I'd let my pride and anger get in the way and now she was gone. I felt a physical pain resonate through my body.

Mind you, that was probably due to Shauna whacking me across the back just now. My God she was strong. I was surprised Jim's nose hadn't broken last night. I tried to see if I could get my hand up to where she'd hit me to give it a bit of a rub. The material of my jacket didn't feel right. There was something stuck to it. I took the jacket off and found a large, yellow post-it note attached. Great, thanks for that Shauna. What was it; a 'Kick Me' sign? I thought she'd realised how down I was.

I peeled the note off and a smile appeared on my face as I read it. Written at the top was, 'This is against the rules, but don't give up, Dirk' and underneath that, was Angela's phone number.

Nothing Ventured

By

Stuart Bone

A few of the locals living in sleepy Ryan Harbour find themselves in need of a change. Whether it's breaking the daily monotony of their lives, making business plans or finding excitement; embarking on a new challenge can be a frightening prospect and positive results aren't guaranteed. However sitting back and doing nothing won't change a thing. Sometimes you just have to go for it. Nothing ventured, nothing gained.

Diana Carlton accepts help with her bucket list from her neighbour, single mum, Lou Turner. They haven't always got along and past squabbles aren't buried too low beneath the surface. Can their friendship survive their very different upbringings, especially when Keith appears on the scene?
Landlord, Jamie Taylor, must find some cost-effective ways to attract the locals back to his pub, but how will his handful of regulars react when the various events don't go according to plan?
With retirement looming, Robert Keane would like to find ways to break out of the boredom of everyday life. Persuading his wife, Grace, to try a little experimentation in the bedroom turns out to be the easy part. Working out what to do proves far more difficult.
Dr Bryant is lusting after his new locum, Dr Moore. As his infatuation grows will he be able to pluck up the courage to begin an affair and will Dr Moore be receptive?

Coming soon, another visit to the county of Tenhamshire as Stuart Bone's second hilarious novel introduces us to a host of new, colourful characters to laugh and empathise with.

Printed in Great Britain
by Amazon